the properties of water

also by ann hood:

PLACES TO STAY THE NIGHT

SOMEWHERE OFF THE COAST OF MAINE

WAITING TO VANISH

THREE-LEGGED HORSE

SOMETHING BLUE

Bantam Books

new york toronto london

sydney auckland

the properties of water

---

ann hood

This edition contains the complete text
of the original hardcover edition.
NOT ONE WORD HAS BEEN OMITTED.

PROPERTIES OF WATER

A Bantam Book / published by arrangement with Doubleday

PUBLISHING HISTORY
Doubleday hardcover edition / July 1995
Bantam trade paperback edition / July 1996

Book design by Gretchen Achilles

Library of Congress Card Catalog Number: 94-46456

ISBN 0-553-37565-2

Printed simultaneously in the United States and Canada

Bantam Books are published by Bantam Books, a division of Bantam Doubleday Dell Publishing Group, Inc. Its trademark, consisting of the words "Bantam Books" and the portrayal of a rooster, is Registered in U.S. Patent and Trademark Office and in other countries. Marca Registrada. Bantam Books, 1540 Broadway, New York, New York 10036.

PRINTED IN THE UNITED STATES OF AMERICA

FFG 10 9 8 7 6 5 4 3 2 1

for sam

acknowledgments

This book came to life with the generosity and love of the following people, all of whom have my deepest thanks: my parents, Melissa Hood, all the cousins—Gina, Gloria-Jean, Becky and Tony—June Caycedo, Lorne Adrain, John Searles, Paul Lombardi, Helen Schulman, Glenn Russow, Marianne Merola, Gail Hochman and, of course, Deb Futter.

spring

week one

East Essex, Rhode Island, had never been beautiful. At least not in anyone's memory. Even in sepia-toned photographs from the nineteenth century, the air was thick with factory smoke and the citizens' faces seemed worn and tired. But to Josie Jericho Hunter, the town had its own unique beauty, not the kind that towns nestled on the bay had, or the rural wooded charm or sweeping ocean views of others. East Essex was hilly, and the view from the top of one of those hills could be, in its way, breathtaking. Looking down from a hilltop, the jumble of trees and houses and mills took on a false grandeur. Smack in the middle, curving and creeping like a large gray snake, was the Pottowamicut River. From up high, it seemed vibrant, like a living thing instead of the way it really was—sluggish and foamy with factory pollution.

Sometimes, when Josie drove the winding road from her house to her parents, she could imagine East Essex as it might have been longer ago than anyone remembered. She could imagine deer in the woods where clumsy modern houses now sat, and thick grass littered with pine needles instead of old roads in need of repair. She could imagine the river alive with fish and frogs, imagine it bubbling across smooth rocks, sparkling under a warm spring sun.

But today, even Josie was having trouble liking East Essex. The soap factory filled the air with its overbearing smell and the town sewer had backed up again, its own foul odor mingling with the soap. The combination was so bad that Josie had to keep her car windows rolled up. The car was too warm, and the smell permeated it anyway. Beside her on the front seat were dozens of party invitations to be addressed, balloons to be blown up, favors to be packaged. By the time she pulled up in front of her parents' small yellow Cape, Josie was hot and cranky. The clock on her dashboard glowed green, reminding her she had exactly one hour before she had to pick up Kate, her youngest daughter, at preschool.

She felt unsettled, disorganized. And it seemed to stem from something more than her being so late. She felt like everything was off somehow. She'd told her husband Will that very morning that if she believed in omens, she'd have to say something was going to go wrong.

"You sound like that fruitcake sister of yours," Will said. He was slipping a pretied tie over his neck, like a noose. He hung them up that way, loosened but already tied, ready to slip on.

"Maybe," Josie had told him, choosing to ignore his remark about Michaela, "maybe it's the party."

He'd laughed then, and kissed the top of her head the way one might kiss a small child. "Honey," he said, "it's a party for five-year-olds. You've got to get a grip."

"Still," she said, "I feel funny."

"Call Michaela and get some astrological advice," Will said, and even though Josie wasn't looking at him, she could imagine the smirk on his face.

On the night before their wedding eighteen years ago, at the rehearsal dinner, Michaela had read them a wedding forecast. Everyone had dressed up for the dinner, but Michaela had worn her usual jeans and a black leotard. She was also stoned out of her mind, but Josie wasn't sure anyone else had noticed that.

"According to the stars," Michaela had read, "this is not a match made in heaven."

She'd gone on to tell them about air fanning flames, Mercury in retrograde, and other things no one understood. Except Josie. Josie understood that Michaela wanted to ruin everything, as usual. That what she was saying was all made-up so that they would feel bad, feel like this marriage couldn't work, that it wasn't in the stars.

Michaela presented them with her reading carefully printed in midnight blue ink on fake parchment paper, a border of carefully drawn angels around it. Every year, on their anniversary, Will reminded Josie of that night. "Should we call your sister," he'd say, "and tell her just how wrong she was?"

But looking into her rearview mirror to readjust her ponytail and wipe off the small dots of mascara beneath her eyes, Josie found herself wondering about her sister's forecast after all. She tried to remember when she had last felt a thrill at the sight of her husband, when she had felt a thrill at anything, really. It seemed her life had settled into a predictable even line, with a few dips when one of the children's fever soared or Will came home unexpectedly late. Josie knew what her mother would tell her: "Thrills are what you get on roller coasters. Not in life. Not in East Essex." She had told her that before, as she lowered Josie's veil and sent her down the aisle of Saint Teresa's church to get married. Then it had been a reaffirmation of common sense, good choices. She'd reminded her of it when Maggie had colic; when Josie considered going back to school to study nursing or child development or sociology or something, anything; when Will turned down a promotion that would take them away, to Arizona, a promotion he had wanted to take and that Josie had fought. Whenever she had tried to imagine them living out west she would see dry flat land, flimsy tract houses painted the colors of sherbert, cactus and snakes and everything else unfamiliar, and her throat would turn as dry as that desert she pictured. Josie had found comfort in her mother's words. She had repeated them to Will. Life isn't about thrills, she'd said. It's about what we have here.

She believed that still. Life—her life, anyway—was the sound of her husband's key in the front door every evening, her childrens' good-night hugs, the comfort of home. Stepping from her car, Josie reminded herself of these things again. Then she saw it—stumbled upon it, really, right there in her path. A big yellow sign. FOR SALE. She tried to catch her breath but only got the terrible combination of sewer and soap. She had been right all along with her feeling of something being off kilter. Her parents were selling the house. Josie's mouth went dry, the way it always did when she panicked.

Still clutching her shopping bags of balloons and Disney trinkets, Josie stepped back, as if she was looking at the house for the first time. It had always reminded her of a storybook house, with its bright yellow paint and sloping roof, its border of rosebushes and startling green front door with the big brass J doorknocker. The house was small, but Josie had always thought of it as cozy instead. The rooms spilled into each other, cluttered in a happy way. Besides her own house, the one she and Will and her daughters lived in, and various dorm rooms when she was in college, Josie had never lived anywhere else. In this house's attic were all her childhood toys, her Easy-Bake oven and Play Do Fun Factory, her photo albums and old records—The Monkees and Bobby Sherman and Paul Revere and the Raiders.

Josie glanced around. After so much time, she still thought of this neighborhood as her neighborhood. Up the street she could see her Aunt Tiny's house, big and gray and stale-smelling from years of her Uncle Frank's cigars. Across the street, behind the Murphys' house, was her Aunt Beatrice's low rambling one. When it was built in the early sixties, it had seemed modern, something the Jetsons might live in. It was bright turquoise then, trimmed in redwood with a glassed-in porch that was always too hot in summer and too cold in winter. More recently they had painted it the slate blue usually saved for Colonials.

Josie pried her tongue from the roof of her mouth and tried to wet her lips. But her mouth was still as dry as dirt. She moved toward the house, slowly. Up close she saw that it needed a fresh coat of paint. And the gate hung crookedly from its rusty hinges. But that was nothing. Will could come over and put it back into shape in a weekend. Less, even. She tried to feel optimistic, as if she could race inside and tell her mother that the house didn't need to be sold, that Will would come by this very weekend and fix everything.

She even smiled as she walked through the gate and into the yard. Until she saw her father, back where their swing set used to sit when they were children. He was walking in what seemed to be a circle, his hands thrust into his cardigan's pockets. He was frowning. A few months ago, trying to be adult about it, Josie decided to talk to her mother. Wasn't that what all the talk show psychologists advised? Confrontation? "Dad seems," she'd started. But then she did not know what to say next. All of the words she'd practiced seemed small compared to the name of the disease. ALZHEIMER'S. She said it to herself once, then again, but to say it out loud might make it true. "He seems tired," she'd said finally. And her mother, relieved, said, "Yes. Tired."

Watching him here in the sunlight, though, Josie saw that it was not fatigue or even a physical ailment that caused him to knot his eyebrows like that, to shake his head like a dust mop. She whispered, "Alzheimer's." Then, panicked, called to him. "Daddy?"

When he looked up, he broke into a smile, and again Josie convinced herself that everything could be put back in order. As her father approached her, she even silently chided herself for being so pessimistic. That wasn't like her at all.

"Hello, there, Ladybug," her father said. He gave her a big wet kiss on the cheek, the kind that used to make her and Michaela run, screaming, from him when they were young.

Lately, her father had started calling Josie by his old childhood nickname for her. Ladybug. Michaela had been My Girl, like that old song, and Josie had been Ladybug. She liked hearing it again.

"What's in the bags?" her father was saying.

Josie linked her arm through his. "Party junk. I thought I could get Mom to help blow up balloons and wrap the favors, but it's so late now and I have to run and pick up Kate soon."

Her father looked puzzled. "Are we having a party?" he said.

"It's Kate's birthday, Daddy," Josie said. She knew she sounded irritated, but she couldn't help it. She had been planning the party for weeks. Will and Maggie were ready to kill her if she even mentioned it again. She added, "We're having Minnie Mouse come."

Her father led her to the backyard. "Do you know what I was thinking?" he said. He didn't wait for her to answer. "I was thinking about that swing set that used to sit right here. You girls had to have a purple one. 'Purple?' I said when your mother told me. 'Where are we ever going to get a purple swing set?' But we did. We found it somewhere in Pawtucket. Violet and lavender, it was. We gave it to you girls for Christmas. 1959. And we had to come out here and set it up right then, that very morning, even though there was snow on the ground."

Josie stood, looking at the empty yard. Around the fence that bordered it the crocuses had already started to bloom. She saw their tips, purple and pink.

"My crocuses haven't come up yet," she said.

Her father sighed. "The thing is," he said, "when did we get rid of it?"

"What? The swing set?"

"Yes," he said. His eyes moved across the small yard, as if he might suddenly discover that old purple swing set there.

"It just sat out here until we outgrew it and it got all rusty and someone hauled it away," Josie said. This was silly. "I'd better go see if I can enlist Mom," she said, trying to sound bright. She held up the bags again.

"What do you have in there?" her father said.

"The balloons and stuff."

He nodded, looking puzzled again.

"Come on, Daddy," Josie said softly, urging him toward the house. "Let's go inside."

The house was rich with the smell of percolated coffee, lemon furniture polish and White Shoulders perfume. Josie followed her father through the small kitchen, with its yellow-and-white gingham curtains and Harvest Gold appliances, into the dining room, where Josie's mother and aunts sat drinking coffee. For as long as she could remember, this was the same scene Josie had walked into whenever she came home.

If she were somewhere far away, like Arizona, and had to close her eyes and imagine home, this was what she would see: Aunt Tiny eating pound cake, dressed in black in honor of a son who had died in Vietnam over twenty years ago; Aunt

Beatrice adding Equal to her coffee, cutting a piece of cake into quarters, then into quarters again, nibbling away at each small bit like a mouse. She always wore something that sparkled—a sweater with colored rhinestones, a sweatshirt handpainted with luminescent pansies. She always wore high heels and lipstick, even when she vacuumed; and finally, Josie's mother, Claire, who had always been known as "the pretty one." She wore white aprons over her size six dresses, and kept her auburn hair shoulder length and curled like a 1940s movie star.

Josie supposed she thought of them all twenty years younger, frozen in time. She was always a little startled when she saw them as they were now, with gray in their hair and deepening lines at the corners of their eyes and mouths. As she made her way around the table to say hello, she hugged them close to her. It wasn't the first time lately that Josie had wished she could slow down time.

"That husband of yours," Aunt Tiny said as soon as Josie sat down, "is a peach. A real sweetheart. He knew I wanted to do my bathroom in sea foam and he put aside a whole set for me—the curtains, the rug, the toilet seat cover and the shower curtain with a liner. 'It's here waiting for you!' he tells me." She cut another piece of cake and put it on her plate. "A real peach," she said.

Josie cut herself a piece of cake, then looked at her mother.

"How could you?" she said, sounding like a pouting child.

Claire did not pretend to misunderstand. "I know," she said.

"Without even telling me?" Josie continued, her voice rising. She saw her mother look to Tiny and Beatrice for help, but did not give them the chance. "Out of the blue I show up and the house is for sale. Just like that?"

"In this market," Aunt Beatrice said, "this house isn't going anywhere anytime soon." She tried to change the subject.

"Elsa Martone's house has been on the market a year and not even one bid has come in. Not one."

"The taxes in this town," Aunt Tiny said, shaking her head.

"Mom?" Josie said.

Aunt Tiny patted Josie's hand. "It's too big," she told her. "Who needs the headaches?"

"I don't see you selling your house," Josie said.

"We put it on the market," her mother said. "That's all. We'll see how it goes. Okay?"

"It looks like I don't have much of a choice," Josie said. But even as she said it, she was thinking of ways to keep the house. She would come over once a week and clean for her mother. Will could help out with yard work. There were ways. She took a bite of cake.

Aunt Beatrice frowned. "I don't think you need those extra calories, Josie," she said.

Embarrassed, Josie put her piece back on the platter. "I really should work out more," she mumbled.

Josie's mother served dessert on the good dessert plates, thin china with small pink roses around the rim. Josie picked up one and traced the roses with her finger. Her grandmother had been so proud of this set, acquired piece by piece, each plate and cup and saucer carefully saved for.

"So," Aunt Beatrice was saying, "Judy says Christy says Maggie doesn't go to cheerleading practice anymore. Is she sick or something?"

"Sick?" Josie said. "No. She's fine." Her cousin Judy's daughter Christy was just like Judy had been as a young girl, prissy, a Goody Two-shoes. Sometimes Josie wondered why Judy and her sister Denise were so perfect, and she and Michaela were so—she hesitated—so imperfect.

"Did she drop out?" Aunt Tiny was saying.

The truth was, Josie had no idea that Maggie wasn't going to practice. Her daughter came home from school late, clutching her pompoms and the megaphone with the double E's on it. But lately, Maggie had been acting odd. "Hormones," Will said. But Josie worried it was something more.

Now, she felt compelled to cover for her daughter. "She's nursing a sore ankle," she said.

Aunt Beatrice narrowed her eyes. "What happened to her ankle?" Today, she wore a glittery purple sweater, long drop earrings, bangle bracelets.

"Who cares?" Claire said. "You don't have enough to do? You have to worry about the cheerleading squad too?"

When Josie had talked to her mother about Maggie's behavior, she had told her to relax.

"She's a teenager," Claire had said.

"But I wasn't like that," Josie said.

"No," Claire said, sighing. "You weren't."

Neither of them mentioned Michaela, but they both thought the same thing, that some teenagers are really troubled, and it has nothing to do with hormones. Maybe Maggie was like that, like Michaela. Maybe her daughter, who for fourteen years had been sweet, good, a straight A student, was suffering from the same restlessness and confusion that had led Michaela away from home and the family into a lifetime of unhappiness.

As if she had read her mind, Claire had put her hands over Josie's and said, "I wish I'd had my children later, so they weren't caught up in the sixties, in all that confusion. These are better times."

Despite River Phoenix and this guy from Nirvana, both heroin users, both mourned loudly and with great dramatics by Maggie, her mother had managed to comfort Josie for a time, until Maggie's next episode, when Josie had been called into school for an editorial Maggie wrote titled "How to Vaporize Your Parents, Siblings, and Other Living Things."

Josie tried to focus on the conversation at the table with her aunts. Already they had moved on to a new topic—a strange family had moved into town and was living in the woods behind the golf course. She tried to make herself listen, to not get stuck on Maggie. Was there a wife? her aunts were wondering. And someone had heard that they raised bees, of all things.

"Really?" Josie said. "Bees?" But her heart wasn't in it. All she could think about was how, just a short time ago, Maggie had been her friend, how just thinking about her daughter would make her smile. Now, every time someone mentioned Maggie's name, Josie wished she could disappear, not have to listen.

"Sometimes," Maggie's teacher had told Josie that day she'd been called in, "even the best kids have rough times. Times when a counselor could really straighten things out quickly."

"A counselor?" Josie had said. She thought of straitjackets, psychiatric wards, troubled teens in TV movies. "Really, I think Maggie is just fine."

She hadn't mentioned any of it to Will, not the teacher's gentle suggestion or the editorial itself. Maybe, she'd hoped, it would all just get better. She would wake up one morning and everything would be back to normal.

Her aunts' voices were swirling in her head, and Josie forced herself to tune in to them. Aunt Tiny was telling them about a dream she'd had the night before. A dream in which her dead son David had returned, twenty years late, from the war. Josie's grandmother had a complicated system for interpreting dreams, a system she'd passed on to her daughters. Everything in the dream meant a different number. Her grandmother had bet on those numbers, illegally, through a man named Vinny. But Josie's mother and aunts played the numbers in the state lottery. Once in a while they won, which made their belief in their mother's system even stronger.

"He looked so handsome," Aunt Tiny was saying. "He wasn't in his uniform. He was wearing a tuxedo with a red bow tie and cummerbund. Bright red."

"240," Aunt Beatrice said. "The dead is 240."

"But wait," Aunt Tiny continued. "He said—"

"He talked?" Claire said. "248."

Aunt Tiny leaned back in her chair. "He told me to play 567."

"Play them both," Aunt Beatrice said, her voice firm. "248. 567. We can't take any chances."

The grandfather's clock began to ring twelve, startling everyone, like an intruder.

Josie jumped up. "Oh, no," she said. "I have to get Kate. I'm going to be late."

She gathered her bags, realizing she had accomplished nothing at all. The balloons were not blown up, the favors were unwrapped, and outside, on the lawn, still sat a FOR SALE sign.

"Buy lottery tickets," her mother called after her. "248 and 567."

As Josie backed up the car, she caught a glimpse of her father, standing alone in the backyard, where their old swing set used to be.

Last year, when Maggie still felt normal, she had spent part of the summer on her back pasting glow-in-the-dark stars and planets to her bedroom ceiling. She had learned about Michelangelo in her summer class, Advanced Art History, and she had imagined herself like him, sweating and planning her design flat on her back. Maggie was Gifted. That's what everyone told her. And she took Advanced classes—Creative Writing and Non-Western Literature and Expression Through Movement.

Great things were expected of her. She knew that. But lately she spent most of her time on her bed staring up at her glow-in-the-dark sky. Her carefully planned design seemed oddly random now and for the life of her she could not remember what she had been thinking when she placed those ridiculous patterns up there last summer. Now she hated it, hated the way Saturn was surrounded by shooting stars and the Earth was right next to Pluto, like she'd played some big cosmic joke or something. In the middle of last night, Maggie had stood on her bureau, reached up and pulled Mars from the ceiling. It had left a big black smudge behind and made everything look even worse. With a hot pink Magic Marker she'd written A BLACK HOLE and drawn an arrow pointing to the smudge.

Still, she hated the stupid ceiling even more than ever. Looking around her room, Maggie took inventory of everything she hated. Her ceiling, of course. And her ugly yellowed bedroom furniture.

When she had told her mother that, her mother's face had crumpled in on itself like wet tissue paper. "But that was my bedroom when I was your age," she'd said. "I had to beg Gran to even give it to us. You know how Gran hates changing anything. But we both wanted you to have it."

"But I hate it!" Maggie had said. "It's old and ugly and it smells funny."

"Smells funny?" her mother said, looking puzzled and even sadder. She'd bent her head to the surface of the bureau and inhaled deeply. "It doesn't smell at all," she said. Then she'd inhaled again. "Maybe of powder. A little."

"Just forget it," Maggie had mumbled. She'd put her pillow over her face and imagined a spare, modern room with a futon and exposed brick and track lighting. She thought about that room until her mother finally sighed and left, her footsteps in her ridiculous aerobic sneakers sounding oddly muted. When Maggie had lifted the pillow she almost thought she'd actually be in that other room—the clean, fresh one of her daydream.

But, no, her room was still cluttered and old. She looked around it now, each object in it something else to make her miserable. Her black-and-gold cheerleading pompoms. Her class picture framed in a silver heart. The big ugly corsage from her ninth grade dance, looking sad now that it was dried up, its colorful ribbons all droopy and long. But that's what all the girls had done the morning after the dance, hung their corsages upside down to preserve them forever.

Sounds of dinnertime floated up to Maggie. She hated what her mother cooked for dinner. It was always some recipe with a title like Elegant and Easy or Quick Casserole that she'd clipped from a magazine. Maggie listened to the sounds of plates being placed on the table, drawers opening and closing, and the *Sesame Street* theme song playing.

"Turn it off," her mother shouted. "Now!"

"No no no no no no no!" That was her little sister Kate, whom Maggie used to endure or ignore but was now starting to hate too.

It was as if Kate was just a crying lump until about a month ago. Suddenly she was this demanding little brat who wanted another story or another game or for everyone to watch her do something like a bad dance step or tell a knock knock joke. Everyone in the world thought Kate was just adorable, all curly strawberry blond hair and frilly dresses. But Maggie had liked her better before, when she did nothing but stare at a bit of light as it moved across the floor.

"Who in their right mind has their kids over ten years apart?" Maggie had asked her mother last week as the whole family sat like morons and watched Kate twirl and twirl across the living room floor like a drunken top. "I mean, this is uncivilized."

Her parents had exchanged a quick look, then turned their attention back to Kate.

"I think we have the next Dorothy Hamill here," her father had said.

"Dorothy Hamill is an ice skater," Maggie told them, disgusted. "Doesn't anyone in this family know anything at all?"

Downstairs, her mother turned off *Sesame Street* and Kate began to sing the theme song herself, screaming it, really. And her father had walked in. Maggie could picture the whole scene as if she was right down there in the middle of it. Her father with his thinning blond hair combed to disguise the fact he was going bald, and his pale blue eyes all rheumy. That was a new word she'd learned and it fit him perfectly ever since they'd gotten a cat because Kate wanted one, had to have one, even though her father was allergic. Maggie had always had pets that died easily, like goldfish and turtles and, once, a tropical bird that got pneumonia. "Non-fur types" her mother called them. But now they had a cat with the embarrassing name of Cuddles that was probably right this minute rubbing against her father because she heard him sneeze, loud.

Kate was still screaming, but now it was the words to "My Favorite Things." They'd had to watch *The Sound of Music* about a million times because Kate loved it so much, loved the mountains and all those singing children. She was probably wearing her pink ballerina outfit; she'd hardly taken it off since Halloween. Kate loved ruffles and sparkles, dainty shoes and shiny tiaras.

"God," Maggie heard her mother saying, "you're home already and the table's not even set because of course that's Maggie's job and the princess has not been downstairs since she got home from school."

Maggie jumped off her bed and stamped her feet hard. "Me? A princess?" she shouted. "Me? I don't get anything in this house except your old smelly bedroom, and no one listens to me, and I could be dead up here for days and no one would even notice I was missing!" She yelled loud, but she knew they didn't hear her because her father was having a full-fledged allergy attack, sneezing like crazy, and Kate was singing "Do, Re, Mi" even louder than she'd been singing before and her mother was banging dinner onto the table.

"I hate you!" Maggie yelled. "All of you!"

Frustrated, she looked around for something to throw or break, but all she could see was her ugly dried-up corsage. She yanked it from the wall and, without thinking, ate it, all the dead petals disintegrating on her tongue, tasting like nothing but dust.

Her mother had made enchiladas as a peace offering.

"I've already eaten," Maggie said. She had pinned the corsage ribbons to her sweater and she tugged on them from time to time, pretending they were high medals of honor.

"She hasn't," her mother said to her father. "She's been in her room all day."

"I'm here, you know," Maggie said. "You don't have to say 'she.' "

Kate was eating her enchiladas. She had on pink blush and blue eyeshadow and one of her tiaras. "These are delicious," she said, enchilada dropping from her mouth as she talked. She didn't care. She just piled more in.

"Isn't anyone going to tell her she can't talk with her mouth full?" Maggie said.

Her mother sighed and added more sour cream to her plate. Just what she didn't need, more calories. Ever since she'd had Kate she'd been looking doughy, softer and rounder, even though she went to a million aerobics classes—step and regular and even Aqua Aerobics. She almost always wore pastel sweatsuits now, to hide her weight. She kept her hair pulled up into a ponytail and was always taking Maggie's scrunchies to hold the ponytail in place. Like now, she had on one of Maggie's favorites, a yellow-and-white polka dot.

"I looked all over for that," Maggie lied, pointing to her scrunchie.

Without saying a word, her mother reached up, yanked it from her ponytail, and slid it across the table toward Maggie. Then she added still more sour cream to her dinner. Maggie imagined hot pink writing, floating in the air: BLACK HOLE, and an arrow, pointing to her mother's head.

"Why are you wearing those ribbons?" Kate asked Maggie.

Suddenly Maggie felt bad. "I didn't say you couldn't wear it," she said to her mother. "I just said I was looking for it."

"Is it for the people with AIDS?" Kate said. She had a way of making her eyes look like Frisbees, all round, practically spinning.

"What?" her father said, like he had just waked up from a dream. He managed a Caldor's at the mall and when he came home he liked to "zone out."

Kate pointed at Maggie. "Those ribbons," she said. "Are they for people with AIDS?"

Everyone looked over at Maggie, who was tugging on her corsage ribbons even more ferociously.

"Why, you smart smart girl," her mother said, and for an instant Maggie actually thought her mother was talking about her for a change. But then she went over and hugged Kate real tight. "You're right. People do wear ribbons for AIDS. But they wear red ribbons. What color does Maggie have on?"

"Blue," Kate said, squinting at Maggie, "and silver and gold."

"Yes!" her mother said. She kissed the top of Kate's head.

"Now why in the world does your big sister have on all those ribbons?"

But Kate had lost interest. She was putting her finger in the bottle of salsa and scooping some out.

"They're from my corsage," Maggie announced. "The one from the dance. I ate the dead flowers."

Her parents both stared at her.

"Why?" her father said finally.

"Because they were ugly and they were bothering me."

"But I thought you girls were saving your corsages," her mother said, looking all crumpled again.

Maggie wondered why her mother took things like this so personally. But instead of asking her, she said, "Maybe we should eat all dead things." She noticed Kate had stopped scooping salsa and was staring at her too. "Like they did in that movie *Alive.* The way the survivors ate all the victims."

"What are survivors?" Kate said.

Kate was doing that thing with her eyes, so they seemed rounder and bigger. Maggie squinted at her sister. "Survivors are the ones who live through a tragedy and victims are the ones who die."

She waited patiently while Kate processed this information. It seemed like her parents were frozen in place, forks in hands, worried frowns wrinkling their foreheads.

Kate opened her mouth, then shut it, then opened it again. When she spoke, her voice rose, all high and screechy. "And survivors *eat* victims?"

Suddenly Maggie felt very hungry. She dug into her enchiladas, nodding solemnly as she ate. They tasted perfect, even though they weren't very hot anymore. Beans—no meat—and lots of cheese, just the way she liked them.

"That was an isolated case," her mother was saying. "Faraway. In South America."

"South America?" Kate said, her voice growing still higher and screechier. "Where the Von Trapps live?"

"No, no," their mother said quickly. "The Von Trapps lived in Austria. In Europe."

"A different continent altogether," their father added.

But the more information Kate got, the more unfamiliar words they gave her, the more panicked she became. Kate, Maggie thought, was clearly not gifted.

"Do you mean," she said, "do you mean that Tiffany Butterfield ate her mother?"

Tiffany Butterfield was in Kate's kindergarten class and her mother had died in a car accident last fall.

Maggie said, "Now you understand, Kate. Tiffany was a survivor and her mother was a victim."

Kate's face turned bright red. She opened her mouth and began to wail, to scream and cry. Both of their parents jumped up and ran over to her.

"Maggie," her mother said. "Honestly."

Maggie smiled to herself. She reached over and put two more enchiladas on her plate. They had just the right amount of salsa on top, and her mother had baked them so they weren't at all mushy. Her father scooped Kate into his arms. She had made her body go real rigid, like a statue. She only did that when she was really upset, like during thunderstorms. As she watched the three of them race out of the room, her mother cooing, "Honey, people do not eat each other," Maggie finished off her second helping and reached for still one more. She thought she could eat a million bean—no meat—and cheese enchiladas.

Josie had cakes of all sizes cooling on her kitchen counter. When that was done, she would assemble them into the shape of Minnie Mouse and frost them. The different-colored frostings sat in bowls, waiting to dress Minnie—bow and shoes and ruffled dress. Sitting at her table, sipping tea, surrounded by the smell of warm chocolate cake, Josie felt as she often did—safe, like she was wrapped in a cocoon, covered with layers of carefully woven silk. From where she sat, she could see the hills of East Essex in the distance, with the river sparkling below. She could see the rough-hewn fence Will had put up years ago as a border for their property, and in front of that, a neat row of daffodils ready to bloom. Josie had planted those daffodils the autumn that Maggie was born, waiting for the first frost before she placed the bulbs in the ground. She had been overcome with the desire to put her hands in dirt, to force life from things. After the daffodils, she'd placed an herb garden in a window box and began to think about growing vegetables in a small patch of the backyard.

"Pack your bags," Aunt Tiny had told her. "That baby is ready to be born."

"Three more weeks," Josie had said, and gone back to her graph paper—the neat rows of tomatoes and lettuce she would plant.

Two days later, Maggie had been born, and Josie never did get around to the vegetable garden. But there were her daffodils, a reminder of that first year of marriage with Will, of Maggie as a baby, all serious and purposeful. Not at all like Christy, her cousin Judy's daughter, who smiled and cooed and moved rhythmically to music on the radio.

On the wall by the back door hung a homemade sign, framed in wood left over from that fence out back. The sign was of a tree, its branches curling, reaching out. And it had Josie and Will's names—William, it said—printed in fancy scroll, with Maggie on a branch beneath them, and Kate, added in just recently, across from Maggie. It was Maggie who had noticed a few summers ago that they'd never added Kate to the sign. "That says 'The Hunters', but we forgot Kate!" Maggie had said, almost delighted. But she was there now, in a different print, but there.

Josie loved this house, even though it was, she knew, nothing very special. It was part of a new development, built to seem more secluded than it actually was—set back from the road and surrounded by trees. She and Will had bought it right before they'd graduated from college, had fallen in love with this blue-and-white kitchen, the sloping barn-like roof, the small stone fireplace in the den. From time to time, after Kate was born, Will said they should move. "We need more space," he'd say.

"Step outside and take a deep breath if you need space," Josie told him. "I'm not going anywhere."

"Yeah," Maggie would mumble under her breath. "Take a deep breath and gag."

"Say the word," Will always told Josie, "and we'll move."

But she knew he didn't really want to leave this house either.

Josie rotated her wedding ring around her finger. It had tightened over the years. At first, she used to take it off and reread the inscription: MORE THAN YESTERDAY . . . LESS THAN TOMORROW. Back then it had seemed daring to get white gold rather than yellow. She smiled. Even though she couldn't easily remove the ring to reread what was carved inside, she knew it was there. Sitting here like this made her feel guilty that just yesterday she'd been thinking about her life as a flat line. Her mother was right. Thrills were for roller coasters.

Josie knew Will better than she knew anyone else in the world. They had been together since they were freshmen in college, had lost their virginity with each other two years later at Phi Sigma Kappa with a party raging one floor below them, both of them nervous, afraid Will's roommate would wander in, or that they would somehow do this thing, this fumbling and moving, all wrong. Above them hung a sign that said, PHI SIGS MAKE THE BEST LOVERS, left over from years before. The Eagles sang "Best of My Love" while the actual sex went on. Only Josie was aware of that, though. She had sung the words to herself while Will moved almost frantically on top of her. The song had soothed her, kept her from thinking about what was really happening, kept her from wondering why she didn't like this as much as her roommates did. When she peeked at Will, he had looked ridiculous, his face scrunched up like he was in pain. She felt relieved when his face finally twisted into an even bigger grimace and he let out a noise that reminded her of the way their family dog Fritz had sounded when he got hit by a Chevy a few years earlier.

She had never really changed her mind about sex. It still seemed silly, and sometimes she still thought about Fritz when Will came. Whenever her friends complained that their husbands wanted too much sex, or not enough, Josie just sat there, listening. She and Will had settled into a routine of sorts, making love once or twice a week on a lazy Sunday morning or an occasional weeknight after the news, during Jay Leno's monologue. He had long ago stopped twisting her into odd positions, insisting they try this or that. There was something almost pleasant about their lovemaking, the way their bodies fit together.

But her friends imagined that she and Will had a great sex life, something wild, even. "Look at her," her cousin Denise would always say, "she's so smug."

Josie would just smile and nod. She wasn't about to tell anyone that most times, during sex, she planned menus, dinners that would satisfy her whole family and still contain something from each of the four food groups.

Suddenly the room grew dark and a hard rain began to fall, startling Josie so much that she jumped up, banging her knee and spilling tea everywhere. Earlier, she had gone from room to room, opening the windows to let in the warm spring air. Now, rain splattered the counters, the cakes cooling there, even the floor. Josie pulled the windows shut, then ran into each room, mopping up the wet sills, closing those windows too.

Upstairs, Maggie lay on the bed, her eyes closed, a Walkman blasting in her ears. She hummed along with the music, a tune Josie could faintly hear but could not make out. The last time she'd asked Maggie what she was listening to, she'd answered Smashing Pumpkins and Josie could not think of anything more to say.

"It's pouring out," Josie said loudly. "The rain was coming in the windows, onto the floor."

Maggie didn't answer her, pretended not to hear at all.

Josie stood over her a moment longer, looking at her daughter's long legs, her thin hips and small breasts. Maggie was built like her aunt. Even though they did not look alike, Josie couldn't help but think of her sister Michaela whenever she got to study Maggie this way.

"I closed them," Josie told her. "It's under control."

Back downstairs, Kate was singing along with *The Sound of Music.* She was just outgrowing a babyish lisp, just losing her baby fat. She too would be thin and tall, Josie thought. She stood in the doorway to the den and watched as the Von Trapp family sang together, happily. Josie had stopped telling Kate not to sit so close to the television. She had stopped worrying about dangerous rays coming through it and zapping her children's blood or ovaries. Josie remembered how the pediatrician had laughed at her when she'd called to ask if six-month-old Maggie could eat table food. Wait until your second one, he'd told her. She'll be eating pizza right after she's born. It was funny how you relaxed into this mothering. Into life, really, Josie thought.

Kate sat there, her face only a few inches from the screen, singing loud. Josie looked around the room. In the corner was the brown corduroy beanbag chair she had made for Will's twentieth birthday. The sofa, worn now, was the first one they'd bought. It had large flowers on it, in autumn colors, and a matching chair that Josie still loved to curl up in to read. She couldn't imagine ever leaving this house. Ever.

That was when she remembered. Her parents were selling their house. The thought made her bend over slightly and hug herself tight. Even though she still had balloons to blow up and the cake to frost, Josie went back into the kitchen and ran her finger down the list of numbers on the pad that hung beside the wall phone. The pad said: PEOPLE WE LIKE TO CALL on top. It used to have a pen dangling from a string attached to it, but the pen was long gone, and Maggie had taken to slowly unraveling the string whenever she talked on this phone, so that it looked like a web coming undone.

Josie's finger stopped at her sister's number in San Francisco, and she punched it in without thinking about what she might say. The copper kitchen clock shaped like a teapot said four-twenty. Only one-twenty in California. While the phone rang, Josie tried to imagine what Michaela might be doing. She had never visited her in the San Francisco apartment. But she had been to see her in Berkeley years ago. That apartment had smelled of incense and pot and laundry that needed washing. There was an Indian bedspread draped across the ceiling, empty jugs of wine covered with melted candle wax scattered everywhere, and a mattress on the floor. Even though that had been almost twenty years ago, Josie still imagined her sister living that way, unkempt and disorganized.

She stopped counting how many times the phone had rung, but clearly Michaela was not home. Josie moved to hang up the phone, then heard her sister's voice.

"Hello?" Michaela was saying.

Josie frowned, her eyes drifting toward the clock above the sink again. Michaela sounded half-asleep, or stoned, or both. At one-thirty in the afternoon.

"Hey," Josie said, forcing her own voice to be perky and clear. "It's your long-lost sister."

"Oh," Michaela said. "Um . . . qué pasa?"

Josie heard her sister shifting, moving about. Before she could answer, Michaela said, "I've . . . uh . . . got someone here. Can I call you back?"

"Of course," Josie said. The false brightness in her voice made her wince. "No problem." Then she added, "A new beau?" and winced again. Beau? It was just the sort of word Michaela would think she used. But, really, she never did. It sounded ridiculous.

"Uh," Michaela said again. "Sort of."

Josie decided she was definitely high on something, her voice all thick and confused.

"Well, great!" Josie said. "Terrific."

But Michaela was already trying to hang up. Josie heard the receiver slide from its cradle, a short ding when it hit, then it slipped into place, firmly.

What had she been thinking? Josie wondered. Michaela had not even been home in years. She rarely returned phone calls, never wrote. The last time she'd been home was for Christmas five years ago, when Josie was pregnant with Kate, all swollen and heavy. Still, she'd had to drive Michaela around all day on Christmas Eve, shopping. "Couldn't you have bought gifts in San Francisco?" she'd asked. "Couldn't you have been prepared for once?" They had fought and bickered so much that by the time Michaela finally left, Josie was relieved.

Their cousins Judy and Denise had hostessed a party for Michaela, an open house, with all of Michaela's classmates drifting in and out. But she had sat in a corner, sullen, drunk. She had made a spectacle of herself finally, stumbling into people, knocking into the Christmas tree and breaking some of Judy's special handblown ornaments, the ones she had bought at a craft store in Vermont. Josie remembered how, as she'd helped Michaela to her feet, carefully removing slivers of glass from the palms of her hands, she'd looked at Judy and Denise and wished she and her sister could be more like them.

On the way to the airport, she'd told Michaela that, too. She'd used that word—spectacle. "Must you always make a spectacle of yourself?" she'd said. She was aware how much she sounded like their grandmother, their mother's mother who, despite a penchant for illegal gambling, liked to quote Emily Post and practiced her elocution every morning after she did twenty deep knee bends. Josie tried to relax her own speech. "Can't you be like Judy and Denise? Normal?" she said.

But what she had meant, she supposed now, was couldn't *we* be like them, hostessing Christmas parties, wrapping gifts together, sharing hairdressers, pediatricians, clothes. On that ride to the airport, and at other times when Josie had felt frightened by things happening around her, she calmed herself by remembering that *her* family—she and Will and Maggie and Kate—was like that. They lived an orderly, controlled life. Josie found herself remembering her grandmother again. Every morning she drank a special herb tea, designed to get her bowels moving. Every evening she allowed herself a small glass of apricot brandy. Well, Josie told herself, our life isn't *that* ordered.

The rain fell hard and fast. The basement would flood if this kept up, Josie knew. It was the one flaw of the house, a basement that filled too easily with water. Will had put in a sump pump, but still, in very hard rain, it couldn't keep up. Almost five o'clock and Josie hadn't even started dinner. They would go to Angelo's for pizza, she decided. A treat. Even Maggie liked pizza at Angelo's, liked feeding quarters into the jukebox and going up to the counter to pick up Will's mug of beer. She lip-synched along with Tony Bennett and Frank Sinatra, hamming it up like a lounge singer with a napkin on her head for a fedora and a straw dangling between her lips for a cigarette.

They would go out and have fun together, Josie thought. She imagined Maggie performing "My Way," and Kate spinning in circles until she got dizzy and walked crookedly back to the table, and Will's arm thrown across her shoulders in a familiar hug as they watched their children. Yes. They would go to Angelo's. But even though the idea of it made her feel a little better, something still nagged at Josie, something she couldn't quite place, that wouldn't go away.

It was a Friday night ritual that Will had come to dread—all his old fraternity brothers meeting for beers at Twin Willows, the same bar they used to go to in college. Lately he'd been ordering Corona with lime and they had started to call him Pepe.

"This is a good news bad news joke, Pepe," Ron Blakely said as soon as Will sat down at the bar and ordered.

Will hated listening to jokes. What he wanted was to have a conversation, to really talk to someone who would listen. The guys were several beers ahead of him, slightly red-faced, talking too loud.

"Moses comes back from a conversation with God and he tells his people—"

"I heard this already," Grady said, already laughing. "This is good."

"Is this about the commandments?" Frank said. He was

laughing too. "I told it to Brenda and she said that it was blasphemy and I should tell the priest when I went to confession. I swear that's what she said."

"If everybody's heard it," Will said, "don't repeat it on my account."

"So Moses says, 'I've got good news and bad news,' " Ron said. " 'The good news is, I've got Him down to ten commandments. The bad news is, adultery is still in!' "

Will forced a smile and finished his beer in one long gulp.

"I love it," Grady was saying. "Adultery is still in!"

Will Hunter did not know when he stopped loving his wife. Like most of the things that changed in his life, it had probably happened gradually. All he knew for sure was that he did not love her anymore, not even a little, not like a sister or a friend and definitely not like a wife. He stayed with her for all the wrong reasons—out of laziness, for security, for the kids; because they had promised to do this (they had promised to be faithful too, and to love, honor, and cherish—he hadn't kept those promises, had he?); for those earlier years when just the sight of her made him happy—in her khakis and bright green turtleneck and snowflake sweater, coming toward him, smiling, the cold sun of a winter day behind her or, later, another winter day, pregnant and off balance walking in the door with snow in her hair, short of breath and red-faced from cold and pregnancy, or kneeling in the garden, dirt-splattered jeans, hair mussed, the tip of her nose sunburned, all of those days, those times when he would see her and his breath would catch and he would think to himself, oh, Josie. He stayed with her because an even smaller part of him hoped he might love her again someday, even though he did not, at all, love her now. What he loved now were other women. He knew he had it ass backwards. While all his buddies in college were sleeping with different women every Saturday night, he was already settled in with Josie. He should have been doing it then, noticing the certain sway of one woman's hips, the ripple in another's hair, the way one stood with her lips parted invitingly, how one's voice rose like musical scales and another's practically whispered.

At first, he kept it at that. Noticing. He tucked each detail away so that when he and Josie made love he could recall something—a glimpse of breast in a shirt unbuttoned too low or a slice of silver earring dangling against a bare neck—that would drive him forward. His orgasms, he noticed, were stronger when he thought of other women.

"Do you ever," he asked Josie one night after sex, "imagine I'm someone else?"

He felt her body stiffen.

"I mean," he stumbled, "during sex."

She had often told him this part—the lying together all sticky and close afterwards—was her favorite part. That had bothered him. He liked the actual sex, plunging into her, moving inside, the building up to something.

"Like who?" she finally answered.

He closed his eyes and recalled his latest fantasy, a saleswoman at Nine West in the mall. She was small and slight, but teetered around the mall on very high heels, like a child playing dress-up. He had never seen someone so flat-chested naked. Her skin was very pink. She had freckles on her arms and cheeks; he found himself wondering if they were other places too. And those high heels! Stilettos, really. Spikes. In college they had called them come-fuck-me pumps. Tonight he had imagined her beneath him, still wearing those shoes, the heels digging into his back.

"Are you telling me that's what you do?" Josie was saying. She had sat up and seemed to be looming over him. "While we're making love?"

Will thought she might be crying.

"No!" he said, too emphatically.

"You are. You're thinking of someone else." She was definitely crying now.

"It's just a question," Will said. He knew he sounded defensive.

She took a deep breath. "Okay," she said. "Do you mean like somebody famous? Like Claudia Schiffer or somebody?"

"Yeah," Will said, relieved.

Josie settled back down, her head on his shoulder. "Once I had a dream that I had sex with Mel Gibson," she whispered.

"Really?" Will said, repulsed by her ordinariness, her predictability. He imagined the woman from Nine West, her tawny hair spilling across his chest. It was long and straight and thick. Sometimes she wore it in a braid that fell down her back.

Josie's elbow poked his rib, sharp and hard.

"What?" he said.

"I said who have you imagined."

"Jackie Kennedy," Will said without thinking.

Josie laughed. "Jackie Kennedy? Really?"

He closed his eyes and imagined unbraiding the Nine West woman's hair, uncoiling it while she sat on top of him, naked except those shoes, letting it spill down her shoulders and back.

One night when Will and Josie were out to dinner with her cousins and their husbands, paying too much money for mediocre food, her cousin Denise's husband James ordering expensive French wine and making a big ordeal out of sniffing the cork and swirling the wine around in his glass, Will saw the Nine West woman at another table with three women. She was all dressed up in something pink and fuzzy—mohair. He watched her study the menu, watched her nose wrinkle at something someone said. He got a hard-on just looking at her.

"These are legs," James explained, tracing the rivulets of wine that clung to the glass. "This wine has excellent legs," he said. His idea of a joke. "And a fine bouquet."

Will reached under the table for Josie's hand and placed it over his erection. She pulled back.

"What is wrong with you?" she said sharply.

Everyone looked away from the glass that James was offering for them to sniff, and at Will.

"Nothing," he said.

From behind clenched teeth Josie whispered, "We're in a restaurant, you know."

He couldn't think of a reply. Instead, he drank too much of the expensive wine and watched the Nine West woman eat her salmon. Later, at home, Josie accused him of gaping at a woman dressed in pink. He was too drunk to argue. All he could do was close his eyes and struggle to remember why, when he was only twenty years old, he had wanted to get married. What was his rush? What had he been thinking? What exactly had he expected to come of it?

Will allowed himself one more beer. Ever since he had stopped merely noticing other women and started sleeping with them, he had learned the pleasures of delayed gratification. He would sit here and have another beer with the guys and pretend to be listening to them, to their reminiscences, their jokes, their complaints, while really he was anticipating the woman he would be meeting in half an hour. He had never actually slept with the woman from Nine West. One day, she was gone. She stopped working there and he never saw her again. But somehow she had motivated him to stop daydreaming and act on his fantasies. That was five years ago, and he had lost count of how many women he had brought into his office after hours, bent over the desk, and had sex with. Or driven to meet on a Friday night while the other guys stayed at Twin Willows until closing.

"Hey," Grady said, "remember Pete Moto?"

"Motown!" Ron said.

"Yeah," Will said, "what about him?" He took a small sip of his beer and wondered what Bonnie was doing right now. Probably in bed, waiting. He had told her he'd be there around ten, and it was a quarter till now. She had already shaved her legs and sprayed her perfume behind her knees and inside her thighs. She had already rolled a joint for them to smoke when he got there.

"He's some fucking big shot at IBM in New York," Grady said. "I ran into him at Aunt Carrie's getting fucking clam cakes. And get this. He's with this knockout blonde, driving a fucking Porsche."

Will felt a twang of envy. You idiot, he told himself. While he was planning his wedding, studying swatches of lavender lace for bridesmaids' dresses and lists of hors d'oeuvres, Pete Moto had been flying around the country interviewing with AT&T and IBM. Pete Moto had been getting fitted for three-piece suits.

"What a douche bag," Ron mumbled. He had spilled some beer on his jeans and it looked like he'd pissed his pants.

Will stood up, dropped some money on the bar.

"Leaving so soon, Pepe?" Grady said.

"Man," Ron said, "are you whipped or what?"

Will shrugged. Fucking Pete Moto, he thought. Driving a Porsche.

■ ■ ■

"You smell like you've been smoking pot," Josie said when Will slipped into bed beside her.

"I was."

"What's wrong with you guys anyway?" she said. "Aren't you a little old for this stuff?"

He didn't answer her. Instead, he settled into the pleasant buzz in his groin and his brain. He wished he didn't have to leave Bonnie. She was the first woman in these five years of other women that he found himself missing. Even though he saw her every day at work. Even though he managed to spend these Friday nights with her. Sometimes he worried that he would give up everything for her—his wife, his house, everything.

"With Maggie the way she is, it's probably an especially bad example," Josie said.

It wasn't just the sex, he decided as he lay there. It was her cool exterior, her efficiency. Josie seemed to him disorganized, overly cheerful, placid. Bonnie was a cynic and he found himself enjoying her view of things.

"Will?" Josie said. "I'm serious."

"I had one little joint," he said.

"We went to Angelo's," she said brightly, without missing a beat. She was a pro at avoiding confrontation.

Will turned on his side, away from her. Maybe there was a way he could spend an entire weekend with Bonnie. It would be like a test. To see how dangerous his feelings for her were. How real.

"Did Ron tell you Cathy's pregnant again?" Josie said to Will's back.

"Again?" Will mumbled. Ron and Cathy were always getting accidentally pregnant.

"What would you do if that happened to us?"

"You're not, are you?" he said, trying to sound calm.

"Don't sound so excited," Josie said, hurt.

Will wondered how many hours of his life he'd spent appeasing Josie, comforting her. He sighed.

"Great," she said. "Now you're sighing."

"I lied," he said, not turning toward her. "We smoked a lot of pot. I'm kind of fucked up."

"Is that any way for grown men to act?" she said, and he could tell she was relieved.

It was a sore topic between them. Josie knew he hadn't been thrilled when she got pregnant with Kate. That was right after they'd decided not to go to Arizona. For months afterward he'd still imagined himself there, in the dry, unfamiliar heat. He didn't know if they had adobe houses there, but that's what he pretended he lived in. And then Josie had put blue booties under his pillow one night as a cute way to break the news. Somehow it was all tied up together—not taking the promotion, not moving to Arizona, Josie pregnant, and the woman from Nine West.

Josie slipped her arm around him and by habit he took her hand. She kept her nails short, filed square, unpolished. He had to guide them to his penis, his balls, when they were making love. She never touched him there without some help.

"Remember Pete Moto?" Will blurted.

"Kind of skinny?" Josie said. "Went out with a DZ?"

"He's some big shot at IBM now," Will said.

"That's good." She sounded sleepy.

What had he been thinking? Will asked himself. All those years ago when he'd gone through the motions of someone in love, when he'd actually, foolishly, gotten down on one knee in the parking lot of Twin Willows and asked Josie to marry him?

"He's not married," Will said.

But he could tell from his wife's breathing that she had fallen asleep.

■ ■ ■

Maggie and her best friend Stephanie were at the mall, looking at boys and CD's and funny cards in the new card store. It was, Maggie decided as Stephanie unfolded a card to reveal a naked muscled guy, another boring Saturday. Her life was like a flat line on one of those heart machines they always showed in soap operas. First the machine jumped and beeped in nice, even rhythms, then it changed to one loud monotone and a straight, unwavering line. In one of her gifted classes—Creative Writing—they had learned all about metaphor, and Maggie decided that heart monitor was a perfect metaphor for her life. For the longest time it had progressed in nice, even rhythms, and now it was totally flat.

Stephanie was giggling and blushing beside her. The store was too hot, and smelled like fake strawberries. "God," Stephanie whispered, "look at his thing."

Maggie rolled her eyes and glanced down. The unfolded man stared up at her. He wore just a bow tie, and some kind of oil that made his body shine. His thing was long and smooth like a sausage.

"So?" Maggie said, and moved away to read the sayings on some coffee mugs.

"So?" Stephanie said, coming up beside her. "So someday one of those is going inside you." Stephanie had gotten a bad perm, and her hair flew out all around her head in tight banana curls. Lately, she'd started to wear too much eye makeup and it made her contacts bother her so that her eyes were always red and watery. Rheumy, Maggie thought as she looked at her. Everyone she knew had rheumy eyes.

"Want to get some ice cream?" Stephanie said.

Maggie shrugged. "I guess."

Stephanie had been her best friend forever, but Maggie

couldn't figure out why. She was silly and not very smart. In class, if the teacher called on her, she looked completely blank, like a piece of paper. When she was bored, she wrote haikus on her hands. Maggie thought haikus were stupid.

On their way to Newport Creamery, Stephanie linked her arm through Maggie's. When Maggie tried to move away, Stephanie said, "What's the matter? You think we look gay?" It was easier to just indulge her, Maggie thought.

They passed The Gap and Express, a blur of colors and SALE signs. Stephanie tried to slow down, but Maggie kept moving. It sounded like all Stephanie was saying was "I want that sweater I want those pants I want that jacket." Maggie was getting a headache.

Then she saw him. A new boy. Someone completely different. A stranger. She stopped walking completely.

"Who is that?" she said. She imagined he was from somewhere exotic and faraway. Barcelona, maybe. Or New Zealand.

"Miles Somebody," Stephanie said. "He's new."

Miles Somebody. No one around here was named Miles. They all had boring names like Michael or David. Or tacky names like Brett or Justin. Her grandmother called them nouveau names. But Miles was a completely different name. He must be from somewhere exotic. He had a shock of hair that fell over one eye. Blond hair. And even from here Maggie could tell that his eyes were blue-green, like some faraway sea. His eyes were not at all rheumy. He was tall, taller than the other boys he was with. And he leaned casually against the wall, his arms folded. But the best thing of all was that he looked absolutely, one hundred per cent bored.

"Finally," Stephanie said, "a reaction." She had dropped Maggie's arm and was standing right in front of her.

Maggie looked down. Her friend was a full head shorter than her, and all those tight curls made her look like she had when they were little. Suddenly Maggie liked Stephanie again.

She got a swift image of her back when they were in elementary school and used to always sleep over each other's house on Friday nights. They had matching footie pajamas, yellow ones dotted with white roses, and they would sleep molded together, knee to knee, stomach to back, arms linked.

"Ice cream," Maggie said, and grabbed Stephanie's arm, spinning her like they were doing a square dance.

When Maggie got home, her mother and Kate were making a map of Europe out of colored rice. Everyone was mad at her, but she didn't care. That morning, her mother had come into her room and said, "Christy has called you three times and you haven't called her back. What is wrong with you?" Then she had stood there waiting for an answer, but Maggie had not given her one. Instead, she sat on her bed and painted each fingernail and toenail a different color. "Why do you want to look peculiar?" her mother had said before she walked out.

Now Maggie went and gave her mother a big kiss on the cheek. "Hello, Mommie Dearest," she said.

She even kissed Kate, a quick one somewhere in the vicinity of her ear. Kate smacked at her like she was swatting a fly.

Maggie got an apple out of the fruit bowl on the counter, then stood behind her mother, peering over her shoulder. All those exotic countries loomed before her in bright Easter egg colors. Hungary, France, Czechoslovakia. Places where boys with names like Miles lived, leaning against ancient walls, brushing the hair from their eyes with a casual motion.

"This is Europe," Kate said. "People don't eat each other there."

"Or anywhere," their mother added, filling in Germany with mint green rice. "Except in very extreme circumstances."

Kate nodded. "Very, very extreme. Right?"

Her mother looked over her shoulder at Maggie. "Are you happy now?" she said sternly.

"Yes," Maggie said, and went upstairs.

Her mother's voice followed her. "Don't lose yourself up there. We're going to Angelo's for dinner."

Maggie kept the lights off so her sky would glow. It used to glow brightly, but it was fading now. She took down her pompoms and shook them. The black and yellow streamers seemed pathetic somehow, and Maggie felt embarrassed by them. Embarrassed by the fact that she actually ran around in broad daylight shaking these stupid things, screaming, "Bzzzzzzz . . . the bees are gonna sting ya . . . bzzzzzzzz . . ." How would someone like Miles feel about someone like her? she wondered. A cheerleader. She remembered how powerful she used to feel in her short skirt and the sweater with the big double E's on it. She used to do the best cartwheels, the highest jumps. Would Miles admire a skill like that? Probably not. He probably liked girls with throaty voices who didn't shave their legs. Girls who talked philosophy and literature. Girls who were atheists. Or maybe that was why he looked so bored. Maybe he wanted a cheerleader. Someone with good strong legs who could flip themselves in the air and still land on their feet.

"Maggie," her mother yelled up to her. "We're ready."

Then Kate shouted, "We're starving!"

Maggie waited for her mother's reprimand, her reminder that they were far from starving, hadn't Kate had a delicious lunch? Starving was what happened in Somalia or Bosnia. Not in East Essex. Not in the Hunter house. But instead of a lesson in humanity like Maggie would have gotten, they were down there playing a game. "I can eat seven pizzas with elephant and olives and daffodils!" "Oh, yeah? Well I can eat ten with pumpkins and Volkswagens!"

Slowly Maggie made her way through her dark room, stepping over the Doc Martens she'd had to beg for last fall, over a pile of schoolbooks, her heap of discarded clothes.

"Oh, yeah?" she whispered. "I can eat twenty pizzas. I can eat all the survivors."

In the doorway she paused and did a slow languorous split. She lifted her arms above her head. "Miles, Miles, he's our man," she whispered. "If he can't do it, no one can."

Claire Jericho first heard about it on *20/20.* Her daughter Josie had been visiting, had stayed late because Will was out somewhere with his friends. When Barbara Walters introduced the segment on Alzheimer's, Josie had stood up and left, mumbling something about leaving Maggie in charge too long. But Claire had sat and watched, even when a frightening numbing spread through her, chilling her. They showed all these people in a special home for Alzheimer's disease, wandering about confused. They showed women who could not recognize their own children, men who thought they were back in the war. During the entire segment, Claire had sat rigid, watching the look on those poor faces, a look that seemed too familiar. She could hear Dan, moving around down in the basement. He would come upstairs and say something that frightened her. "Where are the girls?" he might ask. "Isn't it awful late for them to be out?" Or he might ask her why she was wearing her hair that way, even though she'd worn the same style since 1985. Or she might turn to see him wandering the kitchen as if he was lost, as if he'd never been there before.

The reporter interviewed Rita Hayworth's daughter, the one she'd had with the Aga Khan. "People thought my mother was a drunk," the daughter had said. Claire sat up even straighter when she heard that. It was what people were asking her about Dan. Has he started drinking? they asked her. He seems so confused. And then, just when Claire talked herself out of it, just when she decided Dan was too young for such a thing, Barbara Walters asked the reporter if this was something that only struck old people. "That's the saddest part," the reporter said, shaking his head. "It can strike people in their forties." "That is sad," Barbara Walters had said. Claire did not really trust Barbara Walters. But she liked the reporter, a good-looking man with a mustache who once did a segment on stuttering, a problem he himself suffered from.

It was a mother's instinct to wake frightened when a telephone rang in the middle of the night. But Claire Jericho no longer worried that it was one of her daughters in trouble, or hurt in a hospital somewhere, or worse. Now, it was her husband whom she feared for. At the sound of the telephone interrupting her sleep, she reached first to the place where he slept beside her for over forty years, and then for the phone. In the past few months, Claire had been awakened more times than she cared to remember by police and Good Samaritans who had found Dan wandering around. She'd had to throw on her coat over her nightgown and stumble into the night, her car lurching hesitantly forward as if it wasn't quite awake either.

But this time, when the phone rang and her hand shot out instinctively toward Dan, she found him right there beside her where he was supposed to be. Dan always slept on the side near the window, even when they were away from home. He always hung his towel on the left, took bottom drawers in dressers. These were the small things that people worked out in marriages. Lately, they had become more important, a system that surpassed convenience. Now they helped Dan remember. Claire had taken to arranging everything—toothpaste and floss and mouthwash in a small plastic basket labeled TEETH, a small Post-it on the silverware drawer that read UTENSILS, his own bureau drawer of socks and undershirts and boxer shorts had an UNDERWEAR sign on it. The medicine chest, with its jumble of old unfinished prescriptions and emergency items like Ipecac and Benedryl left over from Michaela's allergy to bee stings, now simply had KEEP OUT written across it in red lipstick, the way lovers in the movies scrawled messages to each other.

Claire reached over her husband to answer the phone. Knowing he was safe, the next thing that popped into her mind was Michaela. She never worried that something would happen to Josie. Josie stayed put, used her seat belt, looked both ways before she crossed a street. Josie was like Claire, steady and reliable.

"Mom?" Michaela's voice was shouting as soon as Claire answered, before she even got to say hello. There was music in the background, the strong thump of a bass.

At least, Claire thought, she was all right. She was making the call herself. She was some place where people were dancing.

"I'm in New York," Michaela shouted. "Can you hear me?"

"Yes," Claire answered, waiting for the bad news. She took New York as a sign that something was wrong. And Claire believed in signs, in the importance of small things, like the appearance of a blue jay in her yard or an itchy palm of her hand. Ever since their long-ago family trip there—the last trip they ever took as a family, Claire realized—New York meant bad news to her.

"I'm on my way home," Michaela said. "Should be there by the end of the week."

It was funny how, at night, familiar objects took on strange shapes. A chair could become threatening. A bathrobe tossed over a doorknob seemed almost spectral. And a daughter returning home took on strange possibilities. In the morning, Claire told herself, this would seem like good news. In the morning, she would feel happy.

"Mom?" Michaela was saying. "Can you hear me?"

"Why didn't you tell me you were planning a visit?" Claire asked her.

Michaela laughed. "It's not a visit," she said. "I'm coming home."

Beside her, Dan stirred, mumbled. He used to make car deals in his sleep, discuss the value of a trade-in, the cost of the monthly payments, quote *Consumer Reports.* Now he just mumbled gibberish, things Claire could not understand.

"Well," she said to her daughter, "what news to get in the middle of the night." She could feel the warmth of Dan's back. When they slept spoon-fashion, she used to press her cheek to that back and soak up its warmth. Dan smelled like spring, like things about to bloom.

There was a click, then another, and then they were disconnected. Michaela had probably run out of change. Claire did not hold on to see if her daughter would come back on. She just hung up the phone and settled back onto her side of the bed.

Dan mumbled again.

"What?" Claire asked him.

She propped herself onto one elbow, facing him in the dark. His form looked strange, too, and she reached out and rested her hand lightly on his back, between his shoulder blades, to remind herself he was someone familiar.

"What?" she said again.

He sighed, moved away from her touch.

Lately, she found herself testing Dan, whispering trivia questions to him, afraid of his response but unable to keep herself from asking. When is our anniversary? How do you get to Josie's from here? What is my maiden name? She tested him now.

"I have a 1985 LTD," Claire said. "Eighty thousand miles.

New tires. What will you give me for it?" Dan had been the top salesman at Reikel Ford for eleven straight years. A record.

She waited, and when he did not answer, she said, "Dan? What will you give me for that car?"

"Lizzie Fratelli," he said. "That's who."

Slowly, Claire lowered herself onto her side. So far, she had kept her head above all this. Many times she had thought of that Rudyard Kipling poem they'd had to memorize back in eighth grade English. *If you can keep your head when all about you are losing theirs . . .* But now Claire wondered what the benefit was of keeping her head, of not breaking down. Lizzie Fratelli was someone Dan had a crush on in junior high. A tall girl with two long black braids that hung down her back and a slight limp from a bout with polio. She had moved away the summer before high school, to Oklahoma or Kansas, and Claire had not thought about her since. When school started again that September, Dan Jericho had walked up to her locker, taken her books from her arms, and led her down the hall to Civics class. They had been together ever since.

Now he was talking about Lizzie Fratelli, someone almost forgotten to Claire. Someone gone from Dan's life for half a century. Yet just this afternoon when Josie dropped off Kate, Dan had frowned and said, "Who's this little girl? A friend of Michaela's?" "Grandpa," Kate had said, laughing, "don't be so silly." He'd laughed too. "Right-o," he'd said, but the look of confusion did not leave his face for a long time.

Claire took long, slow breaths, the kind Josie swore had helped to relax her during labor. "A cleansing breath," she'd explained, demonstrating, "then deep in, deep out." After three, Claire did feel a bit calmer. She sat and nudged Dan.

"Huh?" he said.

"Wake up," Claire told him. She poked his arm, his back.

"What?" he said, struggling to wake up.

"Who is Lizzie Fratelli?" Claire demanded.

"Lizzie? Rings a bell," Dan said. He sat up, yawned. "That little girl with the limp? The one from a million years ago?"

Relief flooded Claire. It was just a dream, she told herself. A funny dream. Nothing more. Didn't Beatrice always tell her she watched too many news programs, *60 Minutes* and the like? "You watch one about lead in some family's water out in Pennsylvania and you think you've got lead in your water," Beatrice had said. And she was right. It was like those old doctor shows on television years ago. If an episode of *Marcus Welby* had a woman with a brain tumor, everyone went around thinking they had headaches and double vision.

"You were calling her name," Claire told Dan.

"Well," he said, sighing, easing himself back into sleep, "you know how weird dreams are. One minute you're in your kitchen and the next you're sitting up on top of a tree. With no idea how you got there. And there's fifty or so strangers with you. And you don't even wonder how that one flimsy branch is holding everyone up."

Claire frowned. Was he babbling? she wondered. Or making sense? Dreams were like that. Confusing. Out of sequence. But kitchens and trees and fifty strangers? That sounded crazy to her. That was why dreams bothered her so much. Nothing in them fit. "You're such a Virgo," Michaela used to tell her. "Even your dreams have to be in order."

"Is that what you were dreaming?" Claire whispered. "Was Lizzie Fratelli up in that tree?"

But Dan just snorted, and pulled the blankets around him tighter.

Once, Claire had a dream in which everyone from her third grade class had appeared in some way. Awake, she wouldn't have been able to name them all, to remember their faces. But in that dream she recalled each and every one—Stanley Kozinsky who smelled of cabbage, Jimmy DiPadua with the bright red hair and long droopy ears, Cynthia Terranova who, at eight, already had large breasts. When Claire had told her sisters that dream, trying to sort out how she could remember people she thought she'd forgotten, and why she'd given them adult occupations—Cynthia was a druggist and Jimmy a motorcycle policeman—and why in the world was she driving through town in a cement mixer, Tiny and Beatrice had only shouted, "Play 661!"

"But it makes no sense," Claire had said, again and again, shaking her head, trying to make sense of it.

Tiny and Beatrice had played 661, and each had won two hundred and fifty dollars when it came out. But Claire had forgotten to play anything at all. Instead, she'd worried about how she could possibly even imagine herself driving a truck of any kind, why those particular people had those particular jobs.

A Virgo, Claire told herself now. Michaela had done her chart once for Christmas, and even Claire had to admit she fit the profile. Methodical, punctual, pays attention to detail. Analytical. Would make a good accountant. She was good with numbers. She always balanced her checkbook down to the penny. She always got A's in math, even geometry and algebra.

Dan mumbled again, and Claire felt herself grow tense. Slowly she moved toward him, pressed her front against his back, dipped her knees into the hollow behind his, and waited. But nothing happened. He was asleep, unaware. Claire rested her cheek on his back and breathed in. She smelled rain. Was it really him, she wondered, or just the breeze from the open window?

Kate always woke up first. She poured herself some Cheerios and ate them in front of the television. When Maggie was a kid, her television time was limited. One hour a day, period. But here it was, not even seven in the morning, and already

Maggie could hear the television blaring downstairs. She knew, too, that Kate would sit there watching until someone turned it off, which could be hours from now.

At seven-thirty, Maggie stormed downstairs. Kate was sitting about six inches from the TV, watching an evangelist shout about Jesus while she ate her Cheerios, dry, no milk.

"Some people," Maggie said, "are sleeping."

Without even looking at her, Kate said, "Not me. It's my party today."

"You are watching junk. Your mind is going to rot and shrivel."

Kate frowned, but Maggie thought it was at something the evangelist said. Frustrated, Maggie went back upstairs. Her parents' bedroom door was closed. She knew what that meant. With her luck, they'd end up with another baby. She kicked the door lightly as she passed. "Perverts," she muttered.

She did manage to go back to sleep, by putting two pillows over her head and reciting multiplication tables. She had read somewhere that doing math kept you from thinking about other stuff.

It was Kate who woke her up again. Only this time it was after ten, and Kate crawled right in bed with Maggie, pressing her cold feet against her and whispering, "Don't you want pancakes?"

"You were not invited in here," Maggie said. She kept the pillows on her face. Recently she had told Kate that she could only come in her room if she had a specific invitation.

As usual, Kate ignored her. She wrapped her arms around Maggie and snuggled. "Do you have a boyfriend?" Kate said, still whispering.

Maggie groaned. "Go away."

"I have a boyfriend. Michael Jackson."

"Right," Maggie said. She thought about the new boy, Miles. He was too cool. That's what Stephanie had told her on the phone last night. She'd said it like it was a bad thing. Maggie used to think she was cool, but now she wasn't sure. She felt like a weirdo.

"Michael Jackson wants to marry me," Kate was saying. "He gave me this." She thrust her hand under the top pillow, right into Maggie's face.

Maggie wondered what exactly Kate did that made her hands eternally sticky. There, on the ring finger, was a mood ring, set in pink plastic.

"Where did you get that?" Maggie said, emerging from the pillows and pulling herself away from Kate.

"Michael Jackson," Kate said. She looked down at the ring. "I already told you." She held the ring up, right in Maggie's face again. "Is that blue? Or green?"

"Blue, you twerp," Maggie said.

"Goodie!" Kate said, bouncing on the bed. "Blue means happy."

"Great," Maggie mumbled and got out of bed. She looked in the mirror, ignoring all the stuff she had tucked in its corners—a picture of her mugging with Stephanie, a Far Side cartoon, a copy of The Prophet's verse on love. Maybe, she thought, she would be cool again if she cut her hair. She held it up, away from her face. "Ugh," she said, and let it fall. She had inherited her mother's mousey brown hair. "It's not mousey," her mother liked to say. "It's dirty blond." "Blond?" Maggie would say, wondering if even her mother believed some of the ridiculous things she said to Maggie. "Fine. I'm a blonde. A dishwater blonde."

Maggie leaned closer to the mirror. She was looking for zits. But her skin was clear and smooth. She held her hair up again. Maybe she would look better as a blonde. A real blonde. Platinum. Like Madonna used to have. She smiled and puckered her lips, threw her imaginary blond self a kiss.

"Why don't you have a boyfriend?" Kate asked her.

Maggie sighed and kept looking in the mirror. She used to have a boyfriend. But, like everything else, she had grown tired of him. And now he went out with Eve Montefiore. Eve had large breasts and always wore tight sweaters, in case you didn't notice her bra size. "If she's anything like her mother," Maggie's mother had said, "she'll drop him in a flash. She'll move on to a new boy, then another and another." She had meant it to comfort Maggie, but instead it infuriated her. "Not everyone is like their mother, you know," Maggie had shouted.

"Michael Jackson is going to be a policeman and then we'll get married," Kate said. She had come and stood beside Maggie and now she was looking at herself in the mirror too. "Want to make up our faces?" she said.

"Why don't you go watch television and leave me alone?" Maggie said. "I mean, I can't have any privacy in this house. And Michael Jackson is not going to marry you. He is androgynous. He is famous. He is like thirty years old or something."

"No, he isn't. He's in preschool. With me."

Even though Maggie didn't want any pancakes, or to look at her parents, she went downstairs anyway.

Her father was reading the Sunday paper. The business section. There was a joke for you. Maggie used to think her father was important, the way everyone at the mall knew him. She used to love going to work with him, sitting in his little office while he did paperwork. On his desk, he used to have a plastic cube and each side had a picture of her in it. Every year, for Christmas, she gave him a tie. Not a lot of fathers wore suits and ties to work. Most of the kids in school had fathers who worked at EB, building submarines for the government, or at the soap factory. Whenever there was an occasion to bring presents to a teacher, those kids gave soap on a rope, or boxed scented soaps. To Maggie, it now seemed ridiculous that she used to believe a father who managed a Caldor's at the mall was somehow more sophisticated.

"Mom's making pancakes," her father said. Then he carefully folded the newspaper, right along the creases.

Maggie tried to imagine her mother kissing him. She tried to imagine anyone kissing him. Impossible.

The first thing her mother said when she walked in the room, carrying a platter of pancakes, was, "Where is your sister?" She said it like Maggie didn't matter at all, like she was a ghost.

Maggie covered her eyes with her hands, leaving just a small slot free to squint through, like she was looking through a camera lens. Both of her parents, she decided, reminded her of extraterrestrials. Maybe their bodies had been inhabited by creatures from outer space, smiling zombies who were planning to take over the planet, to turn everyone else into smiling zombies.

Her father had his head bent over his plate. The better to shovel in pancakes, Maggie thought. She noticed that the bald spot on the top of his head was spreading.

"I read," Maggie said in a loud, authoritative voice, "that men who have this particular type of baldness will most likely die very young of a heart attack." She picked up a pancake with her hands and chewed on it. "This particular type is a circle on the top of the head and it just grows and grows."

Her parents were looking at her with their zombie faces.

Maggie gasped, a big exaggerated gasp. "Oh, no," she said. "You have that type of baldness, Dad." She shook her head sadly. "Poor old Dad," she said.

At Kate's birthday party that afternoon Minnie Mouse danced with all the children, and handed out the party favors Josie had assembled—little bundles with M&Ms and small Disney characters and stickers tucked inside. Even Maggie helped, directing the kids in games of musical chairs and pin the tail on the donkey. More than once, Josie found herself stepping back to take it all in: the cake waiting to be cut with the six birthday candles arranged in a crude heart shape, the Mickey and Minnie paper plates and napkins all lined up, the giggling children rushing to find a chair as Maggie lifted the arm from the record player.

Josie imagined that she, not Will, was the one holding the camcorder, watching, recording, preserving. She watched as Will poured apple juice in everyone's cups, as Kate, dressed in a new pink party dress and a cardboard crown covered in silver glitter clapped her hands and laughed when Minnie Mouse, who had joined in the game, fell loudly and theatrically to the floor. As a little girl, Maggie had hated to wear stiff party dresses. She liked blue jeans, T-shirts with sayings written on them, bright red sneakers. She had worn her hair in a pixie cut. But Kate was just the opposite, always begging for dainty socks with ruffles at the ankles, sparkly shoes and dresses with petticoats.

Josie gave the winner a prize, a box of Mickey and Minnie colorforms, then lit the candles, turned off the lights, and called everyone to their places at the table. Right then, with Will peering through the camcorder and her daughters' faces shining in the candlelight, all of them serenaded by that chorus of children's voices singing "Happy Birthday," Josie wished she could stop everything, freeze time, stay a while longer in this moment. But of course, in a blink, it was over. The candles were blown out, the lights turned back on bright, the cake cut and cut and cut until it no longer resembled Minnie Mouse at all, and finally the parents arriving, retrieving coats and chocolate-faced children.

Josie and Will pried smashed jelly beans from the floor. He saved the bows and ribbons that hadn't been torn apart completely. The dishwasher hummed, but otherwise it was quiet.

Standing there, with everything cleaned up, finished, her house back to normal, Josie let out a small groan.

"What?" Will said, looking up from the pink Barbie convertible he was trying to assemble.

"I just feel so sad," Josie said.

"Sad? But it was a wonderful party. Kate is in the den now, petting all of her birthday presents." He lowered his voice. "Maggie's even being nice."

He was right, of course. But Josie still felt it, an ache of sadness. She shook her head, shrugged, attempted a laugh. Will abandoned Barbie's car to come beside her and give her a hug. He smelled good, like chocolate.

"You have postparty-um depression," he said, patting her back.

She laughed despite herself, and settled into the familiar curve of his body. He had started to go soft. His belly pressed against his belt, his arms did not feel strong like they used to. Both of them should go on diets, Josie thought.

Later, in bed, Will rubbed his foot along her leg. She needed to shave her legs, she knew. It was something she tended to neglect. Josie could hear Maggie talking on the phone in her room, her voice low. She could hear, faintly, Kate's snoring. Bad adenoids, Aunt Tiny had said. Will moved closer, his hand on the inside of her thigh.

"The kids," Josie whispered. Usually she just went along with him. But tonight she felt like slipping into a comfortable position beside him and just going to sleep, his arm resting heavily across her.

He unbuttoned her nightshirt, slipped his hand inside and found her breast. When she was pregnant, he sucked on her breasts so hard, he sometimes left them slightly bruised. Once he had told her that he wished she was always pregnant, he so loved the way her body changed then, the fullness of her breasts, the swell of her belly. Now she was just too pudgy, soft at the hips. His caresses bothered her. She felt sad and fat and unattractive.

"Maggie is awake," she said, pushing his hand off her thigh, where he drew delicate circles with his fingertips.

Will paused, listened. Then he got out of bed and turned on the portable TV they kept in their room but almost never watched.

"Honey," Josie said, fumbling to button up her nightshirt, "she'll know. We never watch TV up here."

He laughed, and got into bed, climbing right on top of her. "Birthday parties make me horny," he whispered. "They make me frisky."

He was all over her, breathing hard, groping. When all she wanted was to be left alone, really.

"You could go to jail for that," Josie told him. "Getting turned on by a party full of five-year-olds."

"It was the hostess who did it," he said.

Saturday Night Live was on the Comedy Channel. They never got to watch it, always falling asleep before it came on. Josie craned her neck to see the screen. Wouldn't you know, it was one of the few she'd seen. There was Dana Carvey, imitating Ross Perot.

Will was sitting up, pulling her onto him. Not only did she not want to do this, but she didn't want to suddenly get so creative.

"What is wrong with you?" she hissed. Afraid she had hurt him, she said, gentler, lying back, "Come here."

She drew him to her. "Here," she whispered again.

"Ahhhhhh," he moaned.

"Shhhhhhh," she said. "The girls." But even she knew the TV laughter drowned him out.

His movements made her thighs jiggle, reminding her

again that they needed to get in shape. She wondered if pasta was fattening. She could never remember if it was or not. It was Kate's favorite. Noodles, Kate liked to call them. She could make some tomorrow, with vegetables instead of red sauce. It was the cheese and sauce that made it fattening, she decided. Pasta primavera and a garden salad. Surely that was low cal. And thinking of it, bright with the green of asparagus, the red of peppers and deep yellow of squash, Josie thought it was the perfect meal to celebrate the start of spring.

Will finished, muffling his moan, thankfully, in her pillow.

She liked this part, when it was over and he held her close. She snuggled against him, listened to his heart as it slowed back to its normal pace.

"Josie?" Will said, his fingers playing with her hair. "Did you enjoy it?"

She felt her body stiffen. He wanted not only to do it, but to talk about it too?

"Did you?"

Her mouth was getting dry. "Of course," she said, hearing her tongue smack against the roof of her mouth.

He cleared his throat. "Do you ever . . . you know?" He waited, but when she didn't answer, he added, "Come?"

"Well, of course," she lied. "I mean, sometimes. You know." Josie had read about men who got together in the woods and talked about things like this. Sensitive men. New Age ones. She felt that feeling again, everything shifting slightly. When the house was brand-new, and they'd just moved in, they would feel the house do that, shift, creak, find a new place. That was how she felt, she decided. Except the house was starting to settle back then, and she was already settled, happy. She didn't need to find a new place.

"I mean, you never seem to—"

"Some of us are just quiet," Josie said, forcing a laugh. She thought briefly of Fritz, the screech of tires, that awful sound he'd made. The vet had put a pin in his leg, and he'd recovered without even a trace of a limp.

"Maybe—" Will began.

But it had gone on too long already. Josie playfully pinched some of the roll around his middle. "Tomorrow," she said, "we start a diet. Both of us. We'll go to the new supermarket and get fresh produce."

He sighed.

"I thought I'd make pasta primavera. Judy gave me a recipe that comes from Le Cirque. In New York."

He rolled onto his side, draped his arm around her. She liked the weight of it there.

"Sounds good," Will said.

Josie lay there, listening to Will fall asleep, to the way his breathing changed, slowed and deepened. What had gotten in to him? She was still awake when the phone rang and she had to slip out from under his arm to answer it.

"I'm calling back," Michaela said, laughing. There were street sounds behind her—horns, a siren, traffic passing.

"It's after midnight here," Josie said. This time, she did not try to sound cheerful. "Some of us have kids, you know," she said, then was immediately sorry she had said it. "It's after midnight," she said again, gentler this time.

"You called me," Michaela said. "I figured something must be up."

Something? Josie thought. How about a million things? Our parents are selling our house. I'm feeling—feeling what? The dull start of a headache began. Was she too young for menopause? Josie wondered.

"I called you yesterday," Josie said too loudly.

Will grumbled in his sleep, pulled the pillow over his head.

Josie debated whether to go downstairs to talk, but then decided to make it short.

"Mom and Dad put the house up for sale," she blurted.

"I know," Michaela said.

"How do you know?"

"Dad told me."

Josie sat up. Why would her father tell Michaela and not her? Or was he trying to tell her that the other day, with all his talk about that old swing set of theirs?

"We have to stop them," Josie said.

"Stop them? Josie, they can't keep the house up anymore. They should move to Florida like everyone else's parents. Get a condo on the beach. Take it easy."

"People die when they go to Florida," Josie said. "It's like a way station before heaven." It was true, she thought. Will's parents had moved there and they called every week to report another neighbor's death. "They should stay here," Josie continued. "Where they belong. In that house."

Michaela laughed. "When will you ever grow up? People get old, move, retire. Et cetera."

"You are so irreverent," Josie said. Et cetera, she thought. She closed her eyes, again tried to picture her sister. She sounded fine tonight, not drunk or stoned, for a change. But Josie could almost not distinguish anymore. When Michaela had left home to go to Berkeley, she went to study science. Astronomy. Josie had believed back then that her sister would be wildly successful, like Carl Sagan or Isaac Asimov. That the name Michaela Jericho would mean something.

There were loud clicks, like a pay phone running out of change, and Michaela mumbling, "Shit! Do I have any more quarters?" Then the sound of coins dropping.

"Hello," Josie said. "Hello?"

"Look, little sister, I've got to go," Michaela was saying. "Mom and Dad should sell that old house of theirs. You should sell that shack of yours too. Everyone should free themselves."

What was that supposed to mean? Josie thought.

"You sound like an idiot," she said. "I'm sorry I called. I actually thought you might care about something. Go out and have fun. I'll hold down the fort here, as usual."

This time, she didn't wait to say good-bye. She just hung up the phone.

Settling back against her pillow, Josie thought about her sister. Not this Michaela, the one she no longer knew. Instead, she thought back to a time before Michaela turned—as everyone referred to it—wild. When they were children together, in that house, and Josie would crawl into bed beside her sister and let Michaela tell her what it was she saw through her telescope. She explained about other galaxies, novas, falling stars.

"I'm going to explore all of it," Michaela would say, and the excitement in her voice would thrill Josie too. "What will you do while I fly around outer space?"

Josie pressed herself against her sister. Michaela smelled of Ivory soap and strawberry shampoo. Sometimes a strand of her long red hair would work its way into Josie's mouth, and Josie would leave it there, hug her teeth around it and close her mouth tight.

"I'll be here waiting for you to come home and tell me all your adventures," Josie used to say. "When you come back, I'll be right here, waiting."

In her whole life, Maggie had never played hooky from school. Not really. Last year, on National Bunk Day, she had gone to the beach with her friends instead of going to school. But that didn't really count because her parents knew she did it and thought it was fun, and besides, no one even expected you to go to school on National Bunk Day. They expected you to go to the beach.

So she felt a little creepy, like a criminal, on Monday morning when she picked up her book bag and pretended to leave for school.

"What's on your agenda today?" her mother asked her as she headed for the door.

Maggie froze in place. "What's that supposed to mean?"

Her mother sighed and rubbed her temples. "What is wrong with you, Maggie? It's a perfectly normal question, for Pete's sake."

Maggie cringed. Who on this planet actually said "for Pete's sake"?

"I have ballet today," Kate called from the living room, where she was glued to the television, as usual.

"Not you, pumpkin," her mother said. "I'm trying to have a conversation with your sister." She didn't wait for Maggie to say anything. Instead, she got up and started to clean the table, to brush away the toast crumbs and wipe up the juice and coffee spots.

Watching her, Maggie got an ache in her chest. What a pathetic horrible life her mother had. Always cleaning up after everyone, wiping away spills. Even a few months ago, Maggie would have gone over to her mother and hugged her good-bye. But now she just stood and watched her, a plump woman in a blue terrycloth bathrobe holding a pile of dirty dishes.

"Aren't you going to be late?" her mother said, resigned.

"I can tell time," Maggie said. She readjusted her book bag.

From the living room, Kate yelled, "We're learning third position today!"

"Who cares?" Maggie yelled back. She made sure to slam the door on her way out.

Josie stared at the tape recorder balanced at the edge of the pool and wondered if the entire Aqua Aerobics class would be electrocuted if it fell in. She looked over at her cousin Denise and tried to imagine her perfectly permed and mahoganied hair standing on end, her Norma Kamali bathing suit singed. It was almost too easy to picture. So easy that Josie glanced again at the tape recorder to be sure it hadn't actually toppled in. But of course there it was, sitting beside a chlorine puddle and way too close to the pool's edge, hovering, it seemed, right over the big black 3 painted on the pale blue tiles.

"All right, Josie, let's move now!" the instructor shouted. Her name was Debbi with an i and her whole face seemed to pout—Brigitte Bardot lips, little pug nose, even her bouncing ponytail.

Debbi was new. Their old instructor, Barb, had been attacked in the parking lot of her apartment complex. No one knew the details, but people hinted at them. Josie had heard the word rape whispered in the locker room. Someone else had heard she'd had broken bones. That complex sat right on the edge of the Essex mall. From the mall parking lot Josie could see its Japanese garden with its small arched bridge and kidney-shaped pond. The pond, she knew, had giant goldfish and lily pads. The whole place looked serene, like something not usually found near East Essex. It did not look like the kind of place where violence would dare to happen.

"Rock . . . Rock steady . . . Rockin' 'til the break of dawn . . . Rock . . . Rock steady . . ." the tape recorder blasted, and Debbi with an i moved her arms vigorously through the water, as if she was really going somewhere. Just watching her made Josie exhausted.

The best part of Aqua Aerobics, Josie decided as she looked around at all the other bobbing women in the pool, was that no one could tell if her legs were moving since they—and half her body, really—were submerged in water. She could stop a moment, like she was right now, and catch her breath, study everyone else, try to figure out if they were all actually doing the strange shuffle-hop-step at the bottom of the pool, or faking it like she was.

Josie looked over at Denise again. She looked perfect. Will liked to tease Denise about her weekly tanning salon sessions and her shiny gold jewelry. Since they were teenagers, Denise wore her jewelry everywhere—even to the beach—and adulthood hadn't changed that about her. Today, three fine gold chains of varying lengths hung around her neck, topaz and diamond rings spiraled around several fingers, and a diamond tennis bracelet clung to one arm. Topaz was her birthstone; the tennis bracelet was an anniversary gift. Josie knew the history of all of Denise's jewelry. Sometimes she told the story of a ring or bracelet to Will like it was a fairy tale. "Once upon a time," she'd say, "there was a lonely topaz and diamond ring . . ." Even though Will laughed, Josie always felt slightly guilty when she did it.

Denise caught Josie staring and winked one of her carefully made-up eyes at her. Her makeup must be waterproof, Josie thought. Her own mascara, bought at Caldor's with Will's employee discount, was starting to clump. She could see small chunks hanging on the tips of her eyelashes, ready to cascade down her face like a mini avalanche at any moment. Her ponytail was sliding down her head too, while Denise's own hair hung just above the water, neat and dry. In fact, everything about Josie seemed to be melting, falling, liquefying, while everyone else, even Rhoda, who weighed close to three hundred pounds, seemed to be light and clean.

"Josie!" Debbi shouted, startling her. "Are you cooling down already?"

Josie looked down and found that she had stopped moving altogether. Her arms hung in the water, her toes gripped at the slippery pool bottom, and all the other moving women were staring at her and laughing, seemingly in rhythm.

"Uh," Josie said, "no. Of course not."

"Then move it!" Debbi shouted.

Debbi bounced over to the edge of the pool where dozens of empty plastic milk bottles lay, and began to toss them into the water. Josie hated this part of Aqua Aerobics most of all—thrusting those milk bottles through the water until her upper arms throbbed while disco music blasted all tinny and loud. She watched Denise squeal happily at the sight of the stupid things.

"Keeps the flab off these arms," Denise said, smiling like an idiot and holding up her toothpick arms.

She attacked the water savagely and with great determination, and Josie let herself hate Denise for talking her into coming to Aqua Aerobics, for having perfect-length hair, and for shaking her milk bottles so effortlessly while Josie's own flabby upper arms burned.

As if she read Josie's mind, Debbi shouted, "Let it burn, ladies!" And everyone except Josie pushed their milk bottles even more furiously.

Josie watched a real swimmer emerge from the locker room. She wore a navy blue Speedo and a tight bathing cap with goggles lifted to rest on it. The swimmer glanced over, amused, at the Aqua Aerobics class while she did her deep knee bends and warm-up breathing. All the real swimmers made Josie feel embarrassed. She did not want to be a slightly overweight housewife bouncing in the shallow end of a pool with plastic milk jugs.

The song ended and Debbi shouted, "Hoo!" then the class shouted, "Ray!" and everyone splashed each other and giggled. For an instant, Josie found herself wishing that the tape recorder had fallen into the pool. She thought again of Denise with her hair standing on end and all that gold burned black. But when Denise bounced up beside her, smiling her Cafe Mocha lips, Josie felt bad for thinking it. She could smell her perfume: Giorgio. She decided that Denise smelled like a magazine with too many perfume inserts. Her teeth were bright and large, reminding Josie of a beauty pageant contestant, which Denise had, in fact, been. Back in high school she had been first runner-up in Miss Junior Miss, Miss East Essex, and Miss Teen Rhode Island. She had acted like being first runner-up was even better than winning.

"So we'll see you and Will Saturday night?" Denise said as she began to glide away.

"Right," Josie said. She tried to stretch her smile the way Denise did, to make her whole face seem open and bright.

Denise stopped gliding. "Are you all right?"

Josie nodded and tried to stretch her smile even more.

"You look like you're in pain or something," Denise said.

Slowly, Josie let her mouth return to normal. She got that melting feeling again. "No," she said, sighing. "I'm fine."

When Maggie was certain her mother was safely at the gym, jumping around in some sort of aerobic exercise, she took the bus to Providence. It was nearly empty until they stopped at the state mental hospital. Then a ragged line of weird people climbed aboard. Maggie tried not to stare at them, but she couldn't help it. Maybe they were dangerous criminals. Maybe she should memorize each of their faces in case one of them went berserk and she needed to provide the authorities with an accurate description. She spent the rest of the bus ride pretending she was being interviewed by a cop, a sexy one with an Irish accent and big muscles bulging under his uniform shirt.

"The woman was about five-five," she told the policeman, whose name happened to be Miles. "Heavy-set. She had a big, ugly mole, like Cindy Crawford, except hers was gross. And her lipstick was bright fuchsia and smeared way beyond her lip line."

The policeman would capture the crazy lady because Maggie's description was so accurate. And then he would swoop Maggie into his arms and carry her off. Maggie closed her eyes. Where would he take her? The squad car? Back to Ireland? Wherever it was, she would let him take off all of her clothes and ravage her body.

Whenever Maggie had thoughts like that, she got a warm feeling in her crotch. The feeling kind of scared her. Maybe she was a sex maniac. A nymphomaniac, like everybody said Tara Polaski was. Maybe that was her entire problem. A nymphomaniac in a cheerleader's outfit, in the gifted program, for Pete's sake.

She opened her eyes and saw that one of the mental hospital people was staring at her.

She pretended to describe him to her policeman. "He looked a little like Kramer," she would say. "From *Seinfeld?* Except he was missing a bunch of teeth on the top."

This time she stopped the fantasy right as the policeman swooped her into his arms. If she was a nymphomaniac, she thought, she would have liked it better when she and Jeff used to go parking. Once, he had taken her hand and put it right on his hard-on. On top of his jeans, but still she felt it, a hard lump. She pulled her hand away, fast, but not before Jeff let out a loud, scary moan. That had not given her the warm feeling. In fact, it had made her feel a little queasy.

The bus pulled into Kennedy Plaza. "Last stop," the bus driver announced.

Maggie let all the crazy people get off first. Then she picked up her book bag and left the bus. It was a beautiful day, cool and clear, the sky a deep blue, the blue the ocean sometimes had. Maggie breathed in the air and looked around to get her bearings. She felt like someone on a television show, someone in a new place, about to undertake a life-changing event. She decided to think of herself as Paulina, like the model. Maybe she'd even use a slight accent.

She took a deep breath again and spoke into the breeze. "Hello," she said, sounding throaty and exotic, "I am Paulina."

The hairdresser chewed cinnamon gum and talked the whole time. Her name was Melissa and someday, she told Maggie, she would have her own salon. In Boston or maybe LA.

Maggie had been under the hair dryer for what seemed like a very long time. Melissa had listened carefully to what it was Maggie wanted done, nodding and chewing her gum the whole time, and running her fingers through Maggie's long hair. Before she began, Melissa said, "This will be great. Trust me." That made Maggie even more nervous.

She had been at the hairdresser's all morning. First they had to strip her hair, then neutralize it, then mix and apply the solution. Then she had to sit under the hairdryer forever. Now, finally, they were washing her hair again, adding conditioner, rinsing. Maggie had a stiff neck and she was sick of listening to Melissa, who was telling her about her rich boyfriend from Jordan.

The salon was called The Hairy Ape, and it was where everyone from Brown and RISD came to get their hair buzzed, dyed, and spiked. Even everyone at school knew about The Hairy Ape. But Maggie was certain she was the first one to actually come here. They all went to Jordan Marsh, or the ten-dollar place, where they got their bottoms trimmed and their bangs feathered. That was where Maggie herself went every ten weeks, to keep her hair healthy. The cheerleading squad was going to die when they saw her.

"Okay," Melissa was saying. She lifted Maggie's head and wrapped a towel around her shoulders. "Now we're going to cut it, just like you said. It's really gorgeous, Paulina." But she wouldn't let her look until everything was done. "You've got to get the full effect," Melissa told her.

Maggie heard the snip of the scissors, but the hair that fell to the floor seemed to belong to someone else. Even wet, it appeared light, like ice.

"Where you from, Paulina?" Melissa asked, cutting and tugging and cutting some more.

"Poland," Maggie said.

"Really? Is that where that special water's from? Poland Springs?"

"Yes," Maggie said. "It's from my own little town, in fact." Her accent sounded unbelievably fake, but Melissa didn't seem to notice.

"Okay, turn your head over," she told Maggie. Then she started blow-drying, curling, geling and spraying.

Finally, she pulled the towel from Maggie's shoulders and spun her chair around. "Da-da!" Melissa said.

Maggie stared at the reflection she saw, trying to believe it was really her. Melissa had done exactly what Maggie had asked for—she had made her look like Madonna. Or, she'd made her hair look exactly like Madonna. The rest of her looked like . . . like a stranger. A stranger with Madonna's hair. The platinum color made her own pale skin look pasty, all washed out. And her eyes, which used to seem almost golden brown, looked colorless against all that pale.

"You'll need to rethink your makeup, of course," Melissa said. She was standing behind Maggie, so that she loomed in the mirror too.

Why, Maggie wondered, had she agreed to let someone with slicked-back dyed-black hair and platform shoes touch her hair? All the women at the ten-dollar place looked like everybody else she knew—long straight hair and feathered bangs. They wore Gap clothes and lip gloss.

"Maybe some red matte lipstick," Melissa said. "For contrast, you know?"

Maggie nodded and smiled, but what she was really thinking was that the worse possible thing had happened—with her new hair and white face and blank eyes, she looked exactly like her parents, like a zombie on the wrong planet.

The last thing Josie wanted to do was spend Saturday night at one of Denise's parties. Especially this one—a black tie affair with a mystery guest of honor. But Will had already rented a tux with a scarlet cummerbund and shiny wing tips. Josie had spent almost two hours after the invitation arrived trying on every fancy dress she owned, only to decide nothing was right. The silver one made her look like a space age sausage, the little black dress was way too little, and the green chiffon looked like something a mother of the bride might wear.

As she drove from the Y to her mother's, Josie tried to imagine herself somewhere else this weekend. Bermuda, perhaps. That was where she and Will had gone on their honeymoon. They had rented mopeds and rode on a glass bottom boat. The sand there was a pale pink. Remembering those five days, the smell of coconut tanning lotion and the sweet taste of rum swizzles, made her start to relax. She had used this same relaxation technique when she'd given birth to both of her daughters, Will beside her describing their honeymoon in Bermuda. He sounded, she'd thought, like Robin Leach.

She would buy a new dress, she decided. Something sophisticated. Something that fit. Really, Denise went overboard on everything, Josie thought. She and Will were always rolling their eyes at Denise's elaborate parties. Why, even the invitation to this one had been ridiculous. Some high school boy had shown up at their doorstep holding a silver tray with two glasses of champagne, two chocolate truffles, and the invitation carefully rolled and tied with a silver ribbon. That poor kid had to drive all over town in someone's borrowed Cadillac, delivering the things. Josie and Will had a good laugh over that one, she standing there in her worn blue terrycloth robe, and Will holding a Rolling Rock, both looking confused by the offerings on the silver tray. The tray itself had a big elaborate W carved into it, for Wykowski. The kid even bowed and said, "I come on behalf of Denise and James Wykowski."

By the time she pulled in front of her parents' house, Josie was laughing to herself. Denise was like a Martha Stewart clone gone bad. A mutant Martha Stewart. Will would like that. A mutant Martha Stewart.

She paused when she walked past the FOR SALE sign. Early yesterday morning she had called her mother to talk about it, but her mother had refused.

"There's nothing to discuss," she told Josie.

"Yes, there is. Like where will you go? And why do you want to go at all?"

"I'm in a bit of a tizzy right now. Why don't I call you back later?" her mother had said.

But she hadn't called back. When she'd first had Maggie, Josie remembered looking up at Will late one night as she fed their daughter and saying, "I wish everything could stay just like this forever." Will had told her that was a bad idea. "It's going to get even better," he'd said. "Why stop here?" Walking past that FOR SALE sign, though, Josie knew that this wasn't going to get better. Her parents would move to a condo somewhere, they would leave their garden, sell their things. They would grow old. She thought of Will's mother on the phone last night. "Remember Mrs. Martone?" She had said. "Died in her sleep. And her sister was the one I told you about just a month ago. Both dead." Josie had held the extension tighter, wondering why people thought of fun when they thought of Florida.

No, Josie decided as she stepped inside the familiar kitchen, breathed in the smell of percolated coffee and the sound of her aunts' voices, things were not going to get better from here. It was time to stop everything now, keep it just like this.

Another voice stopped her.

"And then the boat starts rocking," the voice was saying, "and rocking and rocking. Ferociously. And I look down at the water—"

"Water!" Aunt Tiny said. "Was it clear or muddy?"

And then that other voice. "Why, clear. Yes. Clear. I could see all the way to the bottom."

That other voice was Maggie's, Josie realized. It was noon and Maggie was not in school, sitting in Spanish class conjugating verbs like she was supposed to be. She was sitting here eating Dunkin' Donuts and talking about her dreams.

Then Josie saw Maggie's hair.

"What have you done to yourself?" Josie said. She stood as close to Maggie as she could and put her face right next to her daughter's. Her mind flooded with other things Maggie might have done. Worse things. Tattoos. Body piercing. Even one of the teacher's at Kate's school, a young thing, right out of college, wore a nose ring.

"Clear water," Aunt Tiny muttered, "is bad luck."

Maggie ran her fingers through her hair. She looked away from Josie and at Aunt Tiny. "Well," she said, laughing, "I have had a bit of bad luck today, haven't I?"

Aunt Beatrice shook her head and set her lips into a tight, straight line. Her grandchildren, after all, were well-behaved, normal. Judy's daughters didn't get their hair cut and dyed, didn't have their mother go for private meetings with teachers. And Denise's son was at West Point, no less. He'd gotten letters of recommendation from senators and Boy Scout leaders and even a bishop. That's why Aunt Beatrice could sit there and tighten her lips like that and shake her head.

Josie felt her mother's eyes on her. She would want Josie to settle this at home, quietly. Not in front of the aunts. But Josie didn't care. "Suppose you tell me what sort of bad luck you've had," she said.

Now Maggie looked toward her grandmother.

Claire said, "Calm down, Josie. She got into a little trouble. That's all."

Aunt Beatrice snorted.

"A prank," Aunt Tiny said, but she sounded distracted. She was writing on her napkin with a small pencil, and frowning.

"Maggie," Josie said. Her jaw was starting to ache from being clenched so tightly.

Finally Maggie turned toward her mother. "I got suspended," she said. She didn't even try to look remorseful. In fact, she was almost smiling.

"Suspended?" Josie said. The kids who got suspended from school flunked everything and rode in noisy, souped up cars. They were from bad families. "Oh, Maggie," Josie said, sinking into a chair. "How could you?" She pictured the parking lot at the high school. She thought of loud engines, Led Zeppelin music, heavy smoke, and black leather. Then she pictured Maggie right in the middle of all that.

"It's only for a week," Maggie said. "And I wouldn't have been suspended at all if I hadn't gotten into trouble and sent home Thursday."

"Her teacher thinks her head's in the clouds," Claire said, as if having one's head in the clouds was a good thing.

Josie was having trouble keeping up. "Thursday?" she said, unable to remember anything unusual about Thursday.

"I didn't want you to freak out," Maggie said.

"Well," Josie said, "I am. I am freaking out."

"Christy says—" Aunt Beatrice began.

But Josie couldn't bear to hear anymore. "What is it you've done?"

"She skipped one little class," Claire said.

"Gym!" Maggie shrieked. "I cut gym! To get my hair cut. I

mean, gym isn't learning. It isn't school, really. It's just running around the stupid track."

Aunt Tiny looked up from her figuring. "Physical Education is important," she said. "President Kennedy started that, you know."

"It's just running around the stupid track," Maggie said again. "And when it rains we play crab soccer. Do you know how stupid that is? Crawling around the stinky gym floor trying not to get hit by this giant red ball? And, I mean, I could lie like everyone else and say I've got my period so I should be excused, but I don't want to lie."

"She was protesting," Claire said, almost proudly.

"She should protest something important then," Josie said. "Like social injustice or something."

"This is an injustice," Maggie said. She leaned back in her chair and folded her arms, as if the matter was closed.

"She's just like her aunt," Beatrice said, shaking her head again. "Just like your Michaela."

Josie looked around the table at each of them, at Maggie with her platinum hair and defiant look in her eyes, at Aunt Tiny busily scribbling on her napkin, and Aunt Beatrice shaking her head, and her own mother in a green apron decorated with brightly colored fruit, like a mother from an old television commercial. She imagined what she must look like, with her hair still damp from Aqua Aerobics and her faded sweatpants and Will's T-shirt that said: I CLIMBED MOUNT WASHINGTON. He had a bumper sticker on his car that said: THIS CAR CLIMBED MOUNT WASHINGTON, and neither he nor the car had.

"It's not the end of the world," Claire said finally.

Josie sighed and reached for some doughnuts. A few years ago, Dunkin' Donuts had claimed their doughnuts were fat free, except for French crullers. Josie remembered that, but still those were what she chose now. Two of them.

"Maybe you should have a plain one," Aunt Beatrice said,

pushing the plate toward Josie. She knew the French crullers were the ones that had fat too.

"No," Josie said, "I want this kind." Then, afraid she sounded a bit too curt, she added, "I just came from aerobics so I've burned a lot of calories already today."

Aunt Tiny looked up, smiling. "756," she said.

"What?" Josie said. Her teeth hurt from the sweetness of her doughnut.

"756," Aunt Tiny said, and held up her napkin. "Water is always 56," she explained. "Clear is 556. Muddy is 456. But Maggie was in a boat."

"A rowboat," Maggie said.

"Yes. And boats are 725," Aunt Tiny said.

"Sailboats are 725," Beatrice said, biting into the plain doughnut herself.

"Well, sailboats are something else," Aunt Tiny said, waving her napkin. "You need to take the 7 and you need the 56. 756." She nodded her head for emphasis. "There," she said, and placed the napkin in the very center of the table. "There you have it."

Maggie sat, slumped low, in the seat beside Josie. She was humming to herself again, and had her eyes half-closed. Just as well, Josie thought. It was difficult to look at her with that ridiculous haircut. Josie remembered what that teacher had said. A counselor, she'd said, could really straighten things out. Was it that bad? Josie wondered, sneaking another glance at her daughter. Weren't counselors for kids with real problems—drugs or pregnancy or shoplifting? Josie wasn't even sure what Maggie's problem was, but she felt confident it wasn't that bad. Aunt Beatrice's words drifted back to her. Just like Michaela, she'd said. But Josie refused to believe that. Believe? she thought. Or admit?

Sometimes, she thought of their family in two parts: before Michaela went wild, when she was a skinny tomboy who spent her time studying astronomy books and charts and playing sports—softball, CYO basketball, track and field, and then after that, when Michaela discovered drugs and sex and Josie was afraid to imagine what else. The before parts seemed soft, like the flannel animals in one of Kate's books that begged you to stroke them. The after parts were bright and loud and unpredictable. And ever since, people lowered their eyes when they said her name. Michaela, they'd say, and their cheeks would redden a bit and they would look down, the way people did when they mentioned Aunt Tiny's son David, the one who'd died in Vietnam. She couldn't let that happen to Maggie, who until recently had made them all laugh with her animated personality, her quick sense of humor.

She glanced over at Maggie again, almost hoping to find a younger version of her sitting there. After taking a music workshop for gifted children one summer, Maggie used to make up funny songs. She would ask someone to name a genre, like opera or country western, and then a topic, broken hearts or cloudy days, and right on the spot she'd make up a little song. Maybe Josie could try that now. She'd say, "Rap," so Maggie would know she wasn't totally out of touch, and then she'd say, "Home," and Maggie would come up with something clever.

Josie almost did it, almost called out to her daughter, but up ahead Kate's school loomed and there wasn't time. It was an indulgence, she knew, to send Kate there instead of to public school. But one day a month, Josie was a teacher's aide to help defer the cost. She helped the children on with their coats, exclaimed over their art projects, made sure they formed a straight line before they went outside. She brought in their mid-morning snack that day, carefully cut cookies in the shapes of *Sesame Street* characters colorfully iced in yellow and blue and green. "You are the best mother of all," Kate had told her the last time Josie spent the day there. "You make me very, very proud."

The school was a bright yellow Victorian house with purple gingerbread trim and a yard bordered with rosebushes. Josie could remember when she was young and the house was abandoned. Everyone said it was haunted. Once, on a dare, Michaela and her friends spent the night there. They claimed to hear distant voices and soft footsteps. They claimed to smell the faintest perfume. It reminded them of lilies. Michaela liked to think that something tragic and romantic had happened there. But no one really knew the house's story. Still, whenever Josie spent her day there, she expected to catch a whiff of lilies, or hear footsteps coming from an empty room.

Now, the house looked cheerful and alive. "Like a fairy-tale house," Kate always said. With spring here, it reminded Josie of a fairy-tale house too. Trees heavy with sweet-smelling blossoms dipped and swayed. The path to the front door was sprinkled with pink and white petals, and everywhere she looked Josie saw another burst of fresh-blooming flowers. She smiled at the sight, finding it hard to even remember what the house used to look like. It was gray, she thought. Or maybe a dark green. Certainly it had been thick with weeds and ivy, full of cracked windows and loose shingles.

"Oh," Maggie said, sitting up straight and opening her eyes wide, "the elite private school."

"It's a cooperative," Josie said crossly. "It's not elite at all."

"It looks like the Addams Family house," Maggie said. She made sure to slam the door hard when she got out of the car, and to walk well ahead of Josie with her hands jammed into her pockets and her head bent.

Just as they reached the door, it flew open and a stream of children burst from it. Josie picked out Kate right away, grinning, her face sticky from what looked like a red lollipop. She wore the dirndl skirt and peasant blouse that Josie had found at a yard sale. "Just like the Von Trapp children wear!" Kate had squealed when Josie presented her with it. She had wrapped her arms around her mother's waist and squeezed hard. "Where did you ever find such a thing? You are the very best mother in the world."

"What does she have on?" Maggie said. "She looks ridiculous."

Josie looked over the heads of all the children that separated her from Maggie. How could one daughter think she was the best mother in the world, and the other dislike her so much? She thought back again to a time when Maggie too adored her. Now she was considering sending her to some counselor, getting her fixed.

Kate ran to Josie, shouting, "Mommy!"

Her friend Cory said, "Mrs. Hunter, when are you coming to our class again? We miss you."

"Next week," Josie said. She looked over at Maggie, hoping she had heard Cory. But Maggie had walked back to the car, where she leaned against the hood, her face turned up toward the sun.

"Mrs. Hunter?" Cory was saying. She tugged on the hem of Josie's T-shirt. "Can Kate come home with me? My mom's right there. She'll drive us."

Josie followed Cory's paint-splattered finger to where her mother stood waiting, right beside Maggie.

"Not today," Josie said.

Cory's mother waved at them and Josie waved back. But Maggie, thinking her mother was waving at her, looked right at Josie and stuck out her tongue.

"Isn't that your sister?" Cory whispered.

"No," Kate said solemnly. "She's a stranger."

"You know what?" Josie said, taking Kate's hand in her own and walking back to their car. "You can go to Cory's for the afternoon. I have to go to the mall and I'll pick you up on my way home."

The little girls screamed and jumped up and down.

"We'll play *The Sound of Music,*" Kate said. "You can be Maria."

They skipped ahead of Josie, their voices high and sweet as they sang "How do you solve a problem like Maria?" They would, Josie knew, sing every single song, and act out every scene.

"Where's Julie Andrews going?" Maggie said as she got back in the car.

"I thought you and I could go out to lunch. Go to the mall." Josie tried to seem casual about it. "Have a girls day together."

"Uh-huh," Maggie said. She looked out the window and didn't talk again all the way to Friday's.

Josie knew that Maggie and her friends thought Friday's was the coolest place to eat. Personally, she hated it. The menu was too big and the restaurant was so noisy she could never decide what to order. She always left there unsatisfied and with a headache. But she refused to believe that anything was really wrong with Maggie. At least, nothing that Josie couldn't fix herself.

All the waiters at Friday's wore silly hats. That was something Josie always forgot until she got in there. The noise and the odd things that hung from the ceiling and the hats made her dizzy right away. Their waitress wore a bright beanie with a propeller on top of it.

"Are you ready to order?" she asked them. She wore a lot of

buttons, too. Old campaign buttons and a big smiley face, too many for Josie to read.

"No," Josie said, staring at the giant menu.

"Yes," Maggie said. "An Outrageous and a Banana Bippy."

She said it looking right at Josie, like it was a dare, but Josie had no idea what she was talking about.

"A hamburger," Josie said, happy to close the menu. Her headache was starting.

"Which one?" the waitress said, opening the menu again and pointing.

There was a whole section on hamburgers, all named after a day of the week, with detailed descriptions beneath each one.

"I don't care," Josie said, and closed the menu again.

The waitress smiled and shrugged. "It's up to you."

"Come on, Mom," Maggie said. She had her teeth clenched, and she was looking around, embarrassed.

"Well," Josie said, "it's Monday, right? I guess I'll have a Monday burger." She tried to make it sound like a joke, but she just sounded confused.

"You can have any one you want," the girl said gently.

Josie closed her eyes.

"Just bring her a Monday burger," Maggie said.

"Does she want French fries?" the waitress asked Maggie.

"Yes!" Josie said. She opened her eyes. "Yes! French fries."

"God," Maggie mumbled.

"Don't you just love this place?" Josie said. She knew she sounded like a crazy person, but she couldn't stop herself. "Isn't it just the greatest?"

An Outrageous was the biggest ice cream sundae Josie had ever seen. A Monday burger had things like sprouts and guacamole on it, things that did not belong on a hamburger. Still, she kept smiling and telling Maggie everything was super. "Right," Maggie said, "real super." She didn't talk again until they got to the mall. Then she paused at the entrance to the Gap and said, "Everyone has Gap loose-fit jeans, you know." She was testing Josie, and Josie knew it. But she was determined to get close to her daughter again. If Kate loved her, so could Maggie. She could fix everything. If that meant eating in her least favorite restaurant and buying a pair of jeans, she'd do it. Didn't she spend a full afternoon each month decorating cookies to look like Big Bird and Oscar the Grouch?

She bought a pair of jeans for Maggie, and then, on a lark, bought a pair for herself. That ought to impress Maggie, Josie thought. But as they walked back into the mall, Maggie said, "Don't wear those in front of anyone I know, okay?" and jammed her hands back into her pockets, bent her head, and walked ahead of Josie again.

In Jordan Marsh, Josie decided she would buy a dress for Denise's party and let Maggie pick it out for her. No matter which one Maggie chose, Josie would buy it. Even if it was expensive. Even if it was awful. But upstairs in Better Dresses, Maggie just sat on the floor in front of the triple mirror and made faces. Josie came out in dress after dress. "What do you think?" she asked each time, and each time Maggie shrugged. Until finally Maggie got up and said, "I'll meet you at the bookstore, okay?"

Quickly, Josie picked a dress from the floor of the dressing room. She had hardly paid attention herself, so eager to include Maggie, to make her feel important. The dress on top of the pile was red, with a rhinestone belt.

"Here," Josie said, thrusting the dress and her credit card at the saleswoman as Maggie disappeared down the escalator.

"Are you sure this is the one you want?" the woman said.

Josie looked at her. She was plump herself, with Shirley Temple curls and a fake beauty mark beside her mouth.

"Yes," Josie said, not sure at all.

"Maybe you'd look better in something without a belt?" the woman said, not unkindly.

Deep down, Josie knew she was right. But Maggie was walking away from her, putting still more distance between them, and she felt desperate.

"No," Josie said. "I'll take this one. Please." Some part of her was thinking about Will's scarlet cummerbund and how she could cut away the belt loops.

The saleswoman held the bag out to her. "Enjoy," she said, smirking.

The bright shock of Maggie's hair disappeared completely. Josie grabbed her bag with the dress that was all wrong for her and raced toward her daughter.

Josie showed up at her parents' house with a box of doughnuts and her serious face. Even as a child she'd had this expression. "Like a little old man," Dan used to say.

Claire was upstairs packing. Every day she tackled a new part of the house to dismantle. She had boxes marked JOSIE, MICHAELA, KEEP, and GOODWILL. "Typical Virgo," Michaela would say. But Claire needed to keep order. If she didn't, she would never be able to discard old ballet tutus from some long-ago recital, the sequins sadly dangling from the tulle, or the faded yellow report cards with her blurred signature on the back. When she had signed those she had felt confident, her life stretching before her in a predictable path. Now, if she let herself think about how that path had veered wildly off course, she would not be able to do the simple tasks she wrote down each morning: MICHAELA'S CLOSET, JOSIE'S DRESSER, FILE CABINET IN DEN.

From the upstairs window in Michaela's old room, she spotted Josie, pink-and-white box of doughnuts in her hand, face puckered.

"Shit," Claire said when she saw her daughter approaching. Cursing was something else that was new to her. "Your mother," Dan used to tell the girls, "wouldn't say shit if she had a hand full of it." Watching Josie make her way toward the house, Claire got the crazy notion to hide in the closet. The door was opened and old parts of Michaela's life were spilling from it, a hodgepodge of paisley and colored beads and fringe. Claire looked at the closet, then at the bent head of her daughter below. If she were closer, she would see the two lines that appeared on Josie's forehead whenever she frowned. She would see the turned-down corners of her mouth. "Like a little old man," Claire thought, as she stepped over the curtain of colored beads into the closet. Michaela had strung those beads for her bedroom doorway the summer she was seventeen.

The back door slammed shut, as if to announce Josie's determination. Claire knew why she had come. She wanted to talk her mother out of selling the house. She would have a plan, probably one that involved her and Tim. She would have a backup in case that failed, something that involved a compromise. If in a year you still feel this way, she'd say, we'll discuss this all again.

Claire pushed herself deeper into the closet. It still smelled like that horrible oil Michaela used to wear. Patchouli. She heard Josie downstairs, looking for her. Slumping back, fighting fringe and denim, Claire silently wished they would all go away. Her well-meaning sisters, her efficient daughter, everyone except Dan. She wished he would somehow, miraculously, be his old self again.

A bit of red caught her eye and she followed it deeper into

the closet. Dan's Santa Claus suit. She ran her fingers over the cuff, where white fluff was beginning to break apart, like a dandelion gone to seed. Gently, Claire blew on it, and tiny shreds flew off, fell to the floor. Dan had always been Santa at the car dealership, handing out candy canes and small matchbox Fords. He could make his laugh boom, produce the jolliest Ho-ho-ho's. Children left there convinced he was the real thing.

"What in the world are you doing?" Josie shrieked from somewhere outside the closet.

Caught, Claire thought, and inched her way back out.

But Josie had not found her. It was all those boxes Claire was packing that Josie had discovered and was now, almost frantically, pulling things out of. When she heard her mother behind her, she spun around, clutching an old skirt that appeared to be made of chiffon rags.

"First you put the house up for sale, and now this," Josie said.

Claire shrugged. She felt exhausted, worn down. Obviously if a person moves, they have to pack, she thought. But she kept quiet.

"And what is in your hair?" Josie said, swatting at Claire. A trail of Santa trim flitted down.

"Dandelion seed," Claire said.

Josie sat on the edge of Michaela's old bed, gently laying the skirt, a bracelet of bells, some peacock feathers, down beside her.

"You're packing," she said.

Claire sat beside her and looked at the half-full boxes and cluttered floor. "There's so much," she said. "I do a little every day."

"But you're not selling the house for certain," Josie said. "I have a plan."

Claire picked up the skirt. Each tier was a different soft color, lemon yellow, peach, raspberry. It reminded her of sherbert.

"Michaela wore that one Easter," Josie said. Her voice had a hint of betrayal in it, of How could you?

Claire rolled the skirt into a ball and tossed it into the box marked GOODWILL.

"And what is in your hair?" Josie said again.

"Santa fluff."

"Dandelion seed. Santa Claus," Josie said. "Is everyone going crazy here?" She inhaled sharply, as if to take back this last observation.

Claire forced a smile. "Come on," she said. "I have a feeling you brought something sweet with you."

Josie took one last look around the room, her eyes settling on the places where posters hung and now, removed, left dark rectangles on the walls, then on the boxes, the empty bureau top.

But Claire would not stay there with her any longer. "I'll put on coffee," she said as she walked out of the room and down the stairs.

Kate thought that she was maybe the most loved little girl in the world. Her father liked to swoop her up into his arms and spin around and around until they both felt dizzy. Sometimes he called her Katy-Did, and even though a Katy-Did was a bug, she didn't mind because it was a private little nickname he had for her that meant he loved her.

Kate always watched grown-up TV shows. She did not like *Reading Rainbow* or *Mister Rogers.* She hated Barney. And some of the characters on *Sesame Street* were okay, but just okay. What she liked to watch was MTV and the *Today Show* and all the talk show ladies. If she could not marry Baron von Trapp, she would marry Bryant Gumbel. When Bryant Gumbel smiled it looked like he was smiling right at her. At night, when she said her prayers, she asked God to bless her family, the von Trapps, and Bryant Gumbel.

She saw on *Oprah* how special nicknames were one sign of love. She couldn't remember the other signs. Now, whenever her father swooped her up into his arms and said, "Hello there, Katy-Did," Kate said, "You love me a lot, don't you, Daddy?" Her father called that being secure.

Her mother liked to hug her tight and say, "You are the best little girl *ever.*" To Kate, that was how her mother talked. She always exaggerated words, so that her voice sounded like a song. Her mother smelled like something sweet that Kate couldn't name. And her face was round like a pie. If she took time to fix her hair, Kate thought she looked like a lemon meringue pie. But most of the time she was apple, all cinnamon and brown sugar, all round and sweet.

Everyone in her school loved Kate too. At playtime, they played *The Sound of Music* with her and let her choose who could be who. Kate was fair. She only let herself be Maria sometimes. Last year, during Family Night at her school, her teacher had picked her to be Ariel in *The Little Mermaid* song. Other kids had to be tropical fish and all kinds of boring undersea life. But Kate wore a long red wig and a silvery mermaid suit. She got to lip-sync and comb her hair and her father videoed the whole thing, like she was a star.

This year they were doing a song from *Aladdin* and Kate wanted to be Princess Jasmine. Some boy would be Ali and the other kids would be townspeople. Ali and the Princess got to sit on a mattress decorated like a flying carpet and get pulled around the stage.

"You can't *always* be the star," her mother told her. "You *might* have to be a tropical fish."

"That was *last* year," Kate said, trying to talk the way her mother did. Ex-*ag*-gerated. "The other kids have to be *towns*-people. Or they have to pull the mattress."

"That's what I'm trying to tell you," her mother said. "*You* might do the pulling."

"Mmmm," Kate said.

But she knew that would not happen. Her teacher loved her and would choose her to be the Princess. Her father would call that a fact.

The only person in the whole world who did not love Kate was her sister Maggie. Maggie called her Punk and Pain and other nicknames that were not the good kind.

Just yesterday when Kate was watching *Oprah,* Maggie came in and said, "Don't you know that television rots your brain?"

Oprah had on people who were as skinny as pickup sticks and others who were soft and fat as marshmallows. Before Maggie came in, Kate was thinking about how funny they all looked, even though some of them were crying. But when Maggie said that, all Kate could think of was worms chewing up her head.

"You are so spoiled," Maggie said, and Kate thought of sour milk and cottage cheese that had turned green. She wrinkled her nose. Spoiled things smelled bad. "I was never allowed to watch junk."

Maggie only watched *Mary Tyler Moore* on Nick at Nite.

"Do you wish you lived in Minneapolis?" Kate asked her sister. While she talked, she slowly and carefully sniffed different parts of herself—arm, knee, foot. She was *not* spoiled.

"I wish I lived anywhere else. Minneapolis. The moon. Anywhere," Maggie said, waving her arms. Maggie waved her arms a lot when she talked. Their father called this being melodramatic. Maggie, he'd say, and he'd sigh big and heavy, cut the melodramatics.

"People don't live on the moon," Kate said.

"No shit, Sherlock."

Kate frowned. Another bad nickname plus the S word.

"Why can't you be normal?" Maggie was saying. "Why can't you watch that stupid dinosaur like every other kid in the world?"

Kate thought about that, but could not come up with an answer except, "Dinosaurs aren't really purple, you know."

"Oh, I see," Maggie said, waving her arms again. "You're too much of a realist."

"I am not a realist!" Kate said. She didn't even know what it meant. But she was sure it was awful if Maggie called her one. Maggie was going on and on, about other kids and Barney and all sorts of stuff Kate couldn't follow.

Then Kate got an idea. Maggie would have to love her if she acted just like Maggie. She jumped to her feet and began waving her arms in the air.

"I'm a realist!" Kate shouted. That should make Maggie happy.

"Why are you waving your arms around like that?" Maggie said.

Kate tried to think of something else. Something anyone—even Maggie—would love. "I'm going to marry Bryant Gumbel!" Kate shouted.

But Maggie didn't even hear her. She was walking away, shaking her head, mumbling to herself, waving her arms like a helicopter.

Kate told her mother, "Maggie doesn't love me."

Her mother's apple pie face looked shocked. "Of *course* she does. You're her *sister.*"

That was a belief of her mother's. Sisters loved each other.

"Maggie is going through a difficult time," her mother said. "She's basically a *good* person."

That was another one. All people are basically good.

"She hates me," Kate said. She wondered how she could convince her mother. "She thinks I'm a realist," she whispered, in case it was a bad word like the S word or the F word.

But when she said it, her mother laughed. "Why that's a good thing," she told Kate.

"It is?"

Her mother nodded.

"Maggie doesn't hate me?"

Her mother hugged her hard. "You are the best little girl *ever,"* she said. "No one *hates* you."

Kate felt sleepy. She closed her eyes and thought about running through the Alps like Maria, singing. But then she thought of something else.

"Are Nazis basically good?" she asked her mother. The Nazis had chased the von Trapps out of their beloved Austria.

Her mother hesitated. But then she hugged her tight again and said, *"Everyone* is basically good."

When Josie showed the dress to Will after dinner, he'd grimaced.

"What?" she said. "The belt?"

"No," he said, and she could tell he was choosing his words carefully. "It's just that the invitation says everybody has to wear either black or white."

She held the dress close to her, the rhinestone belt drooping foolishly.

"That's . . . uh . . . red," Will had told her. "Very red."

As she stacked the dishwasher, gave Kate a bath, checked

on Maggie, the dress grew even redder. Until finally she decided to take it back. Even though it was after eight o'clock. She nudged Will hard, to get his attention, never an easy task once *America's Most Wanted* had started. He didn't take his eyes from the television. His hand, warm and a little damp, rested on Josie's knee. A perfect fit, he always said when he settled some part of his body on some part of hers—hand to knee, chest to back, foot to foot.

A face filled the screen, a computer image of a man suspected of murdering his wife in suburban New Jersey. The computer had aged the man ten years, which was how long he'd been missing. He was considered dangerous.

"That does it," Josie said, standing. "I'm going to return that dress. I don't know what possessed me to buy it in the first place." Although she did know. Panic had swept over her and she'd bought it without thinking.

Will wasn't listening of course. He was too busy making notes in a small pocket notebook he kept filled with information on wanted criminals. Will was sure that one day he would catch one of them. Working at a shopping mall, he always said, I see a lot of people. You can never be too sure.

"Maybe you should change careers," Josie told him. "Go into law enforcement."

Will sighed and closed the notebook. "You don't have to be so sarcastic," he said. "You never know."

"Here's something I do know," Josie said. "That dress is going back."

"Now?" Will said, finally noticing that she was gathering her things and getting ready to go. Purse. Dress. Receipt. "I'll come along."

Josie knew that Will hated going back to the mall after he'd been there all day.

"Oh, no," she said. "If I go alone I get to spend all your money. Maybe I'll get a slinky black Donna Karan number."

"Great," he said. He didn't even pretend to know what she was talking about. His eyes had already drifted back to the television and another crime reenactment.

Denise's husband would know who Donna Karan was. And Luciano Pavarotti and Diane Arbus. And Denise's husband was awful. He always talked about things he'd just bought and things he was about to buy. He thought Josie and Will's house was cute. "Faux country," he'd said once, "n'est-ce pas?" He loved using French phrases in conversation. For their honeymoon, that's where he and Denise had gone. Paris.

Josie crawled onto his lap. "I love you," she whispered.

"Uh-oh," Will said. "You *are* going to spend all our money."

Suddenly Josie was overcome by something, a strong feeling that made her grab Will and hug him hard enough that he had to struggle free from it, from her. "You know what?" Josie said, pulling back so she could look Will right in the eye. "You're right. Maybe you will catch one of those criminals. I mean, they do get caught. We hear about it every week."

"Exactly! It's one of those situations where you say, 'It can't happen to me.' But it can."

Now the screen was showing a mug shot of a man who was a carjacker. He had also raped several of his victims. He, too, was armed and dangerous.

"Well," Josie said, "just be careful if you ever do apprehend one of these guys. They're dangerous people, you know."

Will pressed her to him in a bear hug, close and hard. "Don't you worry, little pilgrim," he said in his John Wayne voice. Will could imitate almost anybody. Humphrey Bogart, Jimmy Stewart. Anybody.

Funny, Josie thought, how a man who made goofy faces and imitated old movie stars could make her feel so safe. Walking to her car, she thought that as long as Will was with her, she would be unharmed. Not a very feminist thought, she knew, but it was what she believed.

Josie smelled rain in the air. But the night was clear, with a nearly full moon, a dazzling array of stars. Why not do all of her errands while she was out? she decided. So that by the time she got to the mall there were four grocery bags full of diet food in the back of the Honda. Rice cakes and nonfat yogurt, celery and carrots that Josie would cut into sticks to munch on, skinless chicken breasts and low-fat salad dressings. Just buying it all made Josie feel lighter. That unsettled feeling that seemed to be following her around for so many weeks had disappeared. She felt in charge of her life again.

When she'd left the house, the pale pink poppies she'd planted had burst into bloom. She took it as a good sign. Driving away, Josie had glanced into the rearview mirror and caught a glimpse of her house receding. Watching it she thought, "That is where I live. That is where my family is." She'd had to pull over and collect herself before she continued on. Parked on that hill, with her house behind her and East Essex below her, the dogwoods and magnolias in full bloom, the air rich with the smells of spring and, faintly, soap, Josie rested her head on the steering wheel and cried. She felt ridiculous doing it, but still she sat like that for what seemed a very long time, the cool night air on her neck and the sound of birds and, in the distance, church bells.

Finally she drove on. It was then she had decided to start a diet. A real diet. She would go to the new supermarket, the one where Denise shopped, where the produce was laid out like jewels. Even the peppers there were richly colored—amethyst and topaz and ruby red. But she found herself going a long way around, through the older part of town where the few large, statelier homes were. They were hidden behind a grove of trees bordered by an old stone wall. Josie found herself at Judge Robinson's old house before she realized she should have gone a more direct route, down the hills by her platte and right onto the main street that linked up with Route 2.

Josie slowed in front of the judge's house. It was large and white, with pillars in the front, a rolling lawn, and dozens of rosebushes. She remembered that those roses had won awards. As children in elementary school, they'd taken a field trip to see the roses; in fact, Josie recalled that until she'd seen the judge's roses, she'd thought roses only came in one size and one color—red. But here they bloomed as large as her fist, pale peach and bright yellow and even black. They had not been allowed to touch. There were thorns, her teacher had explained, that could hurt you very, very badly.

A blue Mercedes was parked in the driveway, and beside it a Range Rover. Josie studied the house for signs of life behind the sheer drapes. But everything remained quiet, and so still that she felt a shiver creep up her spine. It wasn't until she drove away that she realized she couldn't smell the soap factory there. Just the clean smells of spring.

Now she stood in Jordan Marsh, the red dress returned, the diet foods bought, paying for a new set of sheets covered with yellow roses. Seeing the judge's house like that, remembering the sight of all those rosebushes, had drawn her to this set. She was buying the dust ruffle and matching comforter, too. She would put up new curtains, she decided. Sheer ones that let in light. A man passed in front of her, someone familiar, and Josie raised her hand in a small wave and smiled at him. He smiled back, a quick smile, and moved on.

In the mirror at the bottom of the escalator, Josie caught a glimpse of herself. She had on her new loose-fit jeans from the Gap, and she'd worn her hair down for a change. Already she seemed to be losing weight, she thought, even though she knew that was impossible. It was the first time in what seemed a long while that she liked what she saw. As she left the store and walked across the parking lot, balancing her oversized bags, she found herself humming an old song, one from when she was young. It was something Michaela used to play over and over, "The Motorcycle Song" by Arlo Guthrie. By the time Josie reached her car, she was singing it softly to herself, the words coming back to her easily after all this time. Funny she should think of that silly song. She hadn't heard it in years.

Josie opened the trunk of her car and dropped her packages inside. The handles on the bags left small red marks on her wrists, like the bracelets she and Michaela used to make out of shoestring licorice when they were children. As she went to unlock her car door, she began to sing that song again.

"Excuse me," someone said from behind her.

She jumped slightly, startled. "Oh," she said, turning, her car keys shining bold and silver in the fluorescent light. She hadn't noticed before how this lighting made everything look so eerie. "You scared me," Josie said.

He smiled when she said that, and the smile seemed familiar. It was the man she'd seen up in the linen department, the one she knew from . . . where did she know him from? Josie lifted her hand to shield her eyes from the fluorescent parking lot light. Will always told her to park under the lights. She glanced around a little nervously. It was amazing how quickly the mall had emptied out. When she'd arrived she'd had to circle several times for a parking space, had considered herself lucky to find one under a light, close to the entrance.

"I'll take those," the man said, moving toward her, reaching out.

Up close like this, Josie wasn't sure she did know him. His face, which had seemed almost baby-like in the store, seemed harsher out here. Maybe he had been one of those boys in high school that hung out in the parking lot with their souped-up cars, Firebirds and Mustangs with wide stripes on the hoods and fat tires. She wouldn't remember one of those boys by name. She thought of loud engines. Heavy smoke. Led Zeppelin music. Black leather.

"The keys," he was saying. He moved closer still, so close she could smell him, a mixture of mint mouthwash and soap. Then, softer, so softly she wasn't sure she'd heard him right, "Bitch."

"Are you from East Essex?" Josie said, pressing against the car door. She could feel the hard edges of the door handle in her back.

The man leaned in to her and, to her horror, Josie felt his erection against her crotch. Ridiculously she thought of junior high dances, of boys with greasy hair and too many pimples doing the same thing, pushing their hard-ons into you while Bobby Vinton sang "Blue Velvet" on the stereo.

"I know you," she said, "don't I?" She was pinned between him and the car. She couldn't get away.

He was twisting her arm now, twisting it hard so that the keys dropped from her hand. She watched them fall, watched him bend and scoop them up. Even if she screamed there was no one to hear her. When the man stood, he took both of his hands and grabbed her breasts in them. His touch was oddly gentle. My God, she thought. My God. He looked right at her, with the slightest trace of a smile. Josie tried to memorize important details, height, weight, clothing, distinguishing features. Like they did on *America's Most Wanted.* Not letting go with one hand, the man took a key, the one that opened the car door, that started the car, and pulled it harshly down her shirt, sending buttons popping off. The key against her flesh was warm—from his hands, she thought, and tugged at her skin, scratching it as it moved crookedly down to the top of her new jeans.

Was it better to scream or to beg or to challenge? Did those crime shows give tips about what to do at a time like this? She couldn't remember. She watched him lick his lips. She thought of Will, probably dozing in the chair. She thought of her daughters' faces. She knew every inch of those faces, the slope of their nose, the way the cheekbones slanted, the particular set of the eyes in the face. Those were the things, she told herself, she should be concentrating on here, on this face peering so closely at her own. A cool night breeze drifted between them and, disgusted, she felt her exposed nipples harden against it. What if he mistook that for excitement? For delight? In that instant she wanted nothing more than to pull her shirt closed. Why hadn't she taken the time to put on a bra?

Without warning, all of the lights turned off—the ones that announced each store's name, the ones that illuminated the parking lot. He could kill her now and no one would see anything at all. The man seemed to hesitate, as if he was deciding something. Then he pushed Josie to the ground. She fell hard, felt the gravel against her face, tasted blood as she bit into her lip. She looked up at him. He seemed so large standing there above her. Once again he seemed to hesitate. Josie tried to get up, but he stopped her, kicking her hard in the side and sending her back to the pavement. He kicked her again, still harder, and she felt the air knocked from her. It was a moment before she realized that the grunts she heard were her own. In the darkness, her breasts flopped, white and hideous, embarrassing her. She tasted blood. The kicks landed randomly, first in her stomach, then her face, then on the softness of her thigh. When finally they stopped she thought he was preparing for some final act—rape or a knife in her chest. She thought this was her last chance to escape.

Before she could move again, he was getting in her car, turning the key in the ignition. He looked down at her once more before he drove off, his face lit up by the sluggish interior light that took too long to shut off. And it was in that moment that Josie finally remembered how she knew him. He was the Mall Carjacker, the criminal she and Will had seen just hours ago on *America's Most Wanted.* He was armed and dangerous, Josie remembered, as she watched him drive away in her car with all the diet food and the new sheets and comforter decorated with soft yellow roses in bloom.

week two

—

The first thing Josie did, after the man drove away with her car, was to stretch out on her back, right there in the mall parking lot, and gaze up at the night sky. She lay like that for a long, long time. She used to do that when she was a child. If she felt sad, she would go out to the backyard and lie on the grass and look at the sky. She would find animal shapes in the clouds or make up her own constellations among the stars. Michaela knew about the sky. She confronted it directly—the Seven Sisters, Orion. Her finger could trace the shape of a belt or a bear; she could tell Josie what constellations were over Australia, and why. But Josie preferred a private sky. For her, it held a certain magic. Clouds could be giraffes or elephants, stars could be castles or princesses. She used to find comfort in that.

As Josie gazed upward from the parking spot where her car had sat a moment ago, she saw clouds drift across the night sky and all she could think of was what they really were—drops of water. It was hard to believe she had ever seen them as anything more. Absently, her fingers moved down her rib cage, to her hip, pressing hard. The hip, she decided, was probably just bruised. But one or two ribs could be broken. It hurt to breathe. When she heard a car moving in the vast parking lot, she thought for a crazy instant that he had come back. To finish her off, perhaps. She'd always heard that criminals return to the scene of the crime.

Josie took a slow, painful breath. He had only wanted the car, she reminded herself. By now, he could be out of Rhode Island altogether, driving north, munching her apple cinnamon rice cakes. What kind of person stole a 1986 Honda Civic, when certainly the parking lot had better choices—new cars, clean cars? Somewhere she had read that the Lexus was the most stolen car. Hadn't there been a Lexus parked anywhere in this whole mall lot? Her car, Josie remembered, smelled like the big cardboard strawberry that hung from the rearview mirror. When it was warm, the vomit from Kate's tendency toward car sickness emerged past the cloying strawberry scent. The tape deck didn't even work, hadn't worked since 1991. In fact, there was still a chewed-up Raffi tape in there that Josie had long ago given up trying to pry out. And then there was that sluggish overhead light.

She would have to go to the police. Give a description. But already the man's face was as wispy as the clouds floating past her. Blue eyes? Green? Not brown, she was sure of that. She was sure he was dressed like everyone else. A tan windbreaker, maybe. Jeans? Sneakers? She couldn't be certain. He had looked so ordinary. He had smelled of mint mouthwash. And soap. She knew he was that mall carjacker from *America's Most Wanted,* but she wasn't sure now how she could possibly know that. A person could not go to the police without anything concrete to say. Criminals weren't caught by the way they smelled.

Slowly, Josie got to her feet. She felt stiff, as if she had lain there for hours. She definitely had a broken rib. The mall, the parking lot, everything, looked different, as if she had never been there before. In the distance she spotted the car she'd heard a moment ago, parked now at a crooked angle. Probably teenagers, she decided. She could almost see them in there, a tangle of arms and legs, of sweat and panting. She considered going over there, knocking on the window, scaring the hell out of them. Running the risk that there weren't teenagers in there at all but a pervert with a dirty magazine and his pants down. Will had told her once that there was a guy like that, an old guy who parked near the mall and masturbated while he read dirty magazines.

It ocurred to Josie that she didn't have a clue what she should do. Even at this hour she would have thought there was some kind of mall security, a car to chase away perverts and teenagers, a few guards to prevent break-ins. She turned toward the mall, but it stood there, seemingly empty. The mall itself, the actual building, that Josie always thought of as festive with its stone and brick and bright blue trim, looked like a pile of useless junk. Like nothing inside was worth anything at all.

She said out loud, "I could have been killed." The hoarseness of her voice surprised her. He had, she remembered, kicked her in the throat, too.

She started to walk across the empty parking lot, trying to formulate a plan.

When Josie was six, a boy threw a rock at her on the way home from school. It hit her on the forehead, between her eyes. Years later, Michaela told her that rock landed on her third eye and robbed her of psychic ability and memories of her past lives. But at the time when the rock hit her, with a loud thwacking sound, Josie had thought she was going to die. She was too scared to cry or chase the boy or get help. It took everything she could muster just to walk the rest of the way home, while her head throbbed and a steady stream of blood oozed down her face. All she had wanted was to live long enough to see her house and her mother's face. When she'd turned the corner at her street, she'd actually stopped to take it all in—the flowers bordering the yard and the yellow dotted swiss curtains that hung in her bedroom window. Blood dripped into one eye and gave everything a funny orange tinge. Her legs felt heavy. She walked in the back door and saw her mother and her aunts at the kitchen table, drinking coffee and smoking cigarettes—they all smoked back then, menthol cigarettes. Their faces, when they finally looked up and saw Josie in the doorway, were horrified, the way people looked in horror movies when a monster comes to town.

Without actually deciding to do it, Josie found herself walking up the street to her parents' house, remembering that other time she'd appeared bloody and frightened. She'd known who'd thrown the rock, though, a boy named Gary DiChristofaro. A boy who liked her. For the longest time she'd been certain that boys who liked you caused you great pain. After walking all this way, it hurt even more to breathe. As Josie made her way up the back stairs to her parents' house, her head throbbed in that old place, between her eyes, where there was still a scar that looked like a wavy letter G, a faint white line that no one except Josie even noticed. For a while, she had felt like Gary DiChristofaro had branded her. She rubbed it as she made her way. It was as if, Josie thought, the scar remembered this same path home.

She was not prepared for what she found inside. Her aunts and cousins, her parents. For an instant, she imagined that she had been wandering for a very long time—hours? days?—and that they had all come to find her the way communities gathered in one central place for lost children. But then she saw the reason they had all come together. There, in the center of everyone, long red hair slightly electric, eyes gleaming, almost wicked, sat Michaela.

Michaela had not changed the way she looked since 1972. She still wore her red hair long, all the way to her rear end. She didn't wear any makeup except clear lip gloss and blue mascara that she only wore for special occasions. She didn't wear underwear or bras or deodorant. She owned half a dozen pairs of jeans, size 4, in various stages of fading and ripping and an old pair of black Tony Lama cowboy boots that she'd bought for two hundred dollars in Harvard Square the summer before she'd moved out here. In her left ear she wore a silver half moon earring, in her right ear a silver sun. They were each from a different pair, their mates lost long ago. Those things were the staples of her wardrobe. She wore them every day, no matter what. Somewhere, she had a couple of long tiered skirts, each tier a different print, paisley or flowered.

Men loved the way she looked. Often they thought she was a kid, in her early twenties. When she told them she was actually closer to forty, they never believed her. She would have to pull out her expired driver's license as proof. More and more, though, that only happened in the dark of a bar. In the bright light, even her freckles couldn't hide the thin lines that had started to form around her eyes and mouth. She had taken to holding her hands to her face, cupping it gently. She was considering wearing more mascara, to bring out the blue of her eyes, which were already a startling clear blue that made people think about ice, about cold places.

Josie did not have time to call out to her sister, to anyone. They all turned toward her with those same horror movie faces —mouths open, eyes wide—and in one giant motion that made Josie think of a tidal wave, they moved toward her, their voices blurring together, "My God, my God, what happened to you, my God."

None of them could believe it, that she'd been attacked at the mall, that her car was stolen, that she'd walked here despite her bruises, her scrapes, her broken ribs. Mostly, though, they couldn't believe that she had somehow neglected to call the police.

"I didn't see the point," Josie told them. She could not find the words for her reasoning, how already the man's face was as blank as a sheet of paper.

"But they would have put out an APB," Denise said. "They would have found him. Or the car, at least."

"Absolutely," James said, nodding his head with great authority.

Claire came over to her, inspecting Josie the way she used to when they were children—touching the back of her hand to Josie's forehead, pressing different places on her arms, shoulders, head. All the while, everyone else talked, and Josie could concentrate only on their mouths moving. They seemed large, larger, gargantuan. All flapping lips and horse teeth. There was a scene in an old movie like that, with Hepburn and Tracy, where people's mouths took over their faces, became exaggerated, overpowering.

"It's not even safe," Aunt Beatrice was saying, "to go to the mall anymore."

They began discussing crimes—murders of innocent people with guns, with crossbows, entire families killed as they slept, snipers on highways, in elementary schools. Michaela didn't speak. She just narrowed her eyes and leaned back in the kitchen chair, the way she used to get in trouble for when she was a teenager. "You'll break it," their mother would insist, and she did finally break one, the spindles popping out all at once and Michaela, surprised, falling all the way back, to the floor, in a cloud of splinters and shards of wood.

Aunt Tiny said, "There was a man who murdered his wife and his mother and five of his own children and got away with it—"

"Here?" Judy said, frightened.

"Somewhere else. New Jersey, maybe," Aunt Tiny said. "I saw him on *America's Most Wanted*—"

"That's where I saw my guy," Josie said. "The carjacker."

Denise's face loomed in front of hers, so close that Josie could see the mascara in her eyelashes, the pencil line around her lips.

"You saw him on television?" Denise said, not even trying to hide her disbelief.

"Just tonight," Josie said. "Will always watches that show—"

Michaela laughed. "A real intellectual, that Will."

Josie's head was really hurting now. She rubbed the old scar harder. "He thinks maybe he'll see one of them at the mall."

She was surprised when her father spoke. "You know what they say? That victims of crime are so eager to catch the criminal that they often point the finger at anyone, no matter how unlikely."

He said it kindly. But still, he didn't believe her. Josie saw that. None of them did.

"This is what happened," Josie said, hearing the desperation in her own voice.

"Well," James said. "First things first. We call the police. File a report. Et cetera."

"Che sarà sarà," Josie said.

Denise, who had turned from her to roll her eyes, turned back and Josie caught a whiff of coconut from her hair. "What?" Denise said, defiant.

Claire was shaking her head. "Isn't there security at that mall? Don't the police patrol the lot anymore?"

"You know," Denise said, waving her manicured hands in the air, "it happened to our aerobics instructor." She looked at Josie. "Barb," she said. She lowered her voice. "She was raped."

Josie clutched at her buttonless shirt. At some point she had tied it into a knot around her midriff but she still felt exposed. Denise was looking at her with what? Disappointment? Like her attack wasn't so bad? Maybe Denise thought she had been saved from rape only because she was so out of shape.

"He kicked me," Josie said defensively. "A lot."

James leaned close to her. "Were you violated?" he whispered. "Your shirt is torn, you know."

Josie did not lower her voice. "He . . . scratched me with his keys."

Everyone followed her own stare down to the ragged red line that seemed to divide her body exactly in half.

"My God," her mother said.

James had decided to take control. "You need to file a report," he said. "Should have been done hours ago, naturally. But you can say you were in shock."

"Wasn't I?" Josie asked him. She thought, Aren't I still? She had taken First Aid after Kate was born. She had learned about shock then. But she couldn't recall anything about it. Stay warm? Face pale, raise the tail, she remembered finally. Was that for shock?

James was frowning. "You can identify him, of course."

She thought of all the police sketches she had ever seen, how they all looked the same to her. His eyes were definitely light, she thought again. Definitely not brown.

"He looked so regular," she said. "Wait," she said. "We can call that show."

Her mother looked about to cry. "I'll get you another shirt," she said. "And I'll throw that out—"

"No!" Judy said, jumping to her feet. In high school, she had been the New England Cheerleader Jumping Champion. She had once jumped all the way to Providence to raise money for the Leukemia Society. She was jumping now, little bouncy ones. "That's evidence," she was saying. "You have to keep it just like that. No washing either. And no douching. It's all evidence."

Everyone stared at Josie but she did not know what was expected of her.

"All right then," James said after he'd cleared his throat several times. The idea of douching had unnerved him. "I'll take you as is then."

Josie stood, eager to follow, to have something to do. As is, she thought as they walked out. Like a used object at a going out of business sale.

The East Essex Police Station was a small stone building on Water Street in a neat line of other small stone buildings—post office, fire station, town hall—that had been built in the forties after the war. A monument, also stone, of a soldier in uniform gazing at some distant point, stood between the police and fire station. Usually, it was spraypainted with bright yellow graffiti by high school boys. The class of '69, Michaela's class, had actually drilled the number 69 into the soldier's helmet. The town council voted to keep it there rather than remove the statue or raise the money to fix it properly.

As Josie made her way up the steps to the police station, she saw that someone had painted GIGI GIVES above the etched 69. She found herself wanting to cry, for poor Gigi, for herself, for all the soldiers who had died in any war. James had to take her by the elbow and help her along. Her legs started to tremble so badly she had to pull away from James. She supposed she was out of shock now.

"I can't," she said. She meant she couldn't go in, but it seemed impossible to say anything more.

Denise and James exchanged a look that Josie couldn't interpret. Then Denise sat beside her, carefully dusting off the stone step with her hands first.

"Josie," Denise said. "Someone did attack you, right? And stole your car?"

The strong smell of coconut and Giorgio made Josie's stomach do a flip. She could taste the spaghetti she'd had for dinner. Dinner, she thought, remembering the casual way she'd placed the salad and pasta on the table, how she'd only half-listened to Kate's description of Oprah's guests that afternoon, how she hadn't even imagined that a few hours later she'd be knocked to the ground, fondled, kicked. Without warning, sobs began pouring from her.

"It was horrible," she managed to gasp.

Denise's hand covered her own. Through her tears Josie made out the oval fingernails, the smooth polish in a color called Seashell.

"Are you telling us the truth?" Denise was saying. "If something else happened . . . I mean, we're your family." She pressed her mouth against Josie's ear. "I won't tell Will," she whispered. "You can tell me anything."

It hurt to cry. Her head, her cheek, her jaw. "Like what?" Josie asked. When she went to push the hair from her face she felt a thick clot of blood.

"Like maybe you had something to drink and ran the car off the road," Denise said, still whispering. "And maybe you remember what happened to Barb and you figured it was a good story."

"You think I made this up?" Josie said.

Now it was James and his expensive French cologne that made her stomach flip. She burped back the sour taste of old spaghetti sauce.

"It looks funny," he said. "That's all. The way you didn't tell anyone."

"There was no one to tell," Josie said, the hoarseness in her voice surprising her again. She wondered if vocal cords bruised. "The mall was closed."

"But weren't there still people around?" Denise blurted.

James shooed her away. "There's a protocol, that's all," he

said, soothing. "You wave down a car. You run into Dunkin' Donuts and have someone call the police."

"You call 911," Denise said.

Josie put her hand to her mouth. They were right. She could have done any of those things. The Dunkin' Donuts was open twenty-four hours a day and sat right across from the mall. And she herself had read tales of incredible courage in which people who had been shot in the head, attacked by a grizzly bear, or nearly froze to death had gotten themselves to a road and flagged down a car for help. She tried to remember what she had been thinking, but even the walk home seemed to have been accomplished by someone else.

"I was in shock," she said finally.

"And honey, I'm sorry, but that story about the man just having been on TV," Denise said.

Josie got to her feet. "Has anyone called Will?" she said.

There was nothing she wanted more than to have him appear on these steps, right beside her. He would know she was telling the truth. He would produce his little notebook and give the police the man's description. Height. Weight. Color of eyes.

James studied her carefully. "Before we walk in the door, you'd better have some good answers as to why you did what you did."

All she had done, Josie thought, was return that stupid red dress. For their party. She continued up the steps. It didn't really matter if Denise and James believed her. The police would, and they would call Will and find the man who'd done this. They would put an end to this nightmare.

The policeman who took her statement was someone she'd gone to high school with. He had the improbable nickname of Dog. His badge said: DOG MCGOVERN. When she first walked in he was sitting behind the desk playing solitaire and he looked up and said, "Holy shit! What happened to you? Car accident?" Josie could just see Denise and James exchanging that same look behind her.

After she told her story, Dog said, "Let me see if I got this right. You say some guy with light eyes came up to you in the parking lot at the mall and ripped your shirt and kicked you a bunch of times, then drove away in your car."

Josie nodded. She couldn't believe that Dog McGovern was supposed to solve this crime. He couldn't even diagram sentences in school. He couldn't even pass new math.

"You say this happened at ten o'clock."

Josie nodded again. The clock that hung over Dog's head read two-twenty.

Dog leaned back in his chair. "Where you been for four hours?"

Still not very good at math, Josie thought. But she didn't correct him. "I lay there for a while," she said. "A long while, I guess. Maybe I blacked out?"

"Laid where?" Dog said.

"In the parking lot." Then she added a lie. "I kept thinking a patrol car would come by, but there were just these kids parking."

James slapped his hands down on Dog's desk. "There was another car there?"

"They came later," Josie said. She had never been a good liar. Why had she said anything new at all? "After the guy drove off."

"Excuse me for asking," Dog said, scratching his head where it met his hat in the back. "But why didn't you ask them to take you to the hospital or something?"

"I was afraid," she told him. "My husband—" she began, then decided not to say anything about the pervert.

Dog shook his head. "Okay. Then what?"

"Then I got up and walked to my mother's house. But it took a long time because it's hard for me to breathe. I think he broke a rib."

"You walked what? A mile? A mile and a half?"

James broke in. "About a mile and a quarter, I'd say."

"Did you pass any cars or anything like that?" Dog asked her.

Josie shrugged.

Abruptly, Dog stood. "Well, we got your license number, car description, pertinent data"—he pronounced it like dada—"and we'll see what comes of it. You know, if car theft is reported right away, we can usually find it. Four hours later . . ." He shrugged too.

"If you think of anything else," Dog said, shuffling the deck of cards, "give a call."

On the way to the emergency room, Josie remembered that once she'd kissed Dog during a game of Spin the Bottle in someone's basement. The thought made her dizzy. Neither James nor Denise were talking to her, so she rolled down the window and tried to clear her head. By the time they got to the hospital, it was dawn and it had started to rain. She had to wait two and a half hours for her X-rays to come back. "Broken rib," the doctor said. But she already knew that.

When she finally got home she was so tired she almost asked James to carry her inside. But she just thanked them and got out of the car.

"We'll call tomorrow," Denise said. "To check in." Her face was all twisted up. She mouthed something—Call me? Trust me? Tell me? Was it that unbelievable to have lost four hours after something like this? Josie wondered.

They watched her until she was safely inside.

Will and Maggie and Kate were all waiting for her. "My Puffalump was in the Honda!" Kate said. "What am I going to do?" Maggie wanted details. "Were you scared? Were you brave? Did he have pockmarks?" But Josie was too exhausted to answer any more questions. She just gave them a half wave and walked by, up the stairs, into her bedroom. It was hard for her to believe that just twelve hours ago she had felt happy. That she had loved this house, these people. Without undressing or folding back the covers, she lay on the bed. She could not remember what that new comforter she bought even looked like. Then it came to her. Roses. Yellow roses. What would that man do with it? she wondered.

Will came into the room and stood over her. From this angle, she could see right up his nose. She looked away.

"I don't understand what happened," he said.

"What?"

"You left here at eight to return one dress. Why would you still be at the mall at closing time? And even then the parking lot is full. There are employees leaving. There's a security car on patrol."

"I went grocery shopping first," she said, knowing it sounded foolish. But she couldn't think of a way to explain to him how she'd been feeling lately, what she'd thought as she sat in the car and looked at their home.

"I was attacked," she added. Was she misunderstanding something? "The car is gone," she added as proof.

"You didn't even call the police."

Josie sat up. Sudden movements made the pain from her broken rib worse, and she groaned. "I have a broken rib," she said. "And my hip—"

"What were you thinking?" Will said.

He was looking at her like she was the criminal. If her rib didn't hurt so much, Josie would have lay back down and looked up his nose all the way to his brain so she could understand what he was thinking. The thought made her smile. Imagine if that was possible! Then a sudden terrible thing came into her mind with great clarity, as if she really had peeked into Will's brain—he doesn't love me anymore, she realized.

"Thank God I'm alive," Josie said softly.

The odd thing was, she didn't feel especially alive. She felt like everything inside her had been sucked out. Last year she had taken a course at Easter time on how to make Ukrainian Easter eggs. The teacher had shown them how to poke a small hole in one end of an egg and suck out the insides. That was how Josie felt right now, like one of those empty shells.

Nancy Caycedo was the realtor for the Jericho house. Claire remembered her as a cheerleader with her niece Judy, a muscular girl who cried when the East Essex team lost a football game. Even now, standing in Claire's kitchen, Nancy looked like she could still turn a cartwheel on a clear autumn day and land firmly on her feet. Imagining her that way made Claire sure that Nancy Caycedo would sell this house.

Already Nancy had a list of potential buyers. Mostly young couples, just starting out. "This house," Nancy said, nodding solemnly, "is ideal for new families."

Claire nodded. She and Dan had bought the house in 1950 from the woman who'd bought it brand-new. When they walked in, the house was full of the smell of cinnamon. Years later someone told her that was an old seller's trick, to make it smell homey. The woman had made them strong tea, and told them about her own children, all grown then and moved away. Her husband, Claire remembered, had recently died of something long and painful. "This house," the woman had told them, patting Claire's hand, "is for young people. People beginning life." The woman still wore her wedding ring, a simple thin gold band that had grown too large for her shrinking frame.

Nancy was staring out, hands on hips, as if she could already see new people there, a fresh coat of paint on the walls, children's toys strewn about. She exhaled deeply and turned on her bright cheerleader's smile. "Let's get to work!" she said with so much enthusiasm Claire felt the impulse to shout and jump herself.

Getting to work meant showing the house right away. "ASAP," Nancy said, studying her list.

"How soon is that?" Claire asked her. She had intended on dusting and putting out some fresh flowers from the garden. Maybe even baking something with cinnamon.

"The Laboissonaires can be here in an hour," Nancy said. She poked her finger at their name on her clipboard. "They both work at home so they make their own hours. She's pregnant with numero uno, even though she must be forty, at least. Why, you might even know her. She went to school with Michaela and me."

"Laboissonaire?" Claire said. "I don't think so."

"Her name was Pullman," Nancy told her. "Cynthia."

"Cynthia Pullman? She was one of Michaela's best friends." Claire could picture her clearly, her horsey face and large teeth. "I thought something terrible had happened to her."

Nancy leaned closer to Claire. "Drugs. She was in and out of rehab centers. Then she got in some kind of awful accident that left her with a limp. She and her husband are in some kind of cult, I think."

"A cult!" Claire said. "I don't want anything like that in my house."

"Not like the Moonies or that Waco thing," Nancy said quickly. "Just some kind of strange religion. Someone told me they have a weird shrine in their living room."

Both women turned toward the Jericho living room.

"A shrine," Claire said.

Nancy stood up, all business again. "They're woodworkers," she said, as if that erased the other terrible stuff. "Isn't that something?"

"Yes," Claire said, unconvinced. She could always say no to them. She didn't have to sell the house to people in a cult, to drug addicts. Like the woman who had sold the house to her, Claire wanted a nice family in it.

Nancy was collecting all of her papers and lists, putting them into her briefcase. "How is Michaela?" she said. "I see Josie all the time. She's like me. Still shops at Freddie's Market. That Super Stop and Shop is so impersonal, I think. And full of stuff I've never even heard of."

"Yes," Claire said, wanting her to leave so she could go and sit in her living room and think.

But Nancy seemed to be waiting for something. "Michaela?" she said finally. "How is she?"

"She's home," Claire said. "She's jogging."

"After all this time," Nancy said. "I guess that's what happens. Everyone goes off and experiments with this and that and finally just comes back home again. Cynthia and Ollie and now Michaela." She snapped her briefcase shut. "I'll be back," she said. "With the Laboissonaires."

"Wait," Claire said, and touched her arm to keep her there. "Ollie Pfeiffer has moved back?"

Again Nancy leaned in toward Claire and lowered her voice. "I heard he has a drinking problem. Isn't that the saddest thing? They bought Judge Robinson's house so at least he saved up some of that money he got from those big contracts."

"They?" Claire said.

In the instant she heard he was back, Claire had imagined that fate had intervened and brought Michaela and Ollie back home again to live out the life they should have had. But no. Here was Nancy Caycedo telling her about a beautiful wife and beautiful children.

"Children," Claire repeated.

"Two at least," Nancy said. "Boys with odd names. But the wife is from down south somewhere. I think they like to name them funny down there, don't they?"

Claire shrugged, even more eager to have her house to herself.

"I guess," Nancy said at the front door, "people just have to come home."

Alone finally, Claire knew she should fix the house up a bit. At least bring some flowers in. Instead, she went into the living room and sat in the rocking chair. It creaked when it rocked. It always had. That creak was comforting and familiar. Claire had rocked both of her children in this chair, holding them close to her in the middle of the night, singing them back to sleep. She used to sing them show tunes, the only songs she knew all the words to.

Claire tried to imagine different furniture in here. Woodworkers, she supposed, would have large, heavy furniture. They would have that bright Haitian cotton on everything, the kind that made you itchy when you sat on it. Where would they put the shrine? She looked over at the grandfather's clock. It hadn't worked in years, was stuck at nine-twenty and missing one of the weights. A funny thing to lose, but they had.

That was where the shrine would go, she decided. In the corner where the grandfather's clock had sat for so long. There would be a purple cloth, those strange candles they sold in the supermarket, the ones that supposedly brought good luck. And incense and a picture of their guru or whatever it was they had. Funny, even though the clock had been silent so long, she could still hear its loud ticking, like a metronome. And the way it bonged so deeply, calling out the hour and the half hour. Maybe she'd get it fixed. There was a dumb thought, Claire told herself. She wouldn't be needing a big old clock taking up room in a condo.

Claire closed her eyes and rocked, singing "I Love You a Bushel and a Peck" softly to herself. That was from *Guys and Dolls.* It had been one of her favorite lullabies. Sitting there like that, remembering, she could almost feel the weight of a baby resting in her arms.

Michaela Jericho had come back to East Essex for a reason: to get on with her life. Despite all her cynicism and disappointments—not only with her life, but with life in general, the bad politicians and the right-wingers and the children in Bosnia and Somalia and pollution and homelessness—despite all of that, there was still a part of her that sounded like a Hallmark greeting card, a part that believed in order to move forward, you had to sometimes first go back.

Years before, she was a young girl with clear skin and long legs, a kid who loved to run, fast. On her softball team, she held the record for the most stolen bases. When she played basketball for her CYO team in the gym of the Catholic school, she could steal the ball from an opponent and run to her team's basket, leaving everyone behind. Since she'd come back, she had spent hours looking through shoeboxes filled with old pictures, staring at her own, younger face, surprised by what she saw there. That was why she was out here in the rain, running again, wearing her old black-and-yellow East Essex High regulation gym shorts and one of her father's undershirts.

Her plan had been to come home and confront her past. She had left San Francisco finally, so she could look her mother in the eye and talk about what had happened the summer before she left. But when she got here, everything was out of place—her father was worse than she'd thought, her mother had grown older, and then there was Josie. Her sister had wandered in last night with a story no one could believe. Four hours lying in the parking lot? each of them had said. But Michaela had believed her. Trauma did strange things to people. In the twenty years that she'd lived in San Francisco, she'd been mugged twice, once at gunpoint and once with what turned out to be a high-heeled shoe tucked inside a guy's jacket; it had looked exactly like a gun to her. She didn't believe she had acted rationally either time. When she had her wet laundry stolen from the laundromat while she'd gone next door to buy Bounce, she'd kicked all the machines and sworn instead of looking down the street for someone dragging ten pounds of wet clothes. When she'd had all of her Beatles' albums stolen from the back seat of her car during a move, she had simply sat on the sidewalk and cried. Michaela believed her sister. What was bothering her was that she hadn't let Josie know that. She couldn't reach out to her sister anymore. Or maybe she couldn't reach out to people at all.

Michaela kept running, the muscles in her legs aching, soft. East Essex unfolded sadly around her. You fix a place in your mind, she thought, and when you see it again, it disappoints. The way a return trip to your kindergarten reveals a duller, smaller room, East Essex had shrunk, gone seedy. All of these years, Michaela had thought of the old stone walls that lined the fields here, the neat rows of mill houses along the river, the river itself—sparkling, gently curving—as if it were all part of illustrations in a fairy tale. She had not thought of East Essex as shabby. But it was. She saw that as she turned each corner, reached the top of a hill, looked down on the town. East Essex was falling apart. Every house needed painting, shingling, a new roof. Potholes gaped at her as she ran down the roads. The smell of soap clung to everything, turned the air a strange yellowish brown. Ocher, she thought. A color she'd never really experienced before. But then, she'd never imagined that the cloying smell of soap would make her want to wash up with very hot water to get rid of it.

Of course, when soap seems dirty and home seems unfamiliar, a person had to wonder if all of her memories had turned the truth inside out. While she jogged, Michaela made herself think of the other thing, the one that had led her away from East Essex and now had brought her back. A few months ago, her friend Belle had thrown her runes. "It's time to complete unfinished business," she'd told Michaela. And Michaela, who had long ago given up on the stars, had seen in her own chart that the time was right to take a risk that would bring harmony and completion. Looking up from the pile of stones she'd thrown for Michaela, Belle had asked her, "What was it that you gave up?" Michaela had thought of this town, of her mother and aunts around the kitchen table and the feel of her sister's head on her shoulder. She had stared down at her runes, laid out before them like a run-down cemetery. "Everything," she said.

Michaela paused to look up at the factory. It seemed almost medieval, like a castle—old and stone. The thing was enormous. Standing beside it, she felt nearly invisible. A speck. Breathing hard, she walked over the footbridge that led to the main entrance. The bridge arched gracefully, and Michaela thought that standing on it someone could easily imagine they were crossing the Pont Neuf, that the river gurgling beneath them was the Seine. She stopped midway across and peered over the side. Looking down at the sluggish yellow-brown foam below, Michaela got that inside-out feeling again. The Pont Neuf. She smiled to herself. The water here was so polluted it reminded her of water after you've done a large load of especially dirty dishes. The river hardly even flowed. Instead, it swirled and burped and sent up a vaguely foul smell.

A loud horn blasted.

Michaela looked up at the factory. Inside, people began to move in some kind of robotic ballet. Despite growing up here, despite all of her various careers, Michaela realized she had never stepped foot in a mill. Here she had grown up in the cradle of the Industrial Revolution and she didn't even know what went on behind these doors. What she knew about factories seemed to be out of a textbook. She imagined children in short pants, women in flowing dresses and hairnets, noisy machinery, rats, fire hazards, assembly lines.

She took a few shaky steps toward the entrance. In old-fashioned script above the door a sign said *Dalton.* Dalton Mill was the last mill left in East Essex. Once, there had been a dozen or more, proudly lining the river. They had made fabric, novelties, luggage, soap. When she was a child, they had all seemed to be alive. People streamed in and out, horns sounded, dark smoke billowed from them into the sky. A few had burned down, long after they were empty. Others still stood, their windows broken, the dates beside the door—1892, 1877—obscured by dust and years. From some long-ago history lesson Michaela remembered that a century ago a sign stood at the border of East Essex: EAST ESSEX MAKES, THE WORLD TAKES.

The doors opened and people began to leave, crowds of them, moving as one. Michaela studied the faces that passed her, hoping to see someone she might know. In school it had seemed that everyone knew someone who worked in one of the mills. For years, Aunt Tiny had headed the payroll department for Montgomery Mill. They made holiday novelty items and Aunt Tiny was always bringing home Christmas stockings in summer, Easter baskets in October, plastic pumpkins stuffed with candy in spring. For a moment, Michaela almost expected to see Aunt Tiny among these people, but of course that was ridiculous. She watched until everyone had flooded past her, their heads bent, the smell of soap on them so strong it became almost sweet. They all wore the same unofficial uniform—sweatpants and sneakers and T-shirts from a vacation spot—Las Vegas and Disney World and Lake Winnipesaukee.

When she was standing alone on the bridge again,

Michaela felt dizzy. Maybe it was that smell. Or the river. She rested against the railing. Or maybe, she thought, it was the way this place—East Essex—had shifted when she wasn't looking.

Back when her name had been Claire Orso and she was considered the "pretty one" of the three Orso girls, Claire's father had been a cobbler. When he returned home at night, he smelled of leather and shoe polish. His hands were stained black, his fingers calloused from holding his tools. East Essex used to have a downtown, a small section of Water Street with shops and restaurants. Her father's shop was there, a tiny place wedged between a woman's store called Ramona's and the five-and-dime. The shop had no name and everyone referred to it simply as Pete's. Inside, amid the racks of boots and high heels and loafers and wing tips, her father hung signs he'd made. WE PUT OUR HEARTS AND SOLES INTO YOUR SHOES. BLESS YOUR SOLE! "You can tell a lot about a person from their shoes," her father used to say.

Now, Water Street was run-down. The old Castle Theatre, where Claire and her sisters had gone every Saturday, where she'd fallen in love with Montgomery Clift and studied the way movie stars kissed so that she'd someday get it right, was now a porn shop. XXX, the marquee read. The five-and-dime where she used to go for a vanilla Coke, where her sister Beatrice once ran the Notions Department, was empty, dusty and bare, its windows boarded up. Ramona's was gone too, just another empty building. For a time, when she was a girl, people came from as far away as Boston to shop there.

Claire parked her car in front of her father's old shop. It was a locksmith's now. At least something with integrity was there, not a bar, not something marked XXX. She took two of the boxes for Goodwill from the trunk and walked down the sidewalk. Water Street reminded her of a ghost town. She half-expected some tumbleweed to blow past, or a stranger dressed in black to appear. At her father's shop she peeked in. Although the store was open, no one was inside. Keys hung in serious rows from the wall that once held everyone's shoes. Bless your sole, Claire thought. But of course the signs were gone. The shop had been empty for a time, and had seen a personalized T-shirt shop, a florist, a card shop before this locksmith had moved in. By the looks of things, this would be gone soon too.

She made her way to Goodwill, a big multi-level store on the corner. Once, this building had been Desjardin's Furniture store. It was where she had bought cribs and changing tables, her daughters' bedroom furniture, the living room set she still had. She and her sisters used to come here just to walk through the showrooms. Now, the store was lit with bright fluorescent lighting. Bins held sad-looking clothes, the showrooms were filled with old sofas, torn Naugahyde easy chairs, lava lamps, and lots of orange knickknacks. It seemed like just yesterday that she and her sisters had stood here and planned their dream houses. Danish Contemporary, Beatrice had wanted. Standing here again, Claire could almost see her sister running her hands over the smooth blond wood.

"You want to dump that stuff?" a skinny boy with a long, thin ponytail asked Claire.

He was holding out his arms to her, ready for the boxes she held.

"Oh," Claire said, blinking a few times to clear away her memories. "Thank you."

He took the boxes from her.

"There's more in the car," she called after him. His T-shirt had the name of a rock group on it, and a picture of snakes. She had recently seen a segment on Satanic cults on *20/20.* A shiver ran up her spine. "That means a ghost walked by you," Beatrice always said. Usually Claire laughed at that notion, but standing under these fluorescent lights surrounded by pieces of people's lives, Claire almost believed it was true.

Miles Pfeiffer got a girlfriend right away. Her name was September and she was new too. Her family had moved to East Essex from Colorado and everyone said they were hippies. They lived in the woods in a house without modern conveniences and only ate what they could grow themselves. For money, they all worked odd jobs. Even September. She brought jars of honey to school and sold them at lunch. September kept bees and got the honey herself. She put it in recycled jars, then added a label she'd made. The labels were bright yellow, each one with a different design. After she gave a talk about her beekeeping in Advanced English class, all the teachers started to buy it. If you returned the empty jar, September gave a fifty-cent discount.

Instead of being jealous of Miles and September, Maggie was fascinated. She began keeping notes on September in her little notebook. She was almost as tall as Miles, with white blond hair and clear blue eyes. She reminded Maggie of Miss Finland in the Miss Universe pageant. Except on her cheek, September had a mark the exact shape and color of a small strawberry. Somehow, this imperfection made her even more beautiful. Maggie decided she wanted to make September her best friend. Already, Stephanie and Christy had stopped asking her to go to the mall or to sleep over at their houses. It seemed to Maggie that she was at some precipice, ready to take a leap.

At lunch one day, Maggie went over to the table in the hallway outside the cafeteria where September sold her honey.

She picked up a jar of honey and studied the label, trying to seem intense the way her mother was. Close up, the label looked like something Kate might have drawn—chubby bees flying above oversized daisies.

"Your presentation was fascinating," Maggie said. She put the jar down and turned her hard stare on September.

Maggie had planned what to wear for this moment all weekend. September always wore clothes that were too big or too long for her. Gypsy skirts, men's shirts, and construction worker boots. If it was cold, she threw on a large moth-eaten blue sweater and didn't even bother to roll up the sleeves. Sometimes, she wore a droopy hat. Maggie had tried to copy September's put-together sloppiness. She'd worn a denim shirt of her father's over an accordion-pleated flowered skirt and her Timberlands. That morning, she'd admired herself in the full-length mirror on the back of her bedroom door. But standing beside September, Maggie felt foolish, like someone wearing mismatched clothes. She wondered what September was thinking. Probably that Maggie was the most uncool person in the whole school.

"Aren't you ever afraid?" Maggie asked her when she realized September wasn't going to say anything.

September turned her head slowly toward Maggie and frowned. "Of course," she said. Even though she was in some gifted classes, September's voice was harsh, like a tough girl's. "Neo-Nazis, nuclear war, radiation."

Maggie felt even more foolish so she didn't explain to September that she'd meant afraid of the bees. She just nodded. She couldn't think of anything else to say, but she kept standing there.

When the bell rang, September gathered her honey and put it in a loose-knit shopping bag.

"Maybe sometime I could come see them," Maggie blurted. "Your bees."

"Uh-huh," September said, and walked away.

· · ·

That afternoon, Maggie decided to go to September's house after school. She knew it was back in the woods near the golf course. Her cousin had told her that September's little brother found stray golf balls and sold them to the golfers for a quarter each. That morning there had been a freak spring snowstorm. As Maggie walked through the woods she saw snow-dusted flowers, icy leaves on trees. She imagined she would stumble upon a log cabin with handmade quilts on the walls and a fire burning in a large stone fireplace. There would be dried herbs hanging upside down in the kitchen, snowshoes on the doorstep, a fat orange cat on September's lap.

The first thing she saw were the beehives. In her presentation, September had said that she never wore protective clothing. The bees, she said, trusted her. Even the sight of the beehives made Maggie jittery. How was she ever going to screw up enough courage to put her hand in one of those? She almost turned around, but then her eyes settled on the house. It was not a log cabin at all. In fact, it was hardly even a house. It was rusty and metal, like an old trailer, with cardboard where windows were supposed to be. Something about the place thrilled her. She thought of her own little split-level, of Christy's grander Dutch Colonial, even her grandmother's tidy square house, and shook her head. This made her feel like Alice in Wonderland, like she'd stumbled upon something extraordinary.

Maggie walked around to the front, staying clear of the bees. The front yard was littered with golf balls. There was a big garden beside the house, with vines and leaves and stalks. But everything was heavy with snow, and Maggie got a strange feeling that September's whole family might starve if their garden was ruined. She imagined herself sneaking back here with baskets of food for them. She imagined herself saving their lives.

Someone had placed stones in front of the door for makeshift stairs. They rocked when she stepped on them, but there was nothing to hold on to for balance. Even with the stones there, she had to take a giant step up to the door, which hung ajar, slightly off its hinges. Maggie peered inside. There seemed to be one main room that served as both kitchen and living room, although there was hardly any furniture in it, just a beat-up sofa, mismatched kitchen chairs, and pillows on the floor.

When she stepped inside, she smelled gas and something sour, like milk gone bad. It was dark in there, and cold. The back door near a rusty sink had no screen or glass in it. A pink shower curtain hung in the one other doorway, and behind it came soft noises. Maggie knew she should turn around and leave. Wasn't this breaking and entering? But she kept moving forward. The shower curtain was the cheap plastic kind and it didn't reach either end of the doorway. When she stood sideways, Maggie could see right into the other room. The room was tiny and completely taken up by a big waterbed. On the bed were September and Miles, asleep. Maggie swallowed hard. She wished they would wake up, move around. She wished they would do it right there. As soon as she thought that, she felt embarrassed, like a pervert. She had to get out of there fast.

In the front yard, she stopped and tried to calm herself, to catch her breath and slow her pounding heart. But it was impossible. Maggie felt like the strangeness that had settled over her house had somehow taken her over. Like everyone around her, Maggie was out of control. For a moment she even missed the old dull days, when everything was predictable. What was going on? she thought, looking around at the incongruous snow on budding trees. She moved slowly away from the house, back into the woods. When she reached a safe distance, Maggie turned around and looked back at September's house. She was startled to see September standing there, out back, in a man's shirt, barefoot in the snow, one arm deep inside a beehive.

The condos at Woodsy Glen reminded Claire of offices in those nondescript buildings along Route 2. Plain white walls, square rooms, the faint odor of cleaning fluids. They seemed innocuous. Benign. Dan, she decided, would be safe there. She found herself remembering those gates they'd had to put up when the children were young—to stop them from tumbling down the stairs, to keep them out of the bathroom. And there were large plastic latches for the medicine chest and the kitchen cupboard where cleaning fluids were kept.

"Mrs. Jericho?" the sales manager said.

"Fine," Claire said to the sales manager. "I'll take this one."

They stood in the middle of an empty apartment that smelled strongly of pine disinfectant. The rain echoed against all that emptiness.

The sales manager, Jim Brown, looked surprised. "This one?" he said.

"They're all the same, aren't they?" Claire asked him.

Couldn't he see that she was weary of this? Ready to get it done? The Laboissonaires wanted her old house. Their baby was due in June and the husband had told Nancy Caycedo he thought the house had good vibes. Already, Cynthia Pullman-Laboissonaire—she'd emphasized that she used both names—had asked if she could send over a Chinese man who was going to tell them how to set up the house, where to put their bed, the baby, even the shrine, Claire supposed.

Jim Brown had a thin mustache that reminded Claire of Don Ameche. He glanced at the xeroxed floor plans.

"I feel it's my duty to tell you," he said, and cleared his

throat, "that some of the floor plans are reversed." He pushed the floor plans toward her.

"Are there forms?" Claire asked him.

He nodded and fumbled through more papers. Claire wanted to get out of there. She wanted to have it done. She wished a fairy godmother could appear and sprinkle magic dust that would finish all this—Claire would open her eyes and the old house would be sold and she and Dan would be all moved in to Woodsy Glen, apartment 2G.

Jim Brown handed her the application forms. She saw that he bit his nails and felt suddenly sorry for him. Claire focused on the forms. Number of occupants. Number of occupants under eighteen. Number of pets.

"I took Josie to the sophomore hop," he blurted.

"What?" Number of automobiles.

"We had a terrible time," Jim Brown said.

Claire had just come across that picture, one of those falsely posed ones, Josie looking miserable in a too-tight green dress, Jim Brown with the same small mustache but long hair—to his shoulders—slouching in a paisley tuxedo.

"Yes," Claire said, "I remember."

"I didn't buy her a corsage or anything," he said, without any remorse or embarrassment, "and I threw up on her dress between dances and it was somebody else's. Her cousin's, I think."

He was right, Claire realized. The dress had been Denise's. Denise had set some sort of record for proms and hops—she went to some ridiculous amount of them, ninety or a hundred, at schools all over New England. Still, Claire thought, feeling guilty, she should have bought Josie her own dress.

"Why did you and Josie go to this dance together?" Claire asked Jim Brown.

"Fix-up."

Claire nodded. Until Will, Josie had not really had a boyfriend. She'd relied on things like fix-ups, blind dates, people's cousins from out of town. "You know what? I think I'll take these applications with me," she said, standing. At the door, Claire turned back to him. "Josie is happily married," Claire told him. "She has two children. Daughters."

She said this with great pride, but Jim Brown merely shrugged. In fact, he seemed to smirk.

"Yeah," he said. "She's married to Will Hunter."

For a long time, Claire had thought Will looked strained. She wondered if Jim Brown had left out the word "happily" on purpose.

After she decided on the condo at Woodsy Glen, Claire found herself driving around town, without any purpose or direction. She knew what she was really doing: avoiding home. Lately, as her car neared the turnoff to the house, Claire became overwhelmed by dread. It was a feeling she used to get when the children were young and she left them with a baby-sitter. While she was out, she didn't give a thought to Michaela or Josie or the young neighborhood girl watching them. But on her way home Claire began to feel something close to panic—who was that girl, after all? Someone who might grow interested in *Dark Shadows* and let the children wander off, out of the house, into a stranger's car? Into the basement where dangerous items lurked? She thought of drain cleaner, mothballs, kerosene. By the time she got to the front door her legs were shaky and her hands were sweaty and she was ready to scream for help. But there they would all be—Josie and Michaela and the baby-sitter—playing Twister or eating chocolate chip cookies, all of them safe and happy. Claire used to somehow manage a smile, a thank you, and carefully count out the dollars to pay the girl. Often, she would add an extra dollar, a tip. Thank you, she would say again. Silently she would add, Thank you for keeping my children safe.

Here was that familiar old feeling again, the near panic, the worry, but there was no relief. No one was watching her husband, keeping him safe. The sound of a distant siren made Claire certain that he had set fire to the house. She felt ready to find anything, imagined the worst each time she went home. Dan hurt, unconscious, missing. She could remember hearing on the news several years ago about a man who had wandered away from home Christmas morning and couldn't be found. He had it. Alzheimer's. His wife had appeared on television, not crying, just worried. He gets confused, she'd explained. He can't remember things. Claire wondered if they'd ever found him. For a while his face had been everywhere—on television, in the newspaper. A grainy Xerox of the man in better days, at his anniversary party, arm around his wife's thick waist, military haircut and too thin tie. There were so many news stories you never heard the outcome of, Claire thought. Like the Tylenol murders. Like a man who wandered away from home Christmas morning. A man who got confused.

Even more frightening on this gray, rainy day was that Claire felt she really had a lot to worry about. There was Dan, of course. There was Josie getting carjacked at the mall. And there was that nagging feeling in Claire, in everyone, that Josie hadn't been carjacked, that something else had happened and she'd concocted that story. Claire hadn't slept all night, even after she'd called Denise to be sure Josie was home and safe again. Instead, she'd replayed the events as Josie described them. No matter how she slowed down the action, Claire could not fill in those four hours. Josie was sensible, she would not simply lie on the ground. Claire was certain of that. Her daughter would run to the police, she would hail a passing car

—wasn't a main road right outside the mall?—she would go to the Dunkin' Donuts and call 911 herself if they didn't do it for her.

If it had been Michaela, Claire would have believed anything—that she had laid on the ground for four hours or four days. Claire sighed. Michaela. Turning up after all these years. And Claire knew what it was she wanted. Last night, when Claire had come home from looking at condominiums, disappointed and sad, she'd turned the corner and her hands immediately went slippery with sweat. The driveway, the street in front of her house, filled with cars. Claire had studied them. All familiar. Tiny's and Beatrice's and Denise's and Judy's. Even the little blue Mazda that Christy and Cassie shared. When Claire had lifted one hand from the steering wheel, it trembled like a hummingbird hovering in front of her. The whole family was there. Claire knew that old adage was true—the only things that reunited entire families were weddings and funerals.

There were so many cars she'd had to park up the street. That walk, past the Madisons' raised ranch with the ridiculous add-ons and the house where the Garibaldis used to live—there was a young couple there now, a young couple with a new baby—that walk down the familiar street, with the pink and white dogwoods showing off and the place in the sidewalk where all the neighborhood kids, her own included, had carved their initials when the cement was wet and freshly poured, to her own house with the FOR SALE sign screaming at her and her family's cars filling every space in front, was the longest walk Claire could remember taking. Longer even than the one down the aisle of Saint Teresa's on her wedding day, everyone watching her, wiping their eyes, her long white train kissing the carpet behind her, Dan ahead, at the alter, smiling, calm, certain. Why, she remembered suddenly, he'd winked at her! As her shaking legs brought her closer to him and she finally could look up at him, he had winked at her and the people in the church had laughed.

Claire stopped, right on her front doorstep. If she turned and walked away, she thought, she could undo whatever was waiting inside for her. But then the door burst open and she knew it was too late to turn around. Denise's husband James stood there in front of her. He was a pompous ass, and the last person Claire wanted to tell her bad news.

"Bonjour," he said.

Behind him people sounded excited. Not at all upset. There was laughter and voices talking over each other.

James held the door open for her, bowing like an idiot. "Madame," he said. A honeymoon in France and he acted like English was his second language. Claire pushed past him and into her crowded kitchen. Someone had laid out trays of cold cuts and cheese and rolls, her good crystal bowls filled with chopped tomatoes and lettuce, mustard and mayonnaise. There were store-bought cookies, jugs of wine. Like the late-night spread after a wedding, or the food served after a funeral. Claire tried to take it all in. The food and wine, the faces smiling and talking. She saw Dan sitting on a folding chair across the room and she grew so filled with relief that she couldn't even walk toward him. Her body would not move. She focused on his face, turned upward, gazing at someone, his eyes filled with— Claire frowned. His eyes were filled with love, she thought.

And Beatrice was calling to her, shouting, "Claire, for God's sake, aren't you even going to go over and hug your daughter?"

Claire looked around the kitchen again, trying to find Josie's face in the crowd. She found it difficult to catch her breath, as if everyone in there had taken all the air. They all seemed to be waiting for her to do something. She looked back at Dan. His eyes, staring at her now, were clear and focused and he was smiling. Claire smiled back, the relief flooding her so that she had to place her hands on the edge of the kitchen table. She breathed deeply, smelled coffee and mustard and perfume. Then Dan did it. He winked. And Claire finally caught her breath and stepped forward.

She heard someone say, "Mom."

Finally Claire could look away from her husband and follow the voice from beside him, where, her hair as bright and red as ever, Michaela stood, clutching Dan's hand, holding court in the kitchen, the way she used to so long ago.

Their eyes did not exactly meet. Claire did not think either of them had looked the other in the eye for twenty-five years. Even when they kissed, they merely brushed their lips against each other's cheek.

But in that instant when Claire opened her arms and her daughter stepped forward into them, Claire could remember how different it once was. Before Michaela left home, this house was full of sounds. She used to bring home friends who played the guitar or the harmonica, who sang Bob Dylan songs, who laughed. When she went away, Michaela took something from this house. It grew quiet and calm. Here she was, just back from California, and already the house was fuller, noisy. Alive, Claire thought, and she wrapped her arms around her oldest child.

They had all come to see Michaela. She read their palms and told them stories about California. Her lips were stained purple from too much jug wine. Claire stood back and watched her. It could be years earlier, she thought. If she didn't look too closely at her daughter, she didn't see the lines around Michaela's eyes and mouth, the strands of white hair against the red. Watching her like that, Claire realized that Michaela had been away from her longer than she'd been with her. She had left them to live her life. What, Claire thought, did she even know about Michaela? Her own daughter, but a stranger.

Funny, but for so many years, when the girls were children, it was Michaela who felt more familiar. Claire could remember the way she had felt inside her, the tumbling and kicking all night. She used to imagine the baby as a dolphin in the Pacific. She did not remember Josie that way, inside her. Claire's own mother had assured her that women always remembered their firstborn best, but that had not given her comfort. Even in the womb, Josie had been placid and good-natured. But Michaela would not let her mother forget.

"I have this recurrent dream," Michaela was saying.

"Oooooh," Tiny said, almost in appreciation. "A recurrent one."

Claire studied her daughter as Michaela talked. Her sweater was threadbare, a thriftshop one, no doubt, cream-colored with scattered beads that no longer made a design. Michaela probably considered it her good sweater, Claire thought sadly. She saw the small swell of her breasts beneath it, almost like a teenager's, the nipples hard. She was braless.

"In it," Michaela said, "I'm on this street, in a city—"

"San Francisco?" Tiny asked. She was taking notes on a paper napkin.

"Actually," Michaela said, and she seemed to be looking right at Claire when she spoke, "New York City."

Tiny began to write furiously.

"And the street," Michaela continued, "is both strange and familiar. Like I've been there before, but a long time ago."

"A lifetime ago," Claire said.

"No, in this lifetime. Just years and years ago. And it's very hot, and I'm walking down this street and, you see, I'm afraid. Terrified. But I know that there's no other way to go." She paused to take a drink. "The street," she said, "is lined with brownstones that seem innocent enough, but I know they really are . . ." She struggled for the right word, wrinkling her nose and brow the same way she had as a toddler searching for a new word.

"Evil?" Beatrice asked.

Michaela shook her head. "Not evil, but not innocent. Dangerous, maybe."

Claire saw that Tiny had stopped writing.

"Anyway," Michaela said, "I keep having this dream. For years."

"But nothing happens?" Christy said. "You just walk down this street and feel scared?"

"Different things happen in different dreams. Sometimes I go inside one of the buildings. Sometimes I climb the stairs but don't actually go in—"

"Climbing means something," Tiny said, sounding almost relieved. "It means you're in turmoil or trying too hard or something. When you dream of stairs, you play 616."

"At any rate," Michaela said, "I went there."

Claire stared down at her own hands. She concentrated on the pattern the veins made, like small rivers flowing, branching out into tributaries.

"You went to that street?" Christy said, not even trying to hide her amazement. "How did you know where to go?"

Michaela shrugged. "I just knew."

"This is like *Unsolved Mysteries,"* Tiny's husband Frank said. "People have these dreams, of Ireland or someplace, and they go there and they know everything. The layout of the town. A particular house. Even the language."

"They speak English in Ireland, Uncle Frank," Christy said.

Frank looked confused. "I don't think so. They speak . . . Irish."

"Celtic," James said.

Denise rolled her eyes. "Michaela," she said, "are you going to try to convince us that you had a past-life experience?"

"Of course not. I went to the street and it was exactly as I remembered—"

"As you dreamed, you mean," Claire said without looking up.

"The brownstones. Everything. And I knew what I would find if I went inside this one."

"Just like goddamned *Unsolved Mysteries,"* Frank said, excited.

"I would find young girls screaming in pain. And there would be blood and people with stony faces and cold hands. If you let them, they would take things from you."

Claire said, "You would let them only if there was no other way. It wouldn't be like that now. These are different times. It would be different."

She felt everyone looking at her, but she couldn't let them see how close she was to crying.

Michaela laughed. "Mommie dearest," she said, "you ruined my punchline. Everything was different. Clean and bright. People were in there living perfectly decent lives. Getting take-out Chinese food and making love—"

"You saw that?" Christy said.

"It was just an apartment building," Michaela said. She sat back in her chair and smiled, satisfied.

When Claire finally did look up, everyone seemed baffled. But of course the story wasn't for them, really. In that moment, Claire understood that Michaela had come home to confront her, to talk about the summer before she'd left home. Claire believed that some things were better left unsaid. Like the decisions made when the world was a different place. She cleared her throat but had nothing to say.

"Well," Tiny said, "we've got a city, and stairs." She chewed her bottom lip, studied what she'd written on her napkin.

"New York City," Beatrice said. "I think that has its own number. 9 something."

Tiny nodded. But she said, "I don't know, really."

"I read somewhere that recurrent dreams come from our experiences in the womb," Christy said. "For example, tidal waves. People who have a recurring dream about a tidal wave were botched abortions."

Tiny covered her mouth. "Christy," she said, her voice low, "that's a sin."

"I read it," Christy said.

"An abortion is dead," Cassie said uncertainly. "I mean, the thing is dead."

"Fetus," Christy said. "And I said botched abortion."

"You can't botch one," Cassie said. "They use this suction device. Like a vacuum cleaner—"

"Cassie!" Judy said.

"I saw it on *Nova.*"

"I don't care where you saw it."

"Back in the good old days," Michaela said, "before abortion was legal, there were plenty of botched ones. Girls would be pregnant and scared—terrified, really—and they wouldn't know where to go or what to do so they would wait too long and then they'd have to go someplace terrible that would do it—"

"I don't want to hear this," Tiny said.

"Really, Michaela," Judy said, "it's not appropriate."

"It's true," Michaela said. "I even knew someone who got a botched one. The baby lived and—"

"Enough!" Claire said. "This isn't very celebratory conversation."

Tiny mumbled, "It's a sin."

Cassie said thoughtfully, "If you wait, you can't use that suction thing."

"Isn't this just like our Michaela?" Denise said, trying to sound lighthearted. "Home only a few hours and already getting everyone all riled up. Discussing controversial topics." She looked at her nieces, sitting in a tight row. "Vietnam," she said. "That's what it was when we were your ages, a million years ago. Michaela was wanting us to wear black armbands and march on the school lawn."

"Like in old movies," Cassie said. She seemed to see Michaela differently, with admiration, in that moment.

"She likes getting people riled up," Denise said again, and patted her Aunt Tiny's hand.

Beatrice stood and began busying herself refilling trays and bowls. "You did it too, didn't you, Michaela?" she said.

"Did what?" Claire said sharply.

"Wore those silly armbands. Marched around like an idiot on the school lawn."

Tiny stood too. "I think we'll be going," she said.

"For Christ's sake," Michaela said, "sit down, Tiny."

"Aunt Tiny," Beatrice said to Michaela.

Claire wished they would all go home. She wished Michaela would go too, though she knew Michaela had nowhere else to go. She'd made that clear on the phone.

"Mercury is in retrograde," Michaela said.

"What does that mean?" Cassie asked her. She'd inched closer to Michaela, as if to see her better.

"Communication sucks," Michaela said.

Claire heard Tiny gasp, but it was Josie who caught her attention. She stood in the doorway, eyes glazed, her face dirty, and her shirt torn and awkwardly tied with scraped skin showing through. She had come in the back door, Claire supposed. And something had happened to her, that was clear. But that wasn't what was foremost in Claire's mind. Instead, all she could think of was that Josie had not been here these past three hours, and Claire had not even noticed.

"She says no one was around to help her," Will said. "Some guy followed her out of the mall and pushed her and took the car."

"Well," Bonnie said, "we know that's not true. There's always a security guard patrolling that lot." She smiled at him. "You and I have left there after hours plenty of times and we always see a car patrolling."

After Josie had left for the mall last night, Will had planned a weekend away with Bonnie. He had called a B&B in Marblehead that he'd read about in the newspaper. Ocean views, it had said. Breakfast in bed. He'd made reservations and come up with an excuse for being gone a whole weekend. Lately, Josie had been telling him he was becoming too sensitive and New Age, just because he wanted her to have an orgasm. He thought that maybe there was something worth saving between them, and that seemed like a good place to start. But she'd immediately changed the subject. What is wrong with you? she'd said. He had planned on telling her he was going to a male encounter group for the weekend.

Instead, she'd somehow lost the car, wandered around for four hours, then turned up at her parents' house. She was even incompetent in reporting crimes. If there was a crime. It didn't make sense to Will. There were too many missing hours, too many holes. Why not go into the Dunkin' Donuts across the street and call the police? Over the past few years, he had begun to see Josie as careless—didn't he always have to remind her to park under the lights at the mall? To lock the car doors? Just the other day he had come home and found an empty coffeepot still on the burner, ready to crack. But even with all that in mind, he couldn't believe there was no security, that she had simply sat in an empty parking lot for all those hours.

He had wanted to come to Bonnie's this morning, to creep into bed with her and tell her his planned getaway. He had come and crept into bed with her, but here he was trying to make sense of Josie's story instead of wooing Bonnie.

Bonnie had let the sheet drop from her, exposing her naked body. "Maybe your wife has a lover," she said, smiling. "Maybe she met him at the mall, drove off in his car, and left her car there. They get back hours later and the car has been stolen."

Will looked away from her breasts. "She doesn't have a lover," he said.

"Listen, the woman is a housewife. Why would she go grocery-shopping at night when she has all day to do it. That's what housewives do—they grocery-shop."

Will felt, suddenly, guilty talking about Josie like this. True, he had been thinking the same kinds of things. But it seemed wrong to say them openly, to say them to Bonnie.

"I didn't mean there was anything wrong with how she lives her life," Bonnie said. "I'm just trying to figure it out. That's all."

She climbed out of the covers altogether and reached for his zipper. "I like having you all to myself in the morning," she said, reaching inside his pants for him.

It was the first time in all these years that Will found himself feeling guilty. Thinking about it later that day, he realized why. Not only didn't he love Josie anymore, he didn't even want to be married to her. This wasn't about Bonnie, he knew. It was much worse than that. Something had happened to his wife last night and it didn't matter to him if it had happened the way she described or if she had been with another man or any other possibility. He just didn't care. All he cared about was getting out.

Will reached for the phone on his desk and quickly dialed

home. But the phone there rang and rang. Not even the machine picked up. Josie had forgotten to turn it on, he supposed. In a way, he was relieved. After all, what was there left to say? What message could he possibly leave?

Josie deliberately parked in the same spot she'd been in the night before. She expected it to be frightening, but everything looked harmless, despite the rain that fell, sending a gray cast over everything. When she'd called her mother for a ride to the mall and got no answer, Josie had decided she'd walk. But when she stepped outside she'd been surprised to find Will's car in the driveway, waiting for her. It was newer than hers, and Will kept it tidy and clean. He vacuumed the rugs, Windexed the windows, always remembered to remove his travel coffee mug when he got out. Like a rental car, Josie decided. At the mall, she stood outside the car for a moment, as if being back in that spot might trigger some details. But nothing came. There was no blood, no footprints, nothing. She dreaded having to tell her story to the security people at the mall, having to look at more doubtful faces. Maybe she could convince Will to at least accompany her. Maybe when he heard her official report he'd understand.

Will's office was empty. Josie had no idea what time it was, but she knew it was too late for lunch and too early for him to have gone home. His desk was neat too, the pencils lined up in a straight, even row, a blank pad of white, lined paper ready to be filled up, his phone messages in one stack, order forms in another. He had one of those plastic cubes of photographs beside the phone. Josie picked it up, turned it around. Kate on Santa's lap. Maggie in her cheerleader's uniform. Both of the girls' baby pictures. Funny, Josie thought. Will didn't have any pictures of her, or of the two of them. He used to, she remembered. He used to have a picture of them on a beach in Bermuda, taken on their honeymoon. Both of them tanned, the sand pink, his arm wrapped around her waist. She wore a silly sarong skirt that she had bought in the cruisewear department at Jordan Marsh, all hot pink and bright orange flowers. Will had on aviator sunglasses. Josie frowned. She was certain he'd had that picture right here beside the IN box. And a smaller family picture from the Christmas when she'd insisted they send out Christmas cards with their picture on them. She'd bought red-and-green plaid fabric and made each of them something from it—a tie for Will, a skirt for her, a vest for Maggie, and one of those small headbands that baby girls wore for Kate. Everyone hated that picture except for her. It was a real family photo, all of them smiling, coordinated.

"Mrs. Hunter?" a voice said behind her.

Josie turned, still holding the plastic cube in her hand. Sheila was standing there, in the doorway. She was the manager of Toys, and her arms were filled with Cabbage Patch dolls. Josie had seen Sheila dozens of times. But she seemed unfamiliar, too. She was too white and too soft, like the Pillsbury doughboy, and her green stirrup pants seemed too green. Josie had to look away.

"Are you okay?" Sheila said. "I heard you had some kind of an accident?" Sheila touched her own cheek in the place where Josie's bruise was.

Those dolls, Josie thought, were scary-looking. She said, "Yes. I'm looking for Will. My husband," she added foolishly.

"He's not here. He and Bonnie are at a meeting in Foxboro."

Bonnie was his assistant manager. Will called her his right-hand man. She always wore suits with short skirts and no blouse under the jacket. She had frosted hair, red lipstick, nails long as talons. Josie was sure she'd had a nose job. At parties, Bonnie always kicked off her shoes and liked to run the panty-hosed foot of one leg up and down the calf of the other.

"That's okay," Josie said. Though it wasn't okay at all. She needed Will right now. "Maybe I'll just sit here and wait for him to come back," she said.

"He's not coming in. He said he'd see us tomorrow," Sheila said. "Can I help you out? You don't look so good."

Josie considered that. But it seemed ridiculous. After all, here she was. Alive and breathing. She'd walked from the car, into the mall, to the store, up the escalator, and right into Will's office.

"It looks worse than it actually is," Josie said. "I'll just go on by myself."

She started to leave, then turned back to Sheila.

"It wasn't an accident," Josie told her. "I was assaulted right out in the parking lot last night. The man beat me up and stole the car."

Sheila's dark eyes widened. She was one of those people who plucked their eyebrows down to a thin arched line so that she always looked slightly surprised anyway.

"In this parking lot?" Sheila gasped.

"Yes," Josie said, feeling a rush of warmth. Sheila believed her, she thought. "And the man is still at large."

"They should put up posters," Sheila said. "Send out warnings."

Josie nodded. Maybe they would do that. Maybe when she talked to the security people here they would take control, warn people, solve the case. She held on to that thought as she walked back through Caldor's, down the escalator, into the mall. It wasn't very crowded today, even though Mother's Day loomed and kiosks with gifts had been set up. Josie moved past them, artificial flowers in baskets and wreaths shaped like hearts, wall hangings with calligraphied poems, country kitchen objects—kitchen witches and refrigerator magnets and pot holders. For a moment, Josie forgot why she was there. She fingered the bow on a gift basket, stopped to read one of the poems about motherhood. She lost track of time and actually began to retrace her steps back out of the mall when a familiar-looking man caught her eye. He was drinking an Orange Julius. When he passed by, she smelled soap.

Josie walked faster, to catch him. He wore a tan windbreaker with a red plaid lining. She forced herself to remember details. The man was around Will's height, muscular. His brown hair needed cutting and hung in a ragged line over his collar. As if he knew she was following him, the man walked faster. It was hard for Josie to keep up. Each breath hurt.

She opened her mouth and began to scream. "Catch him! He robbed me! Catch that man!"

The legs of his jeans were too long and had frayed from dragging on the floor. Were these the things that mattered? Josie wondered, forcing herself to remember everything. Panting, she watched as a security guard appeared right at the man's side and grabbed his elbow roughly. The guard blew a whistle and more guards arrived. They surrounded the man. She was aware of everyone stopping to watch. One of the guards was coming toward her, frowning, a pad in his hand.

"What did he take?" the guard was asking her.

Josie could not take her eyes from the man in the tan windbreaker. Under the bright mall lights, his face seemed too round, too young. He looked like a boy who might go to school with Maggie. There was a fine sheen on his face—oily skin. Josie bit down on her lip. Wouldn't she have remembered if that man had been so young? If his skin had been this oily?

"Ma'am?" the guard said.

Josie shook her head. "I was on my way to the security office," she began.

The guard started to write down what she was saying.

"No," Josie said. "I mean, just now. I was on my way to report a robbery from last night. And I thought . . . this was the man."

The boy began to yell. "She's crazy. I work the night shift? At Dalton Mill? The soap factory? I wasn't here last night robbing nobody. I was working."

The guard with the pad was waiting for Josie to tell him differently. "I don't know," she said. "Somebody took my car last night—"

"A *car* theft?" the guard said. He put his pad back in his pocket. "Last night?"

"He beat me up," she said.

"Fuck you, lady! I never even seen you before. I was working last night."

Josie noticed that he had a shopping bag looped around his wrist. A kitchen witch peeked from the top.

"This isn't the guy," she said softly.

The crowd shook their heads, began to disperse.

"Poor kid," she heard someone say.

At first Josie thought they meant sympathy for her. But then she realized that of course they felt badly for the boy, falsely accused of a crime when all he'd done was come to the mall to buy a Mother's Day present. Embarrassed, Josie slipped out the side entrance. She couldn't possibly make a report now.

The police car was parked in front of Claire's house when she finally got home. At first she thought they had come to question her about Josie's story, her whereabouts last night. Then she remembered that her other daughter was back home, the same daughter who had made a habit in high school of being escorted home by the police. But as soon as she stepped from her car and made her way to the back door, she saw that it wasn't Michaela at all. Sitting on the stoop, flanked by a policeman on each side, was Dan. He was barefoot, disheveled, looking slightly confused.

One of the policemen was Nick Jordan, a classmate of

Josie's. "Hey, Mrs. Jericho," he said. He was embarrassed for Dan, for her.

"Nick," Claire said, shaking his hand. "How are you?"

He only nodded.

"How many children do you have now?" she asked, trying to appear normal.

"Just the two," he said. "Twin girls."

"Twins!" Claire said, trying to catch his eye. "That must be a handful." He did not meet her gaze.

The other policeman, someone Claire could not place, said, "We found him down by the river."

"I was fishing!" Dan said, impertinent as a child. It was then that Claire saw how muddy his feet were.

Finally, Nick looked up at her. "He could have been hurt," he said gently.

"Fishing!" Dan said again, and folded his arms across his chest. His arms were covered in mud too.

"There haven't been fish to catch in that river in a long time," Claire told him. She laughed nervously. "You know that."

He seemed to notice her for the first time. "Of course there are fish there. Bass."

As if by some secret cue, both policemen stood at exactly the same moment.

"We see it a lot," the strange one said, patting her arm. "You know Fran Zbrinski? She's got it too. Wanders all over creation."

Nick Jordan glanced at her briefly, then looked away again. "He used to be a great guy," he said. "I'm real sorry. I guess I didn't know he was this bad."

Claire swallowed hard. Fran Zbrinski had Alzheimer's. Claire's hairdresser, Alice, knew Fran's daughter and she'd told Claire everything the daughter had told her. They've got to lock her up, Alice had said.

The policemen started to walk away. But then Nick stopped. "Hey, Mrs. Jericho," he said. "You know what I remember? I remember when he used to dress up like Santa. Down at the Ford place? He made a great Santa."

"Thank you, Nick," she said. "Thank you for bringing him home."

When she turned back toward Dan, he was smiling up at her. "Lady," he said, "you've got the prettiest hair."

Claire knew she should say something. She knew she should go to him, take him inside. But she just stood there, frozen, looking down at her feet. She was wearing low-heeled pumps. Beige ones. They matched the handbag she had over her shoulder. Slowly, Claire bent her toes inside her shoes. Then she straightened them. Bent them again.

"Lady?" Dan said.

His voice had the start of panic in it. But still she stood there, bending her toes. Someone, she thought, had to keep their feet planted firmly to the ground. She straightened her toes and took a big slow breath. What was it Josie called that? A cleansing breath.

"Dan," she said, "you're home now. It's me." She took another breath. "It's Claire." Then she reached her arms out toward him.

Michaela found her mother sitting in the rocking chair, staring at nothing.

"Do you feel bad that I'm selling the house?" her mother said.

Michaela shrugged. "I'm not very attached to things."

"Or to people," Claire said.

The room was growing darker as the rain increased.

"The river is polluted," Michaela said, wanting to change

the subject. She sat on the couch and turned on the lamp beside it. "The whole town looks dirty."

Her mother wrinkled her nose. "I don't know how you can sit there like that."

"Like what?"

"Without showering," her mother said. "All sweaty."

Michaela drank orange juice straight from the carton, without pausing, in long gulps. Her mother sighed. She expected her mother to say, "You were not raised in a barn, young lady," the way she used to when Michaela was a teenager and might casually toss her dirty feet on the kitchen table, or burp too loudly, or worse. But her mother just sat there.

"It's that soap factory," Michaela said, even though it was obvious her mother's attention lay elsewhere. She went on anyway. "It should be cleaned up."

Her mother glanced up at her. "Yes," she said. "I suppose."

When her father came up from the basement, Michaela said, "Didn't people used to fish in the river, Dad? Didn't we? And then we'd even eat what we caught?"

"Of course, girl," he said. "I was just fishing there . . . I don't know, yesterday, maybe."

Michaela felt her mother trying to get her attention, as if the mere will of her stare could make her turn toward her and —what? Michaela wondered. Share some kind of mutual pity? Roll their eyes? What was there to do about it?

"No, Dan," her mother said. "The river is polluted. There are no fish in it. Nothing can live in it."

That look swept over his face. Michaela didn't know if she'd ever really understood what bewilderment was until she saw it on her father's face.

"There are frogs," he said, but even his voice was washed in bewilderment. "Polliwogs," he added. The word sounded archaic, something from another time and place. "In the summer I can take the girls down there and catch fireflies and we can keep them in empty mayonnaise jars with holes punched in the lids."

Her mother stood up abruptly, her chair scraping against the floor with a force that sent goose bumps up Michaela's arms. "Come on," she said, taking Dan by the arm.

He let her lead him. Like a child, Michaela thought. Their voices grew distant, a faint, almost comforting, hum. Michaela was surprised that she did feel saddened by the thought that this house would be sold. She tried to imagine different people in it, moving about the rooms with the same comfort and familiarity that her family had. But she couldn't. The house even smelled like the Jerichos', their own particular mixture of scents—the food they preferred, the cologne they'd used, the way their clothes carried odors. Another family would bring in other smells—sandalwood or soy sauce or coconut, maybe even the smell of the soap factory. Michaela stretched out on the sofa and looked up at the ceiling. It needed to be painted. The grandfather clock needed to be fixed. Like the whole town, this house seemed in disrepair too. She closed her eyes. The sound of the rain let her imagine the river moving again, clean, carrying her to safety.

Kate's teacher, Pam, was frowning right in Kate's face. Kate could see the dandruff in Pam's eyebrows.

"It's after three," Pam said. "We have a problem."

Kate's mother had forgotten her. School ended and all the mothers came except Kate's. Kate had stood in the parking lot, on tippytoe, looking for the familiar red of her mother's car. And when she didn't see it, she decided it must have broken down because her mother was always saying that it was UNRELIABLE and so she started looking for her father's green Volvo that Maggie called the Revolting. Then Kate remembered—a man stole the Honda and her Puffalump, the one she left in the back seat. Her mother would definitely be in the Revolting. But Kate didn't see that either and pretty soon all that was left in the parking lot were the teachers' cars—one white and one blue—a yellow whiffle ball and Kate.

She walked back into the school extra slow, pretending she was wandering around the Alps. Her mother had let her wear her dirndl skirt to school today, even though Maggie had said she shouldn't be able to. Lately, when Maggie was mean to Kate, Kate made herself think, Maggie has ugly hair, and this made her feel better. Molly's hair was growing back funny. Kate should have COMPASSION, her mother told her, but she didn't.

Kate sang "Eidelweiss" twice, then went back into her classroom. She put her jacket and book bag back in her cubby then sat at her group's table, folded her hands and waited. Her father said she was patient because she had a good imagination. That meant she was good at pretending. Kate pretended she was in jail, like the lady on *Oprah Winfrey* yesterday whose husband robbed a bank, the exact bank where the lady worked, and now she was in jail because she was an ACCOMPLICE. Kate had no idea what jail was like, but she supposed you had to do unpleasant things there, like stay inside and not watch TV and think about your crimes.

She didn't know how long she sat there pretending to be in jail before Pam came in and found her.

Pam had thick thighs but she wore short skirts anyway, usually plaid ones. Cory's mother said Pam should wear mid-calf skirts to hide her thighs. Cory's mother always wanted to make people over. Once she told Kate, "Your mom would look great if she highlighted her hair." Another time she said, "You should suggest to your mom that she get one of those sack dresses everyone's wearing. They're so breezy!"

"I called your mother," Pam was saying, "and there was no answer."

Kate considered this. "So she must be on her way."

Pam frowned more. She also always wore bright blue eyeshadow, just a smear across each lid. Cory's mother said she should wear fawn instead, but Kate had no idea what color fawn was since there wasn't a crayon called fawn even in the super box of seventy-two.

Victoria, the other teacher, came in. Shc was frowning too. Victoria was very tall and skinny and Cory's mother said she was too elegant to be a preschool teacher.

"Kate, was someone else supposed to give you a ride today? Maybe Cory's mother?"

Kate shook her head.

Pam wore penny loafers with shiny pennies tucked into them. She was bouncing up and down. "I have an appointment," she said to Victoria. "What are we going to do with her."

Kate wondered if they would throw her in jail. She started to frown too.

Victoria had long oval fingernails and she always wore clear nail-polish. She tapped those nails on Kate's table.

"I could go to my grandmother's," Kate said.

Pam and Victoria looked at each other.

"You owe me," Victoria said.

Pam wasn't frowning anymore. She put on her jeans jacket and wiggled her fingers at Kate. That was how Pam waved to people. "See you tomorrow," Pam said. Then she added, "Jasmine."

Kate smiled. She was going to be Jasmine in the school play and Michael Jackson was going to be Ali. They couldn't put her in jail.

"Come on," Victoria said, buttoning her own ivory-colored coat.

"Are you going to drive me to my grandmother's?" Kate said, hardly believing her luck. A ride in a teacher's car!

"Do you know the way?" Victoria asked.

Kate thought a minute but all she could come up with was that song: "Over the river and through the woods . . ." That wasn't very helpful. She shook her head.

"Do you know what it's near?" Victoria asked.

Kate thought hard. "It's near Aunt Tiny's!"

"Anything else?"

There were just houses and more houses. "It's for sale," Kate said.

"Well, then, you're just going to have to come home with me."

"To your house?" Kate decided she wasn't just lucky, she was incredibly lucky. First a ride in a teacher's car, then a visit to a teacher's house.

It wasn't until they were on the road, driving through East Essex, that Kate realized a terrible thing—her mother never forgot about her. Her mother loved her. Something very, very bad must have happened to her mother or she would have come to get her at two-thirty like she was supposed to, and right now Kate would be home watching *Oprah Winfrey* and eating graham crackers with a very thin layer of strawberry jam spread on them. If her mother was all right, she would not be in a teacher's car, and the familiar winding roads of town would not seem so scary, like they were hiding something dark, some secret about her mother.

Michaela wanted to talk about it. That's what she said to Claire as Claire tried to pull something together for dinner. She was thinking she should make a recipe that was easy to double so she could bring half over to Josie. Michaela had stood in the doorway of the kitchen and said, "I want to talk about it." There were so many things that Claire could have told her—

leave the past in the past or even simply that she was not ready. But instead she'd fumbled around, opening and closing cupboard doors and finally saying, "I've got to go grocery shopping. Will you keep an eye on your father?" Then she'd practically run out the door and into the car, driving too fast all the way to Saint Teresa's.

Claire paused on the steps that led to the front door of Saint Teresa's church. They were the kind of stairs—steep and abundant—that she imagined people climbing up on their knees, though she had never actually seen anyone do that. Before the handicapped ramp was built at the side door, elderly and handicapped people were carried up them, in wheelchairs or in the arms of men specially placed below on Sunday mornings.

Except for Josie and Will's wedding, Claire had not climbed these stairs herself since 1969, and although she could not actually remember the last time she had, she did have an image of her younger self walking up them with ease, her head dutifully bent, her good Sunday shoes—low-heeled and polished—carrying her upward. She could feel the light weight of her pillbox hat on her head, the hat a creamy yellow, her hair in a soft wave beneath it, and her good Sunday purse—inside, just lipstick and tithe money and a small package of Kleenex—held close to her body. The clasp used to make a loud click when she shut it so she left it opened all the time, and worried about the small envelope of money falling out.

Folk masses were the rage then, songs about flowers and peace, teenagers sitting cross-legged at the altar playing guitars and shaking tambourines. Claire hated those folk masses. Where was God in all of that nonsense about "Blowin' in the Wind" and "Where Have All the Flowers Gone?" She had not even gotten used to having mass in English when suddenly people were showing up in jeans and singing antiwar songs. She had missed the glory of mass, the sound of Latin, the men in suits and ties and the women in gloves and hats and nylon stockings. She insisted that her daughters still dress for church, though in the end, of course, she saw that none of that had really mattered.

Claire was surprised to find herself today in loose trousers—her Katharine Hepburn pants, Josie called them—and a man-style shirt, at the door of Saint Teresa's. Surprised too that the climb had left her slightly out of breath. More than slightly. Enough so that she had to lean against the cool stucco exterior until her heart slowed and her breathing became regular. As a child, she thought that when she stood up here she was nearer to God. She would lean her head back and imagine that the steeple, and the cross that sat atop it, were within the reach of God's hands.

Beatrice and Tiny still came to church here every Sunday. They had finally stopped inviting her along, even for midnight mass or Easter morning. What is wrong with you? they used to ask her. I don't believe in it anymore, she told them, even though that answer did not make sense. After all, she was the one who fought giving up Latin, who kept her head covered inside, the one who had to remind them to get their ashes or their throats blessed. She was the one that their mother had thought, maybe, hopefully, would become a nun. Before she was a teenager, before she realized the power of her beauty and discovered boys and French kissing, Claire used to come to Saint Teresa's after school and help the nuns clean the wax that dripped from the devotional candles. It was impossible for her to have stopped believing in the church. But she insisted, and soon they stopped asking, though they still wondered.

They would never guess, Claire knew, that she'd stopped coming because she had sinned. A mortal sin. She had broken the sixth commandment: Thou shalt not kill. She couldn't ever go back into church again. Even after all this time, she hesitated at the door. She remembered women who had married divorced men and could not enter church, how they walked past Saint Teresa's embarrassed, eyes cast downward, making a quick, clumsy sign of the cross. She had pitied those women once.

In her twenty-five years away, things around Claire had changed. There was mass on Saturday afternoon. There was talk of women priests, of homosexual priests. But Claire had not changed. Her sin still made her feel dirty, doomed. Until she realized that something was wrong with Dan. Then Claire began to think that here was her hell. She was paying for her sin through her husband. She would have to diaper him, feed him, rock him to sleep. He would forget who she was. He would forget why he loved her. Michaela would explain all of this as karma. But Claire knew better.

Without warning, the door burst open and a young man came out. He wore sunglasses, a Notre Dame jacket, jeans.

"I didn't mean to startle you," he said to Claire.

He was handsome. He needed a haircut, a trim really.

"Oh," she said, and shook her head.

He glanced at his watch, then back at her. "Were you here for confession?" he asked.

The question surprised her. Confession in the middle of the week! It used to be on Saturdays, the church crowded, dark, hushed.

"No," she said.

He smiled. "Good. I'm running late as it is."

Claire frowned. Was he the priest? But he was just a boy! And that jacket. That shaggy hair. He was bounding down the stairs already, skipping every other one, like a schoolboy. Her hand lingered on the polished wood of the door. She had come here intending to go inside, to kneel at the altar, to think about the possibility of penance, of forgiveness. Perhaps she had even imagined talking to the priest—though in her imagination it was Father Connelly, gray-haired with saggy eyelids and yellow teeth. Perhaps she had imagined a conversation in which she began to talk about what she had done, about duty to the church and duty to one's family. Sometimes Claire wondered how she would have felt if everything was the same except Michaela was happy. Would she still carry the burden of her sin like this?

Closing her eyes, Claire pictured the interior of the church. The dark magenta carpet, the heavy pews and ornate altar. There had been renovations, she knew. Back in the late seventies. But she liked her memory of the way it was. She could walk in there, walk down the long center aisle—the very one she'd walked down as a bride in her ivory satin gown, clutching a spray of gladiolas; the one she'd carried each of her daughters down for baptism, she in a camel hair suit, the babies in white lace. Claire could walk down that aisle yet again, and throw herself on her knees at the altar, and look up to the face of Jesus hanging from the cross at the front of the church, and ask for forgiveness. Or at least for understanding. Ask, maybe, for Dan to get well.

A car passed, beeping its horn. Claire opened her eyes and looked down, toward the road. But she didn't recognize anyone. A priest so young, she thought, couldn't begin to understand. Holding the railing too tightly, Claire began the long walk back.

Victoria had a cat without a tail named Cleopatra. She kept trying to get Kate to play with it, but Kate thought it was the ugliest cat she'd ever seen. Besides, now that it was dark out and her mother still hadn't come for her, Kate knew that her mother must be dead. She felt scared and sad and she wanted to go home. Victoria's apartment had black furniture and ugly pictures on the wall of people that looked stretched out, like rubber bands. Even her coffee table was black and shiny.

"How do you like it?" she'd asked Kate when they first got there. "It's Art Deco."

Kate knew it was impolite to say what she really thought. But it was a lie to say she liked it. So she just said, "Oh. Art Deco," right back at Victoria.

After a while Victoria asked her, "What do you usually do after school? Crafts?"

"I watch *Oprah* at four o'clock," Kate told her.

Victoria laughed. "Right," she said. She gave Kate some construction paper and scissors and said, "Can you cut out some flowers for me? Tulips, maybe? You know, for spring."

Kate didn't want to. Instead, she cut out aliens, triangle faces with antennas on their heads and bodies shaped like hot dogs.

Victoria called to her from the kitchen. "There's still no answer at your house."

A little while later she called out, "Your father isn't at work."

Kate's mouth felt too dry, like she'd eaten a box of Q-Tips. Her father was probably at the morgue, identifying the body. She'd seen that on *L.A. Law.*

Victoria came back into the black living room. She had changed into clothes that looked like pajamas, but fancier.

"Do you know your grandparents' name?" she asked.

"Claire!" Kate said, happy to have a solution. "And Dan. Daniel," she added.

"Claire and Daniel Hunter?" Victoria said hopefully.

Kate frowned. Her Hunter grandparents lived in Florida, on the Gulf. She told Victoria that. "And their names are Bunny and Buddy." Despite her mother's being dead, Kate giggled. Those were ridiculous names. Even Maggie thought so. Grandpa Hunter—Buddy—had something called a pacemaker in his heart and couldn't go on Space Mountain when they all went to Disney World. She told Victoria that too, in case it was helpful.

"Can you try to remember the other grandparents' last name? Claire and Dan what?"

But Kate's mind was empty.

Victoria went back into the kitchen. When she came out again, Kate had used up all the construction paper and lined up the aliens along the back of the sofa. They were invading the Art Deco. They would take the ugly cat back to outer space with them.

"Kate," Victoria said, "doesn't your mother use her maiden name?"

"Maiden name?" Kate said. She thought of that card game, Old Maid. "I don't think so."

"Her name isn't Hunter exactly, is it? I seem to remember it was something different."

"Josie?" Kate said.

Victoria shook her head and left the room again. The next time she came back she had a bowl of chips and another bowl of salsa.

"We might as well eat," she said.

She didn't look very happy.

"Maybe we should put on the six o'clock news," Kate said. They always put murders on the news, she knew. And car accidents.

"Let's think again," Victoria said. "Your father's name is—"

"William Matthew Hunter," Kate said.

"And—"

"And my sister is Maggie Claire Hunter and it's really Maggie *not* Margaret and my mother is Josie Jericho Hunter and I'm Kate Jericho Hunter."

Victoria was smiling. "Jericho?"

"Kate Jericho Hunter," Kate mumbled. She felt really depressed. And all this black furniture wasn't helping much.

"Now we're cooking," Victoria said, and she left the room again.

Cooking? Kate thought, wondering if anyone would ever come to get her. She did not like to eat other people's cooking. That was what her father called a fact.

"You forgot Kate," Will said when Josie walked in the door.

That was when she realized she had forgotten her daughter.

"Oh, my God," she said, "it slipped my mind." Which was the truth.

She had driven all the way home from the mall when she decided that she had to go back and file that report, embarrassed or not. The security guard she'd spoken to knew Will and acted kind.

"Everything took so much longer than I expected," she said. She glanced at the clock. After seven. The table was set and Will was placing a casserole—from her mother? Josie wondered—in the center.

"Oh, my God," Josie said again. She sat at the table, shaking her head. "I needed someone to help me," she said. "I was looking for you and . . ." The day unfolded in her mind. Josie felt her cheeks redden.

The casserole was tuna, she could smell it.

"I'll call the girls," Will said.

Josie told herself, Now we'll eat dinner, like a normal family. But when they were all gathered there at the table, looking at her like she was an interloper, and her mother's casserole was steaming on her plate, Josie could not do it. She could not eat. She could not pretend that everything was the same.

▪ ▪ ▪

That winter there had been seventeen blizzards. Some schools, Michaela knew, were meeting into July to make up snow days. And now with the steady rain there was talk of the river flooding. That had not happened in East Essex since Michaela's mother was a bride. 1950. Dan had taken photographs of her in the basement, her khaki trousers rolled up to her knees, a man's workshirt tied in a knot at her stomach, as she lifted boxes to higher shelves, to safety. They lost photographs in that flood, and their wedding album, a heavy white one that used to play "Oh Promise Me," after all this time still smelled moldy. When Michaela and Josie were children, their mother would show them the pictures their father took of her rescuing items from the rising water. She would take out her wedding album and show them the water marks around the edges, the mud stains on its back. She would lift it to their noses and have them breathe in its earthy, damp smell.

Still, no one took the talk seriously. In the last four decades there had been plenty of springs with heavy rain. Even Michaela could remember the time a mailbox floated down Main Street, all of the letters inside destroyed. And the spring the old high school's roof caved in from all the water that had collected on it. But a flood was something distant and remote, like a memory.

Michaela wanted to wait for the rain to subside before going down to the river, but it did not let up and she finally decided to go anyway. Ever since she'd gone to the factory that day, Michaela had been haunted by the idea that she could change something. Not East Essex, exactly. But a part of it. She imagined that she could take the river and bring it back to life. At night, in her old bedroom, she dreamed the river alive again —she saw it blue, and moving steadily along. She saw reeds flourishing at its feet, speckled fish swimming through it, children on its banks. She even saw the ruins of an old mill, lost almost a hundred years ago to a fire, rebuilt, teeming with life.

In the morning, it seemed real, as if it actually happened. Michaela felt that if she rose from her bed with its pink dust ruffle and rushed past the dulled black light posters of Adam and Eve and Jimi Hendrix, outside, down the hill, to the river, it would all be there, everything she had imagined.

The rain, she decided, couldn't stop her from the first step, at least. From beneath the kitchen sink, where her mother stored neatly folded stacks of brown grocery bags and empty containers—margarine, mustard, mayonnaise—Michaela took a jar, found a lid to fit it, and placed it in the pocket of her father's old yellow rain slicker. She could not remember when she had last felt such purpose. Perhaps it had been the day she'd walked down this same street with her acceptance letter from Berkeley folded in her pocket. That day she had thought her life was just about to begin. She would move across country and never think of here. She would get to know the sky. She would make a difference. Although her hopes were not so grand now, at least she had hope again. Finally. The rain seeped through her shoes so that her feet made a wet slapping sound as she walked. No matter what you did later in life, she thought, it was impossible to recapture that sense of conquering the world that you had as a teenager. Although that realization should make her sad, Michaela instead felt something settle in her. She could not name what that thing was, or what it meant, but by the time she got to the river she was overcome by a sense of confidence and certainty. This was something she could do—she could save the Pottowamicut River.

Even now, standing there with the gray sky and thick rain, the river somehow uglier, stiller, Michaela knew it would be alive again soon. She *saw* it. The banks were sticky with mud and litter. There was nothing to hold on to as she made her way down, stumbling on half-hidden rocks and rusted beer cans, and she slid the last few yards, the mud splattering her jeans and making its way into her shoes. Where the river met the banks, a thick layer of greenish brown sludge gathered. Michaela took off her shoes and socks and poked her toe in the sludge. It let out a little gasp when her toe broke through. Beneath it were long-dead plants, more mud. When she bent to fill the jar with water, the names of strange diseases flooded her mind. Typhoid, bubonic plague, strep, staph, hepatitis. Surely some of those lived in polluted water. The water around her ankles did not even slap at her a little, it merely clung to her, like anything that was dying might.

"Hey," someone called. "What are you doing?"

Michaela looked up. A man in a yellow slicker like the one she wore was running—or trying to run—toward her. The slippery mud made it look like he was a drunk striving for balance. She ignored him.

"You're what?" he said when he reached her. "Taking a specimen?"

She screwed the lid on the jar and put it back in her pocket.

"I've had it tested," he said.

He didn't have the hood up on his slicker and his hair was a mess of wet curls. The rain poured down his face, reminding Michaela of someone crying hard. Drops dangled from the ends of his walrus mustache, the tip of his nose. She thought he looked and talked like a madman. For a crazy instant she thought he might kill her, stab or strangle her, drop her body in the river.

"It's polluted," the man said.

He gestured wildly as he talked. When he reached inside his slicker she thought he really might pull out a knife, and she heard her breath catch. But all he produced was a small spiral notepad. He began to read off numbers. The alkaline and PH and a dozen more.

"Nothing could live in here," he said, and again Michaela

felt frightened. "Nothing," he added. He seemed to be looking right through her.

She tried to stay calm, turning slowly to begin the long climb upward.

"I'm going to clean it up," he said. "Come down on that soap factory for dumping shit in here."

Michaela had to bend over and push her hands into the sludge and mud to make it back up the bank. It made it impossible to turn around. She did stop, though, and said, "I'm going to clean it up. I am." This was her dream, her town, her river. Who was this guy, this intruder? "My father," she said, "used to fish in this river."

The man was beside her. He didn't have to bend nearly as far. "I have a list. Sign up. Help me."

Funny, she had thought he was an older man. But up close she saw that he was about her age, forty or so.

"No," she said.

"I've been to the EPA, everywhere. They won't even come down and do their own tests. I'm on my own here."

What Michaela had imagined was that she would rescue something herself. Breathe life back into the Pottowamicut. This man, kneeling in the mud beside her, could not know what that meant to her.

"It's mine," she said. Then she began to climb up on her hands and knees.

Will hardly knew Father MacKenna. Josie had been telling him that this new young priest was wonderful. Inspiring, she'd called him. Like the priest at the University of Rhode Island when they were in college there. Will and Josie used to go to mass there every Sunday evening. Now, Will thought as he walked into Saint Teresa's, genuflecting quickly, almost casually, at the altar, it was Josie who held up that part of their life—waking the girls on Sunday mornings, getting them to mass, to catechism, even manning booths at holiday bazaars. He would explain his absence to the priest, Will decided, winding his way to the office tucked into the back of the church. He had a job that required him to work on weekends, he would tell him. It wasn't that he didn't believe or anything.

Father McKenna stood in the office, holding a large feather duster clotted with dust kitties. He wore jeans and a Harvard T-shirt, Nikes, no socks.

Will cleared his throat. His lies were stuck there, gagging him. Even though this guy looked like a college student, he was still a priest. The long-haired one he'd known back in college had made Will nervous despite his sideburns and the way he'd called Will "man."

"Priests," Will said to Father McKenna, "make me nervous."

The priest laughed and held up his feather duster. "Even holding one of these?" he said.

Will smiled, shrugged. He and Josie had gotten married in this church. Had baptized both of their children here.

Father McKenna put down the duster and motioned for Will to sit in the burgundy leather chair that faced the large, heavily polished desk. The priest perched on one corner of the desk and waited for Will to begin.

But Will did not know where to begin. His lie about work seemed unnecessary, foolish. His religious background seemed unimportant. As a child, his family had gone to a different church, Saint Stanislaw's. The Polish church. But he had happily gotten married here, joined this parish, because it was Josie's.

"You know my wife," he said finally. "Josie? Hunter?"

The priest nodded.

Will tried to read his face. Did he have some impression of

Josie that he was withholding? Or did she, as Will had come to think of her lately, leave no impression? But the priest gave nothing away. He was, simply, waiting again.

"How did you know you wanted to be a priest?" Will blurted. "I mean, it's none of my business or anything but I'm at this point in life where I can't figure out how anybody comes to decisions about anything. Careers or where to live or whether to move to Idaho or anything."

"You want a divorce," Father McKenna said.

Will's back went rigid. "I didn't say that," he said, defensive.

"When did you get married, Will?" the priest said, and Will didn't like the way he said his name.

"I was too young," Will said, aware that he was mumbling. How could priests, men who make vows of chastity, understand about marriage? About wanting different women? About love?

"What? Twenty-five? Twenty-six?"

"Twenty-two!" Will said. Maybe he could understand.

"That's young," the priest said. "Right out of college? College sweethearts?"

Will was nodding enthusiastically. "Exactly," he said.

Father McKenna reached behind his back and felt around until he found a thick leather-bound date book with a gold cross embossed on the front. He shuffled through the pages, then looked back at Will.

"Don't worry," he said. "Your feelings of boredom, of exhaustion—"

"I don't love her anymore," Will said. "Maybe I never did. I don't know." That wasn't right exactly. He *had* wanted to marry her. It just seemed now that those feelings happened to someone else. It was difficult for Will to dredge them up, to understand them. He had wanted her beside him every night, had wanted them to have children, had longed for the feel of her hand in his when they were apart, the way she stroked the inside of his palm in a particular way. He had loved her, he realized. Will tried again. "It was like I was bodysurfing, you know? I caught this one wave twenty years ago and I've just been riding it and riding it. Josie. My job. The house I live in. Nothing has changed. I mean, I started working at Caldor's when I was sixteen. As a stockboy. I worked there every summer, every holiday. And I still work there. I mean, I'm losing my hair, for Christ's sake. Sorry, Father. But it's just that I got married in this church. A candlelight wedding. That was the big thing then. Six o'clock. All these thick white candles burning and I felt like I was suffocating, like they were sucking up all the available oxygen. Some cousin of mine that I hardly ever saw sang 'Sunrise, Sunset.' It was all so depressing. And there was no air. I got this weird hum in my head. Not a pounding. A hum. And Josie was standing there beside me in this long white gown with these little pearls sewn all over it and she had a veil and a train and there was so much fine fabric everywhere that I just couldn't breathe and this humming was getting louder and louder and the next thing I know someone has shoved my head between my knees and someone else is telling me to take slow, deep breaths into this paper bag and behind the hum I hear Josie's cousin Denise saying at least he waited until after the I do part . . ."

At some point the priest had gone over to a bookshelf and started pulling books from it. He said, "You hyperventilated."

"Yes," Will said. Father McKenna didn't get the symbolism that seemed so obvious to Will. At the time, Will had found it funny. All those candles, too many flowers. But now it was clear. An omen, maybe even a sign from God not to marry Josie.

Father McKenna handed the stack of books to Will. "These are wonderful," he said. "Couples use them all the time with great success. There are exercises in the back of this one." He tapped the top book. His fingers were long and slender, well groomed. "And we have all sorts of options. A Wednesday night couple's group. Private sessions with me whenever your schedules allow. And a couple's retreat next weekend down at Alton Jones. If the rain ever stops. We do those twice a year and people often go to both."

Will was frowning. "What?" he said.

"I have a basic belief that every marriage can be saved," the priest said, grinning. "Even one where the young groom hyperventilates at the altar."

"I want a divorce," Will said, his voice barely more than a whisper.

"I don't suppose there's someone else involved here?" Father McKenna said, lowering his voice too.

Will shook his head. He remembered going to confession as a kid, kneeling in the dark booth, listing his sins—I lied four times, I stole licorice from Calci's candy store but then I brought it back so I'm not sure if that counts, I hit Jimmy Bottenelli twice and I disrespected my mother twelve times.

"Because," the priest was saying, "that often complicates matters. Confuses the issues."

Their eyes met.

Will used to think nuns and priests could read people's minds. He had gone for six years to Saint Stanislaw's Elementary School, a series of makeshift classrooms in the church basement, and he had sat forcing himself to think good things so the nuns wouldn't know he was really concentrating on bad stuff like the glimpse of Kathy Kowalczyk's underwear he'd caught at recess, or Sister Joseph's mustache, or how fat Sister Michael was.

He tried it now, forced good thoughts into his mind.

But the priest was saying that it had been his experience that during a couple's phase of renewal they should focus on each other and their family. "Especially," he added, "when there are children involved." He tapped the spine of one of the books that sat between him and Will. "I think this one is a real eye-opener. The effects of divorce on children are more devastating than we care to admit."

Again their eyes locked.

"Do you want to talk to Josie?" the priest said, and Will didn't like the familiarity with which he said her name—Josie who comes to church and bakes cakes for the cake sale and helps out at the stupid car wash. "Or should I?" he added.

Will stood up, the leather chair sighing as he did. "Look," he said, "I don't love her."

The priest was answering him, but Will didn't care. He walked out of the office, leaving the stack of books behind, genuflecting sloppily at the altar before he walked up the long carpeted aisle that led out.

Josie could not let go of the belief that Will would come around. He would believe her. He would pull out his little notebook and give her a complete description of the man. She sat and thought about that when she should have been making dinner and checking the sump pump in the basement and sorting laundry—colors, whites, delicates. But as she tried each task she grew distracted. The blank hulk of the carjacker loomed large in her mind. She painted different faces on him: small eyes, round bulging ones, blue, brown, hazel, green. A bump on the nose. A scar on the cheek. Hair curly, straight, blond, black. Bald. Then she'd startle herself by dropping a saucepan, or finding herself in the damp basement, or clutching Kate's white tights decorated with purple hearts.

She called Will at work, left messages. He was at lunch. He was away from his desk. He was not answering his page. "He must be out on the floor," Sheila told her. Something began to nag at Josie. She pushed it away, then pulled it forward. She remembered how once, when Kate was only a baby—two, maybe?—and she had found a note tucked deep into a pocket of a pair of Will's pants. It had said, "Thanks. Call. Carla." Will had looked surprised when she'd shown it to him. He had shrugged. "Beats me," he had told her.

Where was he? Josie wondered.

A face appeared at the kitchen window and Josie screamed, a short bleat, really. Almost as soon as she did, she saw that it was Denise.

Her heart jumping wildly about, Josie went to the door to let her cousin in.

"I've been ringing the bell," Denise said. "Is it broken?"

"You scared me half to death," Josie said.

Denise marched through the house, to the front door, and rang the doorbell several times.

"It works fine," she said, frowning. "Didn't you hear me out there?"

Before Josie could answer, Denise was unloading a shopping bag, listing the items as she put them in the proper place—"refrigerator, cupboard, freezer."

"A rotisserie chicken. Pesto sauce. Tortellini. Mac and cheese for the girls. Smoked turkey. Cole slaw. Dijon potato salad."

"Thanks," Josie said.

"Yeah. Well, you've been through something, right?"

Josie looked at her, angry. "Right," she said.

Denise sat at the table and drummed her long nails against it. "I've done things I'm not proud of," she said finally. "You're not alone."

"I'm not ashamed that some guy attacked me in the mall parking lot," Josie told her.

"No one knows this except Judy," Denise said, looking down at her fingertips, dark against the tabletop. "Once, I had an affair."

"What?"

"All right. There. It's out." She exhaled, long and deep.

"With who?" Josie said. "When?"

Denise looked at her. "That's irrelevant. My point is, you can tell me anything. I know you can't really talk to Michaela and your mother shouldn't be burdened with any more. We're family, right? We have to stick together."

Josie nodded but her mind was racing. Who would Denise have an affair with? She thought about telling Will, how shocked he would be. And then she felt a pang of loss. She knew with certainty that she would not tell Will.

"I even thought of leaving James," Denise was saying. "Can you imagine?"

"I'm going away this weekend," Will said the next night after dinner. He said it as casually as if he was always going away for weekends by himself. As if, Josie thought, it was all right to leave her alone so soon.

He was doing the dishes when he said it, his back to her, his head bent into the steam and detergent bubbles that floated up from the sink. Josie always used the dishwasher, but Will liked submerging his hands in soapy hot water, liked taking the dirty dishes and glasses and scrubbing them clean.

Josie waited for an explanation, but when none came she said simply, "You can't."

He was still for an instant, but then resumed washing. He cleared his throat. "I wasn't asking permission," he said.

When he turned around he held a clean dish in his hand. It was off white with slightly raised cornflowers in the center. Their everyday set that they chose together and registered for before they got married.

"It's kind of embarrassing," Will said, "but it's a men's encounter group."

Josie had heard about that kind of thing. She'd even seen something in the newspaper, men going off into the woods and talking about their feelings. She remembered Will mentioning it not long ago when he got on that kick about how to please her sexually.

"What exactly do they do there?" she asked.

"Talk," he said. "It's just a bunch of guys my age . . ."

"Oh," she said, and laughed nervously, seeking some kind of relief. "A midlife crisis already?"

Will began to dry the dishes again. Josie watched his arms move beneath his shirt. She felt an actual ache to be hugged.

"I don't want to be alone here," Josie said. Although that wasn't exactly true. She just didn't think he should leave her alone.

"Maybe your sister can come and stay with you," Will said, turning back to the dishes.

Josie had been avoiding Michaela. When she'd stumbled into her parents' house the other night, seeing Michaela had made it all worse somehow. There was something about her sister being back that troubled Josie, though she couldn't quite figure out why. Maybe she had enough to deal with already—the police kept calling her with more questions, the insurance company sent long forms to fill out, her own mind replayed the incident over and over, like a record stuck in one spot. The last thing she needed was Michaela right now. But thinking that, Josie knew that wasn't really it. There was more to it.

Will was talking about bonding and sisterhood and the need to strengthen those ties.

"What has gotten into you?" Josie said. He sounded like a New Age guru. And he used to laugh at Michaela and what he called her "touchy feely shit."

She didn't really expect an answer, but Will said, "I think it's important to communicate. That's all." His voice was steady, as if he were trying to keep it controlled.

"Well," Josie said, not trying to hide any sarcasm, "you could have fooled me. You haven't listened to anything I've said about what happened."

She watched his arms move in circles as he scrubbed at something.

"You've only made me feel worse," she said.

"I'm sorry if I've done that," Will said.

"Denise's party is this weekend," Josie said.

He shrugged.

Josie kept her eyes on him, on the way his shirt hung loosely from his shoulders—had he lost weight? she wondered. She had the feeling that, really, he wasn't sorry at all.

Something was very wrong with her mother. Kate was sure of it.

When her father told her that a bad man had stolen their car and knocked her mother down, right at the mall, Kate had asked, "What bad man?"

"Someone we don't know," her father explained.

At school last year, a policeman had come in and taught them about Stranger Danger. The policeman had taught them not to talk to strangers, even if the stranger promised them candy. Even if he promised to show them some puppies. Didn't her mother know about Stranger Danger? Kate wondered what the man had promised to get her mother to hand over their car. Whatever it was, her father was angry at her mother for letting it happen.

"We can't even buy a new car with the insurance money," he said at dinner the night her mother forgot to pick her up. "The book value is zip."

Her mother had only shrugged.

In the morning now her mother slept late. No waffles shaped like Mickey Mouse for breakfast. No careful braids tied with bright ribbons in her hair. Kate kept walking past her parents' bedroom, on tiptoe, pausing at the door. She expected to hear something—anything—but it was so quiet she started to think maybe her mother wasn't really even in there. Maybe she climbed out the window every morning and went off with the stranger, Kate thought. Finally, she couldn't take it any longer and she went into the room. There was her mother, in bed, looking like Snow White in the glass coffin.

"Do you want to hear me sing 'A Whole New World'?" Kate asked. For some reason, she stood a few feet away from the bed instead of going close.

"No," her mother said.

Kate was so surprised she actually gasped. "No?" Her mother never said no. She always wanted to see Kate's art work or hear her sing or watch her dance. Kate waited, but her mother didn't say anything else.

The other night, at Victoria's, Kate had been surprised when Maggie and a red-haired lady came to pick her up. The red-haired lady was her Aunt Michaela from California. Kate thought her Aunt Michaela was a teenager, like Maggie, because in all the pictures of her that her mother had she looked young, with blue jeans and freckles on her cheeks. But she was old, older than Kate's mother even. If Maggie hadn't been with her, Kate would not have believed that this old woman was her Aunt Michaela from California. She would have thought she was a stranger and she would have refused to go with her. The policeman had told her class the three R's—Refuse, Run, Report. Apparently her mother had done none of those things.

"Why did you give that stranger our car?" Kate asked her mother.

"I didn't give it to him," she said. "He took it."

"Did you refuse loudly?" That was part of the first R. Refuse loudly. Scream so others can hear you and come to assist.

Her mother sighed and said, "Kate, you're too young to understand."

Kate gasped again. She was mature for her age. Everyone said so. She thought she might cry.

Kate backed out of the room, slowly. Once, on the Saturday afternoon cable "Creature Feature," these scary pods had gotten inside people and made them act weird. Maybe the stranger was a space invader. Maybe her mother had a pod inside her. She stood outside the bedroom door again and tried to think of what she should do. It took a lot of people in that movie to fight off those pods.

As loud as she could, Kate started to sing "A Whole New World." Her real mother would not be able to resist hearing Kate sing her part from the school play. She would come out of that room and she would be smiling. She would give Kate a big round of applause. Kate sang and sang, letting her voice grow louder with each new verse, but her mother did not come out. Even as she sang, Kate imagined large scary things falling from the sky, pods entering her mother's body, changing her forever.

Kate had sung the whole song, so she started again. Her voice grew hoarse.

Maggie shouted at her from downstairs. "Shut up already!"

Only then did Kate finally stop.

On Friday, Josie watched Will pack. A pair of khakis. The T-shirt he'd bought on their family vacation on Martha's Vineyard last summer. His pale blue chamois shirt, the one that made his eyes seem even bluer than they already were. His navy sweater. Josie frowned. His *good* navy sweater, the one she'd given him for his birthday. The one she'd spent too much money for, that he liked to wear on cool summer nights when they went to eat at their favorite restaurant down at the beach.

On those nights, they had drinks outside. Kir or martinis or Rob Roys. Grown-up drinks, they called them, so unlike the beer with schnapp chasers they used to guzzle at fraternity parties and beachside bars in college. He kept that sweater tied around his neck until the sun set and the ocean air turned cool. Now he was taking it to walk around the woods? And, Josie noticed, a bottle of Polo cologne.

"What do you need that for?" she asked him.

Will shrugged. "You know," he said.

But she didn't know. Men together did not worry about how they smelled. She could still remember the mixture of sweat and old beer and gym socks that permeated all the fraternity houses in college. The pale blue shirt and good sweater and bottle of Polo. Josie repeated those things to herself. A funny list of things to take on a retreat.

Lately, Josie had felt frightened by innocent things—the sway of a branch in the wind, the creak of the floorboards. She'd been suspicious of everyone. Why was there suddenly a new mailman on their road? Who was calling and hanging up before she could even say hello? Paranoid, Will told her. He said it as if it were contagious. "What if I am?" she'd said. "I was assaulted."

She said that again now, sitting on the edge of their bed, her bare feet dangling over the side, swinging back and forth.

"It's been a week," she said, "since the attack."

"You've got to stop obsessing about it," Will said.

"It was so horrible," Josie said, her voice soft. She wanted to tell him all of it, every detail. How she'd smiled at the man in the linens department, how she'd thought she knew him from somewhere, high school maybe. How the smell of mint mouthwash had filled her when he came close.

"Horrible things," Will said as he zipped his duffel bag shut, "should be forgotten. Put behind us."

Josie wondered about that. If she could forget it, maybe her life would go back to how it used to be. Her mind touched on things—her carefully planned menus, the comfortable sex she and Will had—then moved past them. The dark, hulking shape of the crime was too big to ignore. It made those other things not matter. It made her see herself as if for the first time. The feel of cotton and wool, even the plastic of the old bean bag chair in the den against her body, her own fingers on her flesh, these were the only things that made her remember she had lived through what happened in the mall parking lot. These were the things that reminded Josie she was still real.

All week they had eaten grilled cheese sandwiches that Maggie made, Will's American chop suey, some kind of casserole her mother sent over, and they had gotten by. Her turkey meatloaf with homemade cranberry sauce, the roasted garlic mashed potatoes, the mango chutney baked chicken, all copied exactly from cooking magazines, the bright glossy photo propped up for Josie to see, seemed like unimportant things from someone else's life. All week she'd slept alone. It felt like the other side of the bed had never been slept in, rather than filled for so many years by Will.

"I can't believe I'm alive," Josie said, more to herself than to Will.

But he heard her and came to sit beside her on the bed. He took her hands in his. He spoke, finally, gently. "Honey, please. Put it out of your mind."

His hands were mostly smooth, with calluses in one place. The mound of Venus, that place was called. Josie knew that from Michaela, who once studied her palm and told her she would have two lovers, two children, three homes.

When Will released her hands, she quickly reached for his again. She placed them beneath her sweatshirt, on her breasts, wanting those calluses, their roughness, against her own smooth skin. She kept her hands over his, gently forced circular motions that hardened her nipples, made her wet between the legs.

Josie arched her back, pushing against him. Perhaps, she thought, he didn't need to go to an encounter group after all.

But, quickly, Will withdrew his hands, held them out from her like a surgeon inspecting them for sterilization.

"I want to," she said. If she made love to him now, boldly, in the afternoon light, perhaps he wouldn't go.

"You're not ready," he said. "It's so soon after."

"I want to," she said again. Hadn't he just told her to try and forget?

"Let's just lie here a few minutes," Will said, stretching out on the bed, pulling her down beside him.

"Remember how we would cut Earth Science and go to your room and make love?" she said. She rested her head on his chest. Will began to play with her hair, gently twisting it around his fingers, tugging, letting go.

"Do you ever think," Will said, his voice husky, his fingers wrapping her hair, holding on, "that we got married too young? Too fast? What was the rush?"

It was as if she had been waiting for this moment, these words. She was right. He didn't love her anymore.

"No," she managed to say.

"Never?"

"Can we just lie here like this?" Josie said. "Before you have to go?"

Michaela had tried everything.

Drugs. TM. Est. Past-life regression—the woman had told her she'd had an affair with Dickens in her last life. She'd drunk too much, snorted too much, practiced yoga, gone to therapy—group and private. Now, after all this time, she was going to try confrontation. Sitting in her old bedroom, Michaela realized that she'd gone into everything else without fear or anxiety, swallowed handfuls of pills, given herself freely to men, even on two occasions to women, submitted to anything, to everything, without hesitation. But facing her mother, doing this, was scaring the hell out of her.

She'd sat like this that spring twenty-five years ago, terrified, cross-legged on this very bed, and strung long strands of glass beads to hang in the doorway of her room at college. She went to flea markets and antique shops in search of good Austrian crystals in beautiful colors. Her fingers had bled from pushing the needle through enough of them to fill a doorway. Even now she could remember the ache in her hands from working so long at it. She could remember the way the light changed from early afternoon to evening. She could remember her fear.

Michaela closed her eyes and tried to remember the rules for relaxation she'd learned in yoga. Or was it TM? Somewhere inside of a person was a place that could be unlocked, opened. If she opened hers, it would all come out, a flood of memories. A kind-faced man in a black kimono back in San Francisco had told her she needed to let go. Water washes, he'd said. He was a Chinese healer that Belle had recommended. Think of a river, he'd told her. Jump in. See where water takes you.

At first Michaela could only conjure the river as it was now, muddy and polluted, but finally she was able to picture Water Street as it had once been, the shabby shops there where her mother had brought them to buy school shoes and winter coats. The woman in the shoe department at Ramona's who had a hole in her throat from an operation. *Cancer.* Her mother and aunts would say the word as if it were a real, living thing. Both of their parents had died from it, long painful deaths that involved trips to the hospital, whispered conversations, suffering. *Throat cancer.* That was what the shoe woman had. She covered the hole with chiffon scarves. Her voice came from a box in there, mechanical and muffled by the chiffon. Don't stare, her mother used to hiss at her. But Michaela couldn't help it. A hole in your throat, she used to think. Imagine! At night, she would sneak into Josie's room and talk like the shoe lady to frighten her. Josie was always so easy to scare.

After the mall opened and businesses began to leave Water Street, Michaela and her friends used to go there and smoke pot in the empty parking lots behind the stores. She and Ollie Pfeiffer would sit in the back seat of his beat-up VW bug and get high, then make slow love with her sitting on his lap facing him. It was the only way their legs and arms fit. His skin looked golden in the haze of smoke and dim streetlight. Remembering it, she saw clearly the definition of the muscles in his arms, the way the veins in his hands bulged as he held her tighter and tighter. More than once, the police had caught them, forced them out of the car clutching their clothes to cover themselves. The policemen would avert their eyes until Ollie and Michaela were dressed, then follow them home. It was all so polite. They never even told their parents what they'd been caught at, just dropped them off silently with the blue light on top of the police car spinning. The only reason they avoided real trouble was because Ollie was the town baseball star. "You two weren't doing anything," her mother would say, "were you?" Michaela might shrug or mumble an answer. But Oliver always looked right at her mother and said, "Of course not."

The sound of footsteps coming up the stairs made Michaela jump off the bed, as if she were still a teenager caught doing something wrong. She laughed to herself, almost expecting her mother to appear in the doorway, frowning, demanding to know what was going on up here. But then she decided that would be good if her mother was on her way upstairs. Michaela was ready.

It was Josie who came in, though, frowning, asking, "What are you doing up here?"

"Thinking," Michaela said. She was surprised to see her sister standing there, an adult.

Josie hesitated, then walked in. As children they'd had a rule—you can only enter if invited.

"I haven't meant to ignore you," Josie said.

"I've been kind of wrapped up in stuff anyway," Michaela told her. Her sister, Michaela realized sadly, had not grown into a lovely woman, the way their mother used to promise her she would.

"What stuff?" Josie said finally.

Michaela felt, surprisingly, disappointed. She reached over and traced Josie's scar on her forehead.

"What?" Josie said, stepping back.

"The river," Michaela said. "I want to get it cleaned up. I even thought the empty mills could be renovated, turned into apartments, businesses. Anything, really."

Josie laughed. "In East Essex? This town is not interested in anything like that."

"It's being done all over the country with great success," Michaela said.

Josie pointed a finger at her. "I thought that maybe you'd come back here with your head out of the clouds."

For an instant, Michaela almost told her. After all, hadn't they once believed that together they could conquer anything? The world, the heavens, and beyond? That must include the past as well.

But Josie was talking about something else. She had dismissed Michaela's plans and was on to more practical matters.

"I can pick you up and we can go over together. And don't look at me that way. I'm dreading it too."

It took a minute for Michaela to catch up. Denise's party. "I'm not going. I've got a meeting set up with this asshole who thinks he owns the river. Hopefully, he'll butt out and let me get on with my plans."

"You're serious?" Josie said. "Where are you going to get money for this? You'll need engineers and architects and builders." She laughed. "Think about what you're saying."

"I have thought about it," Michaela told her.

"Have you thought about how insulted Denise is going to be when you don't show up?"

"This is important to me," Michaela said.

Josie lifted her arms in defeat. "Fine," she said. "I tried."

Watching her sister leave, Michaela wondered who she was, this person who worried about things that did not matter. How had Josie gotten so planted in the mundane? So caught up in rules? Michaela was overcome by the urge to grab her and tell her everything. She ran down the stairs, chasing after her sister, calling to her.

"Remember," Michaela said at Josie's car window, "remember when we all went to New York that summer?"

"It's pouring out," Josie said, "in case you hadn't noticed."

"Dad wanted to sell that game? At Macy's?"

"You're getting drenched."

"Remember?" Michaela shouted.

"Before you left for California," Josie said. "You stayed there for that NYU precollege thing."

"Yes," Michaela said. She always thought that summer day in 1969 should have been like this one, gray, stormy. But it had been hot and humid, the sun bright, the tar sticky beneath her feet. She remembered how the small heels on her mother's shoes had sunk when she walked, like they were on quicksand.

"It was a family trip," Josie said. "A day in New York City."

Funny how, looking back, each of them had a secret agenda that day, except for Josie, who was only twelve and really just excited to see the sights, the Empire State Building and Yankee

Stadium. "Where Ollie will play someday, right, Michaela?" she'd asked, but Michaela had not answered her. Their father had gone to sell a game he'd invented to Macy's. It was to be his big break. No more selling Fords. No more working on weekends. He was going to sell his game and make a million dollars and buy four round-trip tickets on Pan Am Flight 001, the flight that went around the world.

"The game," Josie said, laughing.

It had dominated their lives for as long as anyone could remember. Late at night their father stayed in the basement planning, carving, painting. He would come up with an idea, make a prototype, then have them all play. It always amazed Michaela how difficult it was to play a game, to make up rules, to declare a true winner. The basement grew littered with discarded ideas and old game parts—brightly painted spinners, wooden markers, pieces of boards and questions without answers.

"That summer he was convinced he'd finally found the one that would sell," Josie said. "Why don't you get in the car?" she said softly.

Michaela shook her head. The rain felt good. "I don't remember the details of the game," she said, "but I can still clearly see the board. It was painted like a Peter Max poster and it had these hot pink dice that Dad actually carved himself."

Josie nodded. "It involved words and definitions, an intricate system of color-coded cards and markers. On the ride to New York, he kept practicing his pitch." She dropped her voice. " 'Hello, sir, I'm Daniel Jericho. My family and I would like to play a round of the game that will knock Scrabble off the shelves.' "

That was exactly what he had said, too. He had strode off the narrow escalator, past expensive dolls dressed in costumes from foreign countries, the game tucked under his arm, straight to the manager.

"Hello, sir," he'd said, extending his hand for a handshake, "I'm Daniel Jericho and my family and I would like to play a round of the game that will knock Scrabble off the shelves."

The manager had too-small features that got lost on his oversized face, eyes and nose and mouth like the plastic pieces of a Mr. Potato Head game. "I'd be happy to hear a simple explanation of the game," he said. "If you can't explain a game in one line, well, then, you don't have a game."

But their father was already removing toys from a countertop and setting up the board. "Nonsense," he said. "This is fun. You'll see."

The manager was frowning. "Really, sir," he said.

Dan began to hand out word cards, assigning markers.

"Please," the manager said. "You should be able to explain a game in one sentence without having to play it. I mean, it should be obvious. For example, Monopoly—"

"Absolutely. But my game defies description. Watch. Claire, you go first. See, she'll roll the dice and land on either a Give or a Get spot. Ah! Okay, she landed on a Give."

Michaela had stood slightly back from the others, watching. Under the bright department store lights, her father's game looked exactly like what it was—homemade. He was sweating, his hands moving over the board like a conjurer. Her mother clutched her Give card, frowning in concentration. But by the time she figured out what to do next, the manager was gone.

The memory sidetracked Josie. "They have home care, you know," she was saying. "He doesn't have to be put away or anything."

Michaela looked at her sister sitting in the driver's seat, dry, certain that things could be fixed, taken care of.

"So much has been lost," Michaela said.

"No," Josie said, reaching out her hand, taking Michaela's wet freckled arm.

Michaela let Josie hold it for a moment. Then she moved away from her.

"Change your mind," Josie said. "Come with me tonight."

It was the thing Josie always wanted, for the two of them to still be united in some way. Michaela supposed she would like nothing better than for them to arrive at Denise's smiling, their arms linked, posed in some idyllic version of sisterhood. But there was too much unsaid between them for that.

week three

—

Josie tried to remember the last time she had gone to a party without Will. But the only thing she could come up with was a haze of college socials, she and her friends in pressed khakis, bright Izod shirts, hair ribbons and lip gloss, walking across campus to some fraternity's rec room lined with kegs of beer, Bruce Springsteen or Boz Scaggs playing on the stereo. Even then, Will would be waiting there for her. They used to jitterbug. He would twirl her and dip her and throw her into the air.

Sighing, Josie parked the car and moved unsteadily toward Denise's in her high heels and slightly too tight black dress. She hadn't worn that dress since before Kate was born. If only Michaela had changed her mind, Josie thought. She liked the idea of the two of them bursting into Denise's, smiling, as if they shared secrets, as if they had a special intimacy between them. The sound of footsteps behind her frightened Josie and she quickened her pace. She had been robbed of so much, of the comfort of being alone at night and the certainty that footsteps and smiles would not hurt you.

But it was only a couple on their way to the party too. Josie let them pass. A man and woman, he guiding her by the elbow, even though her step was sure. Or perhaps, Josie thought, that was why her step was so confident. Because he was there beside her.

Josie missed Will.

She missed the way the bed dipped at night when he got in it. She missed the knowledge that at the end of the day, despite everything, he would be there with her. Right now, standing at Denise's door, Josie missed how Will would lean into her and whisper something about Denise's husband or this foolish party. He would tell her that she looked great, and he would say "Great" the way Tony the Tiger used to talk about Frosted Flakes.

Another couple climbed the front stairs and opened the door. Josie followed them inside.

Denise and Judy wore identical dresses, one black, one white. Judy's daughters, dressed in short black party dresses, passed the hors d'oeuvres, and tiny white Christmas tree lights twinkled on all of the taller plants—yucca and rubber and ficus.

"Everything looks beautiful," Denise's husband James said. "N'est-ce pas?"

Josie nodded stupidly then moved away from him and toward the bar set up in one corner of the room.

There, as if holding court, stood the woman from the pool last week. The real swimmer with the big green eyes. She wore an emerald dress, and her hair, which had been hidden under her bathing cap, tumbled down to her shoulders now, a soft honey blond.

One of Denise's neighbors, a lanky woman named Jill, touched Josie's arm.

"I heard you had an accident," she said.

"No," Josie said, confused.

Jill wore a man's tuxedo, her hair in a knot at the back

of her neck. She was frowning. "But I heard you did," she said.

Josie wasn't paying attention. She looked past the swimmer to the tall man at her side.

"At the mall?" Jill said.

Josie studied the man. He still had the same shock of blond hair that fell in his eyes, the same earnest smile with a dimple in his chin, like a handsomer Archie from the comics. He had a considerable paunch now, but otherwise he seemed unchanged.

"It's Ollie," Josie said. "Ollie Pfeiffer."

For all the years that Michaela and Ollie had been together, Josie had hung back, watching the two of them, loving them both. She used to fantasize that when they got married, she would live with them. When she went with Michaela to watch Ollie play baseball, she would pretend he was her boyfriend. She would imagine sitting in the stands at Yankee Stadium, at Fenway Park, and everyone watching him pitch. Even imagining it would make her warm and excited. Over the years, though, she had only seen him on television, a tall stranger on a pitcher's mound.

Now, here he was, standing in Denise's living room, real again.

Ollie's eyes settled on Josie, then moved on. In another instant they returned to her, though, and he broke out in a grin.

"Can it be?" Ollie said. He reached over and seemed to pluck her right into his arms, as if she were weightless. "Josie Jericho? Can it be?"

Ollie held on tight, and Josie felt that old familiar feeling, the rush of warmth, the red cheeks and dizziness.

"Can it be Josie Jericho all grown up?" Ollie was saying to the crowd.

From her new height in his arms, Josie saw everyone's faces clearly—Jill's confused one and Denise and Judy's shared frowns and the swimmer with the lovely eyes and green dress laughing, tilting her own face up toward Ollie's.

"Oliver," Denise was saying, moving toward him, her topaz-and-diamonded fingers plucking the air. "Josie's husband couldn't join us tonight. You'd love him."

"Husband? But you can't be more than sixteen, can you?" he said, peering into Josie's face, not letting go of her.

He had fine crinkles around his eyes, Josie noticed. And a chipped tooth she didn't remember. She touched his face with her hand, the way someone would reach out to feel a ghost. But to Josie, she felt she was reaching back, through the years, that perhaps if she turned around Michaela would be behind her laughing, and their mother would be young again, chuckling and saying, "Oh, Oliver, put her down" and she herself would be just a child again.

Then Oliver was putting her down, though, and around her everyone was grown up, like her and Ollie and her sister. Josie rested her head against Ollie's arm, still slightly dizzy. The swimmer was right beside her, nodding and talking in a rich southern accent.

"I've heard all about you," she was saying. "But you aren't a pip-squeak now, are you? Why sometimes I think Ollie is stuck in time, talking about a grown woman like she was still a child."

Denise led Josie away, saying, "Now that you've met Pamela and seen Ollie again, you don't want to monopolize them, Josie, do you? Everyone wants to hear all the big league gossip and just catch up."

"Why is he here?" Josie said, trying to catch a glimpse of him again as Denise led her farther away.

"He's moved back," Denise said.

"To East Essex?"

Denise nodded, happy to have all the information. "They bought Judge Robinson's old house. I heard he had a bit of a problem," Denise said, and tipped her hand to her mouth as if she were drinking. "You know."

Away from all the guests, in the coolness of Denise's kitchen, Josie finally caught her breath.

"Want to hear the saddest part?" Denise whispered. "I heard he's going to teach gym! At the high school! Can you imagine what a fall that must be?"

When Josie didn't answer, Denise leaned closer to her. "What I want to ask you about is Maggie. Why didn't she come? I bought her one of those cute little pouf dresses like Christy and Cassie have on. I'm paying them for helping out. And she plain old doesn't show up. What's wrong with her anyway?"

Josie hadn't heard anything about a pouf dress or Maggie helping out. She felt like things were moving too fast, out of her control. She tried to remember back to a time when she'd felt steady, when Maggie was normal and Ollie Pfeiffer lived only in her TV set on Saturday afternoons.

Josie thought of lies. She could say that Maggie had a date, or went to a sleepover. She could say anything. But the truth was, Maggie was up in her bedroom staring at her own private sky again.

"I don't know," Josie told Denise.

Above all the party chatter she could make out Ollie Pfeiffer's booming laugh. "I don't have a clue what's wrong with her," she said.

It was too much for Josie. The party. The people staring at her, wondering, she supposed, where Will was, what had happened to her, to Maggie, to all of them. And Ollie Pfeiffer was back, with a wife. A wife in a green dress when you were supposed to wear black or white. Josie went into the kitchen and out the sliding glass doors to the backyard. The rain seemed to have stopped finally. Just that morning she'd read in the paper that there was a flood watch in effect. Unless, the paper had said, the weather cooperated.

Josie kicked off her shoes. The grass was damp from so much rain. The floodlights across the tarp on the pool illuminated a large puddle of water right in the middle, causing the tarp to sag. From behind her, Josie heard the sounds of the party, a woman's shrill laughter. Jill's, she thought. Jill had a reputation for drinking too much at parties and making out with other people's husbands. Josie used to be surprised that so many husbands were willing to make out with her. Many times she had asked Will what had happened to loyalty, to faithfulness. "Maybe we've cornered the market, Jo," he'd said.

Will.

He was the only person she let call her Jo, or anything other than Josie. Everything else seemed too close to her real name, Josephine, an ugly old-woman's name. It had been Will who reminded her of Napoleon and Josephine and who told her the story of how Josephine had loved violets so much that Napoleon had worn some pressed into a locket when they were apart.

Josie missed Will so much that she ached all over.

Was he really off in the woods with a bunch of men, getting in touch with some hidden part of himself? She thought of the blue chamois shirt and felt foolish.

A slow voice drifted to her from beside the pool house.

"Are you hiding too?" the voice said.

Josie had read once that a voice is never forgotten once it is heard. She believed that now because that was Ollie Pfeiffer's voice she was hearing and after all this time she recognized it immediately. She made her way across the wet grass to him.

"I come out at night and lie in the grass and watch the sky," he said.

"You probably learned that from"—Josie hesitated, not

willing to say Michaela's name—"my sister," she finished finally.

Ollie propped himself up on one elbow and patted the grass beside him for her to sit. She did, feeling the wetness seep through her dress. Despite the cool night, he had taken off his tuxedo jacket and bow tie and had unbuttoned and untucked his shirt, revealing a jumble of dark blond hair on his chest and stomach. The air smelled of chlorine and rotten leaves and, from Ollie, stale liquor.

"Do you know," he was saying, "that if you stare at one place in the sky long enough you will see a falling star?" He held up two fingers in some kind of sign. "Truth," he said.

Josie stretched out beside him and looked up. Her eyes settled on one dark spot and she kept her gaze there.

Ollie eased back down beside her and, as if he had done it a million times before, took her hand and laced his fingers through hers.

After a time he said, "Someone told me that once. I don't know who. But it seems they were full of shit."

They lay that way a while more, Josie remembering a time when Ollie had taken her—just her—to Goddard Park and they had played a game of Frisbee together. She remembered how aware of herself she had been that day, aware of her body, the way her breasts moved beneath her green pocket T-shirt and how her hair swayed as she ran to catch the Frisbee. Later, he had gotten them frozen lemonades and brought them to her on the Frisbee, holding it out and offering it to her like something valuable on a silver tray.

"Can I tell you what happened to me?" Josie asked him. Her voice sounded not like her own adult one, but rather like some long-ago voice of hers.

"Yes," Ollie said.

And she told him.

She told him how she'd bought the red dress with the belt

and decided to return it. How she'd seen the guy on *America's Most Wanted.* She told him about going to the supermarket, about buying the linens, about the man in the linen department. She told him every detail. All the way up to walking to her parents. Deliberately, she left out Michaela and Will. But she told him that people didn't believe her. Denise and James. Everybody, she said vaguely.

When she finished, Ollie leaned over her, looked her right in the eye.

"I believe you," he said. "What a terrible, terrible thing."

Then he took her face in his hands. She felt the calluses from years of pitching fast balls. He kissed her, a long deep kiss. He did not taste the way she'd imagined he might. Instead he tasted sour, of too much alcohol. Still, she was certain she had never had a better kiss.

There was the sound of high heels on cement, stumbling in front of the pool house. Then Denise's neighbor Jill said, "Ssshhh" in a drunken exaggerated way. "Come here," she whispered too loudly.

Josie was about to explain how Jill always did this at parties. Got drunk and then went off with other women's husbands. But then she realized that she too was off, hidden with someone's husband. She had kissed him. His hands still cupping her face told her she could kiss him more, do anything with him, everything.

"You grew up so pretty," Ollie whispered to her.

She knew that was a lie.

A loud rhythmic thumping began against the pool-house door. Embarrassed, Josie shook free of Ollie, got to her feet. She felt she should say something. She could still feel his kiss, could taste him and smell him. But what did a person say at a time like this? She wished Will would just appear and take care of everything. Josie mumbled something—an apology? an excuse? She wasn't sure herself. Then she made her way past the pool house where Jill stood, panty hose around her ankles, dress lifted, legs wrapped around a man whose own pants were down around his ankles. They grunted and banged against the door. Despite herself, Josie glanced into their faces as she slipped past them. It was Denise's husband James that Jill was screwing, right there in Denise's own yard.

How much had happened, Josie wondered, that she did not even feel surprised? She licked her lips, again tasted Ollie on them. How much more was there? she thought. The hard asphalt road against her feet made her realize that she'd forgotten her shoes back on Denise's lawn. Carefully, Josie walked to her car. She got inside, and tried to make sense of everything. But she could no longer figure out when everything had started to change. She could only wonder when it was all going to stop.

The rain began in earnest that Sunday morning. When Josie awoke to the sound of it beating down on the roof, for a moment she believed that everything that had happened lately had somehow been erased by the violent storm. This house, her and Will's home, had always been a good one for storms. In winter, snow piled up perfectly on the windowsills. The windowpanes acted as an ideal canvas for frost patterns. Wind rattled the house; they had never fully caulked them tight enough. The result, though, besides a slight draft in the family room that was easily taken care of with afghans tossed over laps, was a kind of comfort in being inside, away from the cold. And there was something in the slant of the roof that lent itself to rain.

Will and Josie were slow on home improvements. For years she had leafed through decorating magazines for ideas to remodel the kitchen. Often she tore out pictures of especially lovely ones—a kitchen with hearts and songbirds stenciled on the walls, a re-creation of a Colonial kitchen with a stone hearth and wide-planked oak floors. But then Kate would find the photographs and cut out the furniture for her paper dolls, or Will would scribble phone messages across them, and eventually they were gone. Josie didn't mind, though. True, the cabinets were too dark, the windows too small, the floor would look better and stay cleaner with tile rather than the faded linoleum. Like other things that were worn and tired in her life, Josie couldn't really let go of the kitchen, which, she thought, hadn't seemed so bad when they first moved in.

What Will had managed to get done, before they had children, was to raise the ceiling in the small upstairs bathroom and put in a skylight. Whenever a storm hit, Josie and Will would take a bath together, the rain or snow dancing above them on the skylight. Waking to such sounds now, Josie could almost believe that Will was somewhere in the house, and that he would draw a warm bath—no bubbles, they both hated the film bubble bath left—and the two of them would climb in and enjoy the bad weather together. In movies, couples placed lit candles all around the tub, but Josie and Will both thought that looked dangerous. When lovemaking began, they'd worry about their hair catching on fire, a burned arm or leg.

Josie rolled onto Will's side of the bed. Without him, she could see how compatible they were. They were practical people, slow to move, unhappy with big changes. For a time, years ago, Josie had joined a reading group that focused on women's literature. The discussion that followed always surprised her. They talked about masturbation and *The Joy of Sex* and multiple orgasms. Once, fed up, Josie had blurted, "What about love in all of this?" and the other women had looked at her as if she were crazy. "Love is beside the point," one of them said finally. Even though Josie had dutifully read the next book—Jane Austen, no less—she had not gone back.

Maybe love was beside the point, she thought as she tried to curve her body in a way that would match Will's, if he were home in bed with her. She thought of Jill with Denise's husband James last night. That had been something more primal than love happening. "They were fucking," Josie said out loud. Was that what Will had been doing all weekend? Fucking someone? She could forgive that, perhaps. But she couldn't forgive him loving another woman. She let herself remember her kiss with Ollie last night. Touching her lips, searching for some kind of mark there, Josie considered taking it further. A ridiculous euphemism from her high school days popped into her head. Going all the way. She could go all the way with him, teach Will a lesson. Clichés crowded her mind. It takes two to tango. Two can play this game. All is fair in love and war.

Imagining where it could take them both, Josie began to cry. Will with someone else in his blue chamois shirt, she and Ollie Pfeiffer, all of them sneaking around, fucking. How was it even done? Motel rooms, behind pool houses after dark, in each other's beds when the spouse was out. Slowly, Josie became aware that there were two different water sounds. The rain, of course, but also water running in the upstairs bathroom. In her new, frightened state, Josie first thought someone had come into the house as she lay there. After all, her house keys had been on that key ring. Even though Dog had told her the carjacker was highly unlikely to also come into her house, she had not completely believed him. She thought there was, at least, the possibility. No, Dog had told her, that's a different kind of criminal mind. As if a policeman in East Essex knew anything about criminal psychology outside of what he saw in *The Silence of the Lambs.* However, Josie told herself that although the carjacker might let himself into the house, he certainly wouldn't come in and take a shower, which was, she decided, what someone was doing. With Maggie and Kate at her parents', that someone had to be Will. Maybe she had wished him back to her. Maybe he was filling the bathtub for her, for them. Maybe starting today, things could go back to normal.

Feeling oddly vulnerable and, almost, shy in her nakedness, Josie pulled on one of the oversized T-shirts that Maggie liked to wear to bed. It lay on top of a pile of clean laundry that Josie still hadn't gotten around to putting away. Wrinkled and smelling of too much detergent, it said CRASH TEST DUMMIES across the front, the strange name and strong smell making Josie feel slightly queasy as she made her way down the hall to the bathroom. She caught herself about to knock on the closed door and just walked in. That was their bathroom etiquette before the carjacking.

Will stuck his head around the shower curtain, a clear plastic one with a neon-colored map of the United States on it which they thought would help the girls with geography. He looked surprised to see Josie standing there, and even clutched the shower curtain, wrapping it around himself protectively.

"Oh," he said. "You're here."

He was avoiding her in the eye, Josie thought. She noticed two long thin scratches running from his shoulder down his back as he ducked back into the shower.

The Plains states hid his penis from her. Iowa, Nebraska, Kansas.

Josie decided to pretend everything was normal. She said, "How did it go? All that male bonding."

When he didn't answer, she continued, "Did you really beat drums and chant and stuff?" Her voice, in an effort not to sound suspicious or cynical, sounded ridiculously cheerful, the way it often sounded when she spoke to Michaela.

She watched him turn around, his ass appearing off the coast of California, then disappearing again.

"Just this morning," Josie said, "I was remembering my reading group, how they always used to embarrass me. That one woman, the really skinny one? Dolores? She told me I should get a vibrator. That everyone should have one."

The water turned off, making the rain against the skylight seem like background music.

Too late, Josie slipped the T-shirt off and climbed into the shower with Will. Awkwardly, she reached for him, but he was as slippery as a baby after a bath, and seemed to pour through her hands.

"I missed you," she said. "At the party last night. All weekend."

She realized as she said it that they had never been apart, really. When Maggie was born he had slept in the small hospital bed with Josie. After she'd had Kate, she'd come right home, eager to be a family.

"I'm done," Will said.

"You sound so somber," Josie said. "I almost think you mean with us."

His Adam's apple jumped a few times, something Josie had never noticed before. It meant something, but what? He was facing her, his penis limp, quiet, his hands hanging at his side as if they had no place else to go. Josie reached over and touched those two long scratches. She imagined some faceless woman raking his back in pleasure.

Will flinched. "Thorns," he said.

"Yes," Josie said, nodding.

The steam was dissipating so that everything grew clearer, sharper.

"We have children," Josie managed.

"I've thought of that," Will told her. "I've thought about everything." He gripped her shoulders, looking straight at her now.

"Where have you been?" she said, her voice sounding squeaky, child-like, embarrassing her.

He shrugged.

Funny, Josie thought, how hands that held her for so long could seem unfamiliar. She thought of all these hands had done —stroked her head when she had morning sickness, cut the umbilical cords from their daughters. Touched someone else, she thought. Another woman. She recoiled.

"I'm imagining crazy things," she whispered. "Terrible things."

Will moved away from her. He stepped out of the shower, wrapped a towel around his waist. The towel was pink. He had kidded her when she'd bought the set. Pink, he'd said, is not manly. I want black, he'd told her. Battleship gray.

She was crying and did not want him to see. Josie turned toward the wall. She cleaned these tiles with a toothbrush, scrubbing, scrubbing, making everything sparkle.

"I don't know what else to say," Will said.

Hearing his voice made her cry harder. Did he want a divorce? Was that where this was going? Words crowded her mind. Custody and alimony and visitation.

From the corner of her eye, Josie caught sight of a flash of pink as he walked out of the bathroom.

"Will?" she said, turning and tripping over the bathtub ledge as she tried to catch him. "Will?" She heard the panic in her voice. It was so strong that it stopped her. She stood in the hallway, looking at all the closed doors, wondering if it were possible to hurt any more than this.

Kate liked to listen to her aunts. They weren't her real aunts; they belonged to her mother. They are your *great-aunts,* her mother had told her when her mother acted like her mother. Kate liked that idea, because these aunts were great. Not at all like her real aunt, Michaela, who was too skinny and looked like her red hair needed combing. When her mother dropped her and Maggie off at Grandma's last night, she'd explained that Kate must be very patient with Aunt Michaela because she never had children and didn't really understand them. Kate just kept away from her.

Instead, she huddled around the *great-aunts,* Beatrice and Tiny. Why do they call you Tiny when you're so fat? she had asked Aunt Tiny back when she was a little baby girl. Once, a long time ago, Aunt Tiny had told her, I was called Tina, short for Christina, and my hands and feet were so small that somehow Tina became Tiny. She had held up her feet, which looked like doll's feet, and said, See? They're still so dainty. Only a size four.

Her aunts told stories about when they were little girls. Her grandma and Aunt Beatrice and Aunt Tiny were sisters, like she and Maggie. And they had lived in East Essex forever. They had grown up in a white house with a big porch that they called the wraparound porch. The house was gone. It was torn down when Route 95 was built. They all hated Route 95, and Aunt Tiny still drove to Providence the old way just to avoid it. When they were all little girls their last name was Orso and their father was a cobbler—like the song "Round and Round the Cobbler's Bench the Monkey Chased the Weasel!"—which meant he fixed shoes. Their mother—Kate's great-grandmother—gave birth to twins—more girls!—and the little twin baby girls died, one that same night and one the next morning. Each of them remembered a piece of that story—their mother wailing in pain (Why? Kate needed to know, and they had all looked at each other and nodded and said, It hurts to have babies, Sweetie) and the tiny cries of those little babies, like kittens they sounded, and their father with shoe polish on his hands, smelling of leather, holding his three living daughters close to him. After that, Aunt Beatrice explained, their mother got on a health kick. She drank a special tea to keep her bowels regular. She walked one mile every day. In the morning she did a particular series of stretches and bends, for her circulation.

Her *great-aunts* knew stories. And they believed that telling stories was important. That is how we keep history alive, they told her.

A woman who lived up the street from them had a baby that was born with gills. Like a fish! And she kept it in the bathtub for three days and then it died.

A little girl named Angela who lived next door and was Aunt Tiny's best friend—Like Cory? Kate needed to know and they all nodded yes—was set on fire bending over a lit candle. She went up in flames. They all saw her, running down the street, on fire.

These stories frightened and mesmerized Kate.

Whenever she slept over at her grandmother's, she had vivid dreams. She dreamed she was being chased by the fish baby. She dreamed she was being chased by a girl on fire. She dreamed she heard babies crying as she slept.

When she came downstairs on Sunday morning, her aunts were sitting at the kitchen table drinking coffee and eating daffodil cake. That was her favorite. Aunt Tiny made it for her special. Angel food cake with bright yellow spots in it.

Kate curled up on her grandmother's lap, trying to wake up. But her head felt fuzzy. She yawned.

Maggie said, "At home she gets up at the crack of dawn and wakes up the entire house with her singing."

"Did you have sweet dreams?" her grandmother murmured in Kate's ear.

Her grandmother smelled good, like coffee and perfume.

"I dreamed—" Kate began.

But Aunt Beatrice interrupted. "Don't say a word until you eat!"

That was how you kept bad dreams from coming true.

Kate ate a large piece of daffodil cake that Aunt Tiny handed her. Then she said, "I dreamed about babies."

"Why, that's news coming," her grandmother said. "Good news."

Kate shook her head. "These were bad babies."

Her real aunt, Michaela, came downstairs and poured herself a cup of coffee. She didn't even say good morning. Aunt Michaela was a grump.

"Bad how?" Aunt Beatrice was asking Kate.

"They chased me," Kate said.

Aunt Tiny laughed. "You could run faster than a baby, couldn't you?"

Kate took another piece of cake and considered that.

"Were they girl babies or boy babies?" her grandmother asked.

"Girls," Kate said. "Can I have some coffee?"

Her grandmother gave her coffee in a big red ceramic cup with no handles. It was mostly milk but still Kate felt very grown-up drinking from it.

"Coffee?" Maggie said. "I'm not allowed to have coffee. There is caffeine in coffee. Jesus."

"We always have girl babies, don't we?" Aunt Beatrice said. Then she added quickly, "Except David."

David was Aunt Tiny's son and he was dead. In a box on their coffee table Aunt Tiny had letters from him when he was in Vietnam and medals he won there and his high school graduation picture and prom picture and some of him in his uniform. By now, Kate decided as she sipped her coffee, he was a skeleton with no skin on him at all. She shivered.

Michaela said, "Denise has a son. We have sons in this family."

Everyone looked at her like she had surprised them.

Aunt Beatrice said, "Well, yes, of course. There's David and there's Lawrence."

Lawrence went to West Point. He wore his hat so low on his head that Kate used to think he didn't have eyes. She giggled, remembering.

Aunt Tiny sighed. "Maybe we could play 229. Babies."

Kate closed her eyes and leaned back against her grandmother. Sometimes she thought she could sit in this kitchen and listen to them forever.

It took Michaela over an hour to find Leo Day's house in the woods. This was the kind of man she would have fallen in love with at one time, she thought, when she finally spotted the rusted trailer he lived in. Years ago, back in Berkeley, she had lived in a tepee in the woods with a man who called himself Ho. She had stayed with him for three months and never even learned his real name or where he was from. Or, she decided as she skirted a big mud puddle, maybe she had learned it and lost it in the haze of hallucinogens she'd favored in those days.

Closer to the trailer, it was impossible to avoid the mud. Michaela just stepped into it and plodded up to the front door.

The cardboard that took the place of real windows had disintegrated in the rain. Leo Day stuck his head out and said, "What do you want?"

"I heard you took renovation plans to the town meeting Thursday night," she said.

"What of it?"

"I have plans of my own," Michaela said. The steps were actually just a pile of stones that wobbled with her anger.

"It was an open meeting," Leo said, then stuck his head back inside.

Michaela saw that the door did not fully close, so she pushed her way in. The trailer was dingy inside, dark, moldy smelling. A little boy with straight white blond hair sat on the floor, pushing a piece of cardboard around like a truck. "Vroom, vroom," he whispered in a froggy voice.

"You have a kid?" Michaela said. She had imagined Leo Day to be some kind of crazy recluse. A burnout from another era. Her era, she reminded herself. "Look," she said, softening, "it's hard for me to explain why cleaning up the river is so important to me."

"Why don't you give it a whirl," Leo said.

Michaela saw that something was missing from him. There was an emptiness, a place that needed to be filled. He'd had a tragedy, she realized. He'd lost something too. Her eyes adjusted to the darkness and for the first time she glanced around. The sofa Leo sat on was lumpy, covered by a maroon-and-green paisley blanket, the kind she'd once hung on her ceiling. She was certain if she pressed her nose to it, she would smell incense, marijuana, the musty smell of thrift shops. She sat beside him, felt a broken spring press into her, and shifted away from it, closer to Leo.

"I know you," she said softly. At the river, he had seemed like a madman. When she'd heard he'd gone to that town meeting and made a presentation, he'd seemed like an interloper. But sitting beside him in this sad home, Michaela saw that he was someone just like her, fighting for something, trying to save himself.

"I came here because it's where my wife was from," Leo was saying. "Maybe you knew her? Laura Robinson?"

He pulled a tattered photograph from his shirt pocket and handed it to Michaela. It was tattered, she saw, from being held so close. The face that peered out had the same white blond hair as the boy's, a pretty heart-shaped face. It was a studio photograph, the kind found in old high school yearbooks.

"Can you believe that's the only photograph I have of her?"

Leo said. "Her high school graduation picture." He laughed. "We never took pictures, that's all." He placed it back in his pocket, tenderly.

"I thought I knew everybody in this town," Michaela said, shaking her head.

"Her grandfather was some big-time judge—"

"Of course. Judge Robinson."

"A tyrant," Leo said. "Laura's mother was a beauty apparently. Posed nude for *Playboy* back in the fifties and got disowned. Had Laura, then promptly killed herself, and Laura grew up here. Well, in boarding schools."

Michaela could vaguely remember the judge having a granddaughter who rode horses. She recalled fuzzy newspaper photographs of a young girl standing by a horse collecting ribbons and trophies.

"When Laura got killed, I didn't know where to go," Leo said.

He gulped a few times, remembering, and Michaela wondered when the sharp pain of bad memories diminished, disappeared, or at least turned into a duller, more distant thing.

"She was thrown from a horse," Leo was saying. "One of those bizarre one-in-a-million accidents. The kind you think don't really happen."

"Or don't happen to you," Michaela said.

He nodded. "That happen to someone else. Someone in a newspaper story. When she died, we'd been living in Colorado, Montana, here and there. I had these two kids and I thought I should put down roots, for them. I was an Air Force brat, so the only place to call home was Laura's hometown. Even though she hated her grandfather and hardly lived here, really, she talked about it a lot. The hills. The river." His big hands were spread out on his knees and as he talked he studied them. "Then when I got here and saw what a mess it was, I figured making it better would somehow even things out. Karma-wise," he added, chuckling.

"Well then we'd better join forces," Michaela said, "because I'm after the same thing."

The little boy was gone and the room seemed to take on a special quiet. Michaela felt that she could simply sit here beside this man and listen to the rain for a very long time.

Too soon the mood was gone. A girl, who looked very much like the photograph of his wife, burst in, bringing wind and rain and afternoon storm light.

"I've lost all the bees," she said.

She had the calm of an older person, of someone who has lost many things and knows what can be replaced.

"And there's a flood watch out," she continued. "They're getting sandbags ready at the fire station." She seemed to take a certain amount of exhilaration from the crisis at hand. "I volunteered us for tonight. To go down there and help."

Leo nodded. He didn't look at Michaela, but she understood he was asking her when he said, "Is that okay with you?"

Michaela stood. "I'll go home and get some foul-weather gear," she said.

What she decided as she walked through the mud, over fallen branches and piles of wet leaves, was that what she had come home for did not matter anymore. It mattered more what she did from now on. She stopped and looked back at Leo Day's house. From where she stood, it was just a fleck of silver against the trees and gray sky. She could hear her own breath being lifted, taken, carried away with the wind. If she'd had more time to sit there with him, she would have told him her story. She would have said that back in the days before abortion was legal, she'd been a frightened pregnant seventeen-year-old with a boyfriend who wanted nothing more than to play in the big leagues.

▪ ▪ ▪

It was 1969, and there was no legal way to get it done. Cynthia Pullman had given her the name of someone in Puerto Rico, but how would she get there? How would she come up with all the money?

In the car, they told her father she had an interview at NYU.

"NYU? But what about Berkeley?" he'd asked.

"She wants to make sure she's doing the right thing," her mother told him.

After his failure at Macy's, Dan forgot all his questions. He looked like a deflating balloon, the air slowly leaving him. Michaela imagined that when she saw him later, he would be all loose, sagging flesh with all the insides gone. They left him with Josie at Rumpelmayer's eating hot fudge sundaes out of silver bowls, the game between them like an unwanted relative. Something in Michaela made her want to stay, to squeeze inside beside her sister or father and eat one of those expensive sundaes, to rest her head on the cool marble tabletop. But she smiled at them brightly and waved good-bye, the way she imagined she would in just a few weeks as she boarded the plane for California, for college and a new life.

She and her mother did not speak in the cab. They stared out separate windows. When Michaela did glance at her once, her mother's lips were moving slightly, and Michaela imagined she was praying. She wished she believed in prayers. When this all began five months earlier, she had prayed. Every time she went to the bathroom, she said, "Please, God, let it be here."

But there was no pink stain, no cramps, nothing except the increasing nausea, the tender breasts, and finally the hard lump above her groin that began to grow and swell until she could no longer button her jeans. Sometimes, she looked at herself after a shower, when the bathroom was steamy and the mirror fogged. She ran her hands over the roundness of her stomach, over her large brown nipples and veiny breasts. When she allowed herself to do that, she liked what she saw, how her own body seemed strange and wonderful under her roaming fingertips. She would lock the bathroom door and stretch out on the damp floor and touch herself, imagining what was happening inside her body, the growing baby, the milk beginning to ready itself. She would touch herself everywhere and not stop until she brought herself to an orgasm. When Ollie was inside her now she felt crowded and uncomfortable. But alone like that, wet and hidden, she could pretend that what was happening was all right.

In her purse she had three joints. She had thought she would need them to get through this, to dull it. But now that she was in it, she did not want to be so easy on herself. She should feel it, she thought. She should know. She became hyper-aware, and it was then that she felt it, the baby moving inside her, rolling, kicking. Before, it had seemed like indigestion. Or at least, she had pretended that was what it seemed like. Sitting in that cab, the backs of her legs sticking to the seat, the smell of the driver's sweat strong as a basketball game, overpowering, she tried to imagine what the baby looked like. A monster from one of those old Japanese horror movies, she decided. Grotesque and misshapen.

When she'd finally told her mother, Michaela already could no longer squeeze into her old clothes. She had taken her mother into her bedroom one night, closed the door, and undressed. It was all she knew to do. There seemed to be no words that made it right, certainly none that undid it. Her mother's face . . . Everyone always said she looked like Grace Kelly, and she did, in a way, but that night her face hardened as she studied her daughter's body, and she too said nothing. She just turned around and walked out of the room.

A few days later, she was waiting outside the school when

Michaela came out. Graduation was a week away, and Michaela had her rented cap and gown with her. She saw her mother and got in the car. They still hadn't spoken of it.

In front of Doctor Winter's office, her mother said, "Does Oliver know?"

Michaela shook her head. On those nights in the back seat of his car, she kept her loose peasant blouse on. She didn't know what to say to him. They had plans together that seemed, somehow, suddenly inappropriate. He was off to baseball camp, she was going to California. She used to think, "I'll study the stars, he'll be a star." She used to think they would, of course, be together. Even when they were little they were together, practicing pitching and batting, racing each other, shooting baskets until it grew too dark to see the hoop. "I'm going to marry you," Oliver had told Michaela when they were nine. She never stopped believing that.

Inside, her mother stayed in the room while the doctor examined her. He had taken out her tonsils when she was five. He used to make house calls, arriving late at night with his black doctor's bag and a lollipop. Now he could not look her in the eye.

"Why did you wait so long?" he asked her mother.

Claire shrugged.

Michaela lay there, exposed, her breasts and belly bulging, like they belonged to someone else. She felt her real self was underneath them somewhere. He should have asked her why she'd waited. Didn't he know there was no way out of this? Didn't they realize what she had gone through, imagining herself sent away to a home somewhere, having to actually have it and give it away to some bland, faceless couple? Or keeping it herself, staying in East Essex, rotting there, wearing housedresses and going on food stamps while all of her friends left and had real lives? Or marrying Ollie now, keeping him with her in some small apartment by the river. No baseball. No stars. Just this, until they grew to hate each other for what they'd missed. She wanted to tell them she had talked to Cynthia months ago. She'd thought about Puerto Rico. But all that money, all that way away.

"Can't you take it out?" she blurted. "Just take it out."

Gently, Doctor Winter placed a large piece of tissue paper over her, to cover her. It was the kind they usually put under you on the examining table. He took out his prescription pad and began to write. Addresses, she would learn later, and affidavits saying she was fourteen weeks pregnant, when really she was more than twenty.

On graduation night, she and Ollie went with a group of friends to the beach and dropped acid for the first time. Now she would have to get rid of it for certain. She'd read about genetic damage, about mutations from this stuff. While they were tripping, she'd stood in front of him completely naked for the first time, and he dropped to his knees and pressed his face to her belly. "We can have it, you know," he said. He said, "I love you." He never mentioned it again, and Michaela always wondered if he had thought it was part of his trip that night, a hallucination. Or maybe what he'd said was a part of her hallucinations.

Before she came back this time, she'd stopped in New York, not knowing what she expected to find, but hoping there would be something. She stood on the street where she had come that summer day, where she had left a part of herself and changed forever. She remembered the gray buildings, all identical, with five steps leading up to a double door and inside the small black and white chipped tiles in the hallway. The doors, all shut. The hushed voices, the bowed heads. That was what Michaela had done when she went back, climbed the five steps to the double doors, bowed her head.

They were apartments now. She stood in the same small foyer where her mother had left her that day, and instead of the strong sweet smell of anesthesia, Michaela smelled food being cooked. Curry. Tomato sauce. The wall had a row of metal mailboxes with names taped on each one. She read them out loud. J. Martin. Deb Brown and Steven Prescott. Greg David Worst. People were living their lives here. The thought chilled her. She imagined those lives: J. Martin a single woman bringing lovers there on Saturday nights, making love in one of those rooms; Deb Brown and Steven Prescott, cooking together, making curried chicken, falling in love, being in love; and Greg David Worst with his Ragú spaghetti sauce, his six-pack of beer, his briefcase filled with papers, his weekend girlfriend.

She saw the rows of beds, of small narrow cots, the fourteen-year-old girl from Delaware with the straw-blond hair and acne, the stern-faced nurses—if they were even real nurses—the fluorescent lights, the secrecy, the way everything, everyone looked guilty, looked dirty. She saw herself in one of those beds, rolled into a tight, frightened ball.

The girl from Delaware, Eleanor, said, "If it was legal it wouldn't be so bad, it'd be in and out, they use a vacuum cleaner thing and suck and you can have sex again with a rubber in like a week. But this way, by the time you find someone who will do it and you get the money and everything you're like really pregnant and they have to do it this way and it's like incredibly dangerous and painful and stuff."

Two of those phony nurses had sat on Michaela's bed and put an IV into her hand and shook their heads and clucked their tongues and said, "What you are doing is immoral. Fourteen weeks my ass." They give her something, maybe Demerol, that made her throw up, made her dizzy, like she was too drunk or stoned or dying maybe. She said that out loud, "I think I'm dying," and the girl from Delaware laughed. "Just wait," she told her. "The fun hasn't even started yet." The girl from Delaware had had two second-trimester abortions already.

A doctor came in—maybe he wasn't real either?—and talked loudly so that everyone could hear. He examined her in front of everyone, too, under those bright, humming lights, exposing her, prodding her, his hands jabbing up her, his hands pressing hard on her stomach. She thought of Godzilla. She thought of Oliver at baseball camp, trying to make the Red Sox. That seemed so simple compared to this. Compared to this doctor with the uneven mustache, like his razor had slipped, leaning over her and saying something about an injection that would kill the fetus. "Fetus?" Michaela had said. He'd tapped her belly sharply. "This," he said. "Your baby." He told her she would go into labor. You're too far along for an easy way, he told her. "Your doctor fudged the dates. Not that it matters to me," he said. "Someday they'll legalize this and they'll make rules and regulations and there won't be any money to be made in it." She tried to picture Rhode Island, to picture home, but she couldn't see anything but this room, this man's face, this. He was telling her she would deliver the fetus. "Dead?" she'd said. The girl from Delaware had muttered, "If you're lucky. If it works." Later, she'd whispered to Michaela, "Do you think these are real doctors? They make mistakes, you know."

They gave her another shot, and she became enveloped, covered, shrouded completely in pain. She tore out the needle in her hand, left a trail of blood as she roamed through the maze of rooms looking for help. There were dumpsters in back, and someone was heaving garbage bags into them, dozens of garbage bags, and Michaela knew for certain they contained babies. That was when she began to scream and they came for her, dragged her through more rooms to what looked like the operating room on *Ben Casey,* stripped her naked, strapped her to a cold metal table, hoisted her legs into stirrups and told her to push. She wondered where her mother had gone, how many hours had passed, where her father and Josie were.

A nurse whose breath smelled of coffee said, "Don't look. You won't want to see."

"See what?" Michaela said.

"Try to picture something pretty," the nurse said.

So Michaela did. She tried to picture Scarborough Beach on a sunny summer's day, the ocean, the sailboats, the smell of Coppertone. She tried to picture Ollie in a Red Sox uniform, winding up, throwing a fast ball.

Someone said, "Chin to chest."

She sat halfway up, pressed her chin to her chest, and saw the blue bruised baby pulled from her.

"A boy," the doctor said.

The nurse pressed her head back. "You didn't look, did you?"

"No," Michaela lied. "No."

"Good girl."

Someone said, "She should have. Maybe she'd keep her legs closed if she saw."

The doctor's hands were in her. She felt metal scraping. Cramps. She felt a cold place where something warm used to be —used to be just yesterday. A place that never felt warm again. A place she kept trying to fill up, for years and years, but that just kept growing bigger, harder, colder.

Before she left she heard that the girl from Delaware's baby had lived, brain damaged, and she would have to go home with it. Everything went wrong. For Michaela too. There had been the hemorrhaging. A visit at home from Dr. Winter. Infection. She had told Ollie she didn't love him anymore. "That's impossible," he had said. He'd made the team. Was off to Mississippi or someplace to play double A ball. He wrote her letters at Berkeley and she simply threw them away. She dropped out of school before Thanksgiving. She stopped going home. She stopped using birth control and never got pregnant. Everything had gone wrong. Even getting signatures on petitions and marching in Sacramento for legalized abortion did not fill that place. She never became an astronomer. There were no victories. She felt the empty spot in her that fighting and blaming could not fill. From here, she would have to fill that place herself.

Maggie had stopped going to school.

What she thought was that September had caught her trespassing and told Miles. Everyone who was cool knew about it by now. Her old friends thought she had lost her mind, the cool ones must see her as a pervert, a criminal, a loser. That only left the assorted weirdos—the dumb kids, the smelly ones, the druggies, the car jocks, the pregnant girls who took parenting instead of history. Maggie was in an orbit all alone. She thought of that Russian cosmonaut whose tether to his spaceship broke and left him alone in space, drifting forever.

Every morning she dressed for school, ate breakfast, threw books into her backpack and left the house. Sometimes she took the bus into Providence and sat in a café on Thayer Street, pretending to be an art student at the Rhode Island School of Design. Sometimes she went down the muddy slopes that led to the river and sat there, hidden by the bridge, watching the river clean-up project. Once, she saw her Aunt Michaela jog past her. But her aunt did not see her. In a way, Maggie felt like she was growing invisible. She wondered how long it took that Russian cosmonaut to die out there.

At night, if anyone was around, she made up lies about her day at school. She pretended to be having trouble with algebra two. She said she was writing a paper on the Russian space program. Her parents just nodded and went on fighting. She noticed her mother was losing weight. Her cheekbones were more prominent, her clothes baggy. She saw that her father was growing a mustache that looked like an upside-down smile.

When she tried to fall asleep at night, all she could see were white naked bodies. She had nightmares about bees.

Miles Pfeiffer cut school a lot too. Maggie saw him down by the river. He would sit there and smoke and play an old beat-up guitar. The songs he played sounded vaguely familiar, though she could never put words to them. It was when she started to see him down there that Maggie decided to follow them. Most of the time he spent at September's. When she saw him turn into the woods, Maggie turned around. She wouldn't go back there again. But he also rode his bike to a bookstore in Garden City and spent afternoons browsing there. He smoked a lot of dope.

She wrote down everything Miles did in her little notebook.

When she had to stay at her grandmother's on Saturday night so her mother could go to Denise's stupid party, she spent the whole night in her room writing her impressions of Miles. On Sunday morning, after her grandmother told her she could be civilized and join everyone downstairs, Maggie put the notebook away and tried. But then Kate got up and everyone was so excited to listen to her stupid dream and watch her eat Aunt Tiny's dry-as-dirt daffodil cake that Maggie went back upstairs and started to read the page filled with what she headed MilesSpeak. He said java instead of coffee, smokes instead of cigarettes, cat instead of person. Then her Aunt Michaela drifted into the room and asked what she was writing.

"Nothing," Maggie said. She didn't like her aunt very much. She smelled like she needed to wash up more and she always looked angry.

"Poems?" her aunt said.

Maggie shrugged. Let her think she was writing goofy teenage poems. "Haikus," she said sarcastically. Anyone who knew her knew she scorned haikus. Once, she'd written a villanelle that even got published in a national high school student magazine. It was called "East Essex Spring" and the first line went "The mill spits soap at us, no bubbles, just the neverending sweet smell of failure."

"Five seven five, right?" her aunt said. She looked behind herself nervously, like she was being followed. Then she closed the door and went and sat right beside Maggie on her bed.

Maggie inched away from her. Now the sheets were probably going to smell bad.

"You're a pretty cool kid," Aunt Michaela said. "Aren't you? In school?"

If she only knew the truth, Maggie thought, but she just shrugged again.

"Sure you are," her aunt said. She was talking real low, but her tone was one an adult might use on Kate. "I've been here a month and I'm going out of my mind."

Maggie wondered if she was really a cool kid if she'd catch on to what her aunt was talking about.

Michaela took a breath. "You must know how to get your hands on some pot, don't you?" she said. "I'd pay you for it."

Maggie didn't answer. She didn't know what to say. For an instant, she'd been cool, and she didn't want to blow that image too quickly.

"I won't say anything to your mother," her aunt added quickly. "Don't worry about that."

Maggie remembered what September had said when Maggie told her she'd like to see her bees. Uh-huh.

"Uh-huh," Maggie said.

"No, really." Her aunt's eyes drifted across the room. "God," she said. "Time warp."

That was what her father used to say her Aunt Michaela was in. A time warp. Maggie smiled.

"So . . ." her aunt said. "You going to help out your old aunt or what?"

"I can't," Maggie said finally.

"That's cool. I mean, with your mother and all. But maybe you could tell me someone who would," Michaela said.

The words just popped out of her mouth. "Miles Pfeiffer."

Her aunt looked almost sick. "What?"

"He's always got some," Maggie said.

"Pfeiffer?"

"He lives in Judge Robinson's old house," Maggie said. She wasn't feeling so great herself. Pervert. Loser. Stalker, she thought.

"That's impossible. That family had all girls. The only kid whose last name could be Pfeiffer would have to be Ollie's kid."

Her aunt was talking to herself, Maggie could see that. The room was starting to smell like her too. "Could you leave now?" Maggie said, not feeling so well herself.

"What?"

"Could you leave? Please?"

But instead of leaving, her aunt sat back on the bed. What if her crazy aunt went to the Pfeiffers demanding drugs? What if Miles got thrown in jail? Why did she open her big mouth?

"Have you met him?" Michaela was saying.

Maggie shook her head. "He goes to my school," she said.

"I mean the father," her aunt said.

Her voice could break your heart, Maggie thought.

"You know what?" Maggie said. "I don't know why I even said that. He's not a drug dealer or anything."

"I was in love with his father," her aunt said. But she still seemed to be talking to herself. "That boy could have been ours."

Maggie hated when adults said things like that. Didn't

they know about genetics? Her aunt and Miles's father would have made an entirely different person.

Her aunt stood up. "I'll let you go back to your haikus. Teenage girls should write haikus. And sonnets. Do you write sonnets too?"

"Absolutely," Maggie said. Anything to get her out. When the door closed, Maggie got up and opened her window. The moon was low in the sky, punctuated by Venus. She remembered that her aunt had once wanted to be an astronomer. It was sad the way things turned out.

Michaela stood beside Leo Day at the East Essex fire station, filling bags with sand. If the rain continued, they would have to place these sandbags at the river to try and stop flooding. Michaela believed that would happen. She felt disaster in the air. The fire station smelled like mildew and nervous sweat. She tried to concentrate on Leo's soothing voice. He told her that he was one of those Ph.D. students who did everything except the dissertation. Maybe someday I'll get around to it, he told her. Meanwhile, let's save us a river.

She liked watching him move, the way his muscles flexed when he hefted the filled bags into a pile. Knowing that Oliver Pfeiffer was back in East Essex made the empty space in her seem bigger somehow. Would losing herself in someone like Leo, someone needing to fill his own place, help her? Michaela wondered. She saw his daughter come in with a long-haired boy. She could not get used to the way teenagers looked like she had when she was their age. It made time seem skewed.

Leo waved to his daughter.

The girl walked with such confidence it made Michaela slightly uncomfortable. When she reached them, she gave weather updates.

"Basically," she told them after reciting meteorological data, "it's fifty-fifty." Almost as an afterthought, she pointed to the boy at her side. "You know Miles," she said.

Leo shook his head distractedly.

But Michaela stepped forward and studied the boy's face. It was angular, full of dips and planes like the faces of young men in underwear ads. He wore a small hoop earring in his left ear. His eyes were a bright green that Michaela imagined girls his age found disarming. Most of all, he looked nothing like his father. He was the creation of another woman altogether, probably a green-eyed stranger. She realized that his very existence had given her a ridiculous hope. But seeing him erased it, just like that. Ollie Pfeiffer had a wife and a son that were not a part of her.

Michaela held her hand out to him. "I knew your father," she said.

Miles remained unfazed. "Cool," he said, and shook her hand without emotion or ceremony. Then he bent to lift a sandbag, one more to add to the growing pile.

Josie lay awake considering change, how one act of violence could alter her, how one kiss could make her see so many things differently. That was the way with everyone, she supposed: the mothers she saw each night on the eleven o'clock news who had lost children to stray bullets; the couple she read about who shared an umbrella during a rainstorm and fell in love. It frightened her, the power of these random acts. It made her wonder. If she hadn't gone to the mall that day, would she be her old self still? Baking cakes? Planning dinner menus? Searching for poblano peppers, Keds on sale, *Aladdin* on video?

She got out of bed and wandered through her house again. Like a vampire, she thought, or a crazy character from a Victorian novel. The sound of muffled snores from the living room startled her. Funny how easily everything shifted. A weekend away—only two nights, really—and it was Will's absence that had grown familiar. Here he was back on the couch, huddled beneath one of the afghans Aunt Tiny was always making and giving as Christmas presents.

When Josie touched his arm, he jumped and gasped. "Jesus," he said. Then, when he made out her face in the darkness, "Josie."

"I want to find him," she said. "My carjacker."

That was how she had been thinking of him, as hers. Like the kiss from Ollie. Hers. Mine.

"Sure," Will said, running his hands through his hair. It was a habit she used to find endearing. Josie smiled. It seemed so now too. "Let's rustle up a posse. Right now. We can get a piece of paper and draw a blank face on it and go from door to door. Have you seen this guy?"

"You have his description," Josie told him. "You wrote it in your little notebook."

Will dropped his feet to the floor, holding the afghan tight around his waist. His skin shone, white. "What the hell time is it?" he muttered.

"He was the guy from television. From your show."

"No, he wasn't, Jo," Will said gently.

She could feel the hair on his arms, smell the sleep on his breath. "If it's so ridiculous," she said, "then why do you bother to write it down every week?"

He didn't answer her, just made a sound like the soft whinny of a horse.

"You expect to catch one of them, don't you?" she said. "Well, this is the one."

In the minute that passed in silence, with Will beside her, naked under the afghan, Josie imagined him as a hero. There would be an award from the town, the state, maybe from the president. He would be mentioned on the show, at the end, when they tell about the criminals the program has helped to catch. She was giving this chance to him. Will would find the mall carjacker and somehow rescue her, them, their family.

"If you catch him," Josie said, "everything will go back to normal." Even as she said it she wondered if she believed that herself. Or if she just hoped it desperately, the way a child hopes her wish comes true when she blows out her birthday candles, or wishes on the first star of the night.

"I want to move out," Will said.

It was easier, Josie supposed, to say things in the dark.

She swallowed a few times, the air in her throat feeling real and large as golf balls.

"Like the trial thing?" she managed. "You'll go away for a little while and think or whatever and then you'll come home again?"

She was thinking maybe she could live with that. He'd come back with a new haircut, a sports car, a suntan. At some distant point in time, their twenty-fifth wedding anniversary perhaps, they'd be able to laugh about it. Remember when you left that time, and grew your hair long and bought a cherry red convertible?

But Will was talking, his voice low, his face shadowy. "I don't think I'll come home again, Jo," he was saying.

Josie had started to cry. She felt her shoulders shaking, her whole body trembling. "No," she said, over and over, as if that one word could stop him.

"I don't even know what happened," Will said. "I don't even know why."

"We could move," she said, reaching for him, his hand or arm, but unable to find any part of him. "I'd go to Idaho. Or Texas. I'll go anywhere."

"Maybe that's what I need," he said. "To go away."

He meant alone, she knew that. But still she tried. "Yes.

We'll pack up and move and things will be better. You'll see. I'll get a job. There are so many things I could do."

"We don't have to rush into a divorce," Will said. "We'll take our time. Get used to being apart."

She felt him standing, moving away from her.

"Okay?" he was saying.

She couldn't give him the okay to leave her there, by herself, in the dark. So she just sat, stiff, hands folded in her lap, until he walked out. Then she continued wandering through the house, visiting each room, searching.

Never once in all the time that Josie and Will had been together had she felt their relationship was in trouble. Now she was sitting at her kitchen table, with the radio announcing flood updates every thirty minutes, wondering what had gone wrong. And when. Wondering how to save her marriage. Last night she had gone to him with a gift. That was how she saw it. The opportunity to put everything back together again. She had offered to give up everything, to move away even. But he hadn't listened. When she woke up this morning, Josie had called Father McKenna. He's already come in, the priest had told her, and before she could orient herself—Will had been to talk to Father McKenna?—he was telling her how Will wouldn't listen. I tried everything, Father McKenna told her. He's made up his mind.

In front of her on the kitchen table, Josie had the Yellow Pages opened to COUNSELORS, Marriage. Her ordered life was falling apart. As she turned the page to continue reading the list—three pages of marriage counselors! What was going on? —she saw that her hand trembled badly.

The phone ringing made her get up, happily, to answer it. She imagined it was Will, that he had reconsidered.

"Dog McGovern here."

Josie stretched the cord taut so she could sit back down.

"Did you find him?" she asked. The familiar nervous habit of her throat going dry made her voice sound harsh.

"Whoa," Dog said. "Don't get worked up. What we need is for you to come down to the station tomorrow at six for a line-up."

"Yes," Josie said, waiting for more information.

"Good," Dog said, as if he'd been waiting too. "See you then."

"No!" Josie shouted. She got up, stretching the phone cord again, this time to go to the sink and get a glass of water. The sink was full of dirty dishes. The cupboard had no clean glasses. She turned on the faucet and cupped her hand beneath it, then splashed the water she gathered there into her mouth.

"Are you okay?" Dog asked her.

"No," Josie said softly, her throat still dry, her T-shirt, another one of Maggie's, wet.

"Uh," Dog said, "are you coming or not? To the line-up?"

"Have you caught him?" she said.

Dog laughed. "That's what you're going to tell us."

When she hung up, she filled a dirty glass—there were flecks of orange pulp stuck to it—with water and sat back down. She closed her eyes and tried to fill in the blank circle of the carjacker's face. But she only came up with movie bad guys, with famous criminals, even with a face strangely like Will's.

The voice on the radio announced, "They are asking the people who live close to the river to evacuate at this time. The authorities feel it's important to move to higher ground and safety."

Josie got her raincoat from the mudroom, where it hung, still damp, and got in Will's car. He was getting rides to work with employees, he'd told her. Some of the streets were flooding, and it was difficult to navigate through them. Twice, Josie was rerouted by policemen in bright orange slickers who shouted at her, "Road closed!"

The mall parking lot, except for a few huge puddles, was relatively dry. Josie parked in the same spot she had the night of the crime. It was a new habit of hers, parking there. She walked inside, and into Caldor's, where she took the escalator up, her eyes searching for Will as she made her way, at last, into his office. It was empty again. For a moment, Josie considered the idea that Will no longer even worked here, that maybe he was leading a double life.

"He's at lunch," Sheila said, poking her head around a shelf of car seats.

Josie glanced down at her watch. "So early?" she said.

Sheila shrugged and went back to writing on her clipboard.

When Josie didn't leave, Sheila called to her, "Is there a message, Mrs. Hunter?"

Josie thought about all the messages she could leave. Yes, Sheila. Could you tell my husband to go fuck himself? Or better yet, could you tell me who it is he's fucking? She took a few steps toward Sheila.

"Remember," Josie said, "how I was attacked? In the parking lot?"

Sheila looked at her blankly.

"Well, I have to go to a line-up tomorrow night and Will has a written description of the guy. I wanted to go over it with him."

Now Sheila was frowning.

"Do you know where he went for lunch?" Josie asked her, feeling desperate.

"Uh, no." Sheila cleared her throat, then tapped her clipboard. "Inventory," she said.

Josie nodded and thanked her. Then went out of the store,

into the mall. There were only two places to eat there. In the garish Food Court—egg rolls or nachos or fast food pizza—and the Newport Creamery. She went to both, moving slowly among the people eating, studying them, even though she would easily recognize the back of Will's head, the particular way he slouched. He wasn't there.

Back outside, she walked quickly to her car, holding her key pointed out, in case someone approached her. She'd read that somewhere once, never dreaming she'd find it necessary to actually do it. There were some chain restaurants near the mall—Bennigan's and Chili's and Chi-Chi's. Josie began to drive to each of them, to circle the parking lots, unsure of what she was looking for. After all, employees picked him up. Did they drive him to lunch too? At times the rain came down so hard, the windshield wipers did not help to clear her vision. So that in Chi-Chi's parking lot, where she almost didn't go because Will did not even really like Mexican food, ate it only to appease Maggie at home, she almost missed him walking out of the restaurant, into a hard downpour. He was with his right-hand man, Bonnie. They were laughing, standing under the dry safety of the restaurant awning, heads bent at a strangely similar angle. Bonnie wore a bronze-colored trench coat, belted tight at the waist. Her waist, Josie thought, was as small as a Barbie doll's. Even in this weather, she wore high heels, navy panty hose. Josie glanced down at her old lime green duck boots and red slicker. She looked like a Christmas tree, she thought.

As if a mutual decision had been made to go for it, Bonnie and Will bent their heads and stepped out into the rain. Josie saw how his hand cupped the small of her back. He unlocked the passenger door first, holding it open for her. The car was a late-model Honda, the same type Josie's had been but in a happy shade of bright blue, newer, sleeker. She watched her husband as he walked around the back of the car, to the side. The door popped open before he put the key in. Josie imagined Bonnie leaning across the seat and unlocking his door for him, letting him in.

There were dozens of people at the river, piling the sandbags against the rising water. At times, Michaela thought it seemed useless, the notion of holding a river back. But then there were times—like now, under this almost full moon—when she felt it was possible. These people could do it, they could keep the Pottowamicut from flooding East Essex. She thought of junior high English classes—man versus nature. In those stories, did nature always win?

Leo Day touched her shoulder.

"Relief," he said, pointing to a fresh group of people making their slippery way toward them. "Why don't you take a break."

At the fire station, there was coffee and doughnuts, donated sandwiches and fruit.

"Maybe you could come back to my place," Leo was saying. "With me."

He had not taken his hand from her shoulder. In fact, he had increased the pressure there. Michaela looked up at him, then past him at the sky.

"I was going to be an astronomer," she said. "I got sidetracked. But I could still tell you what's up there right now, even though we can't see it."

"Or," Leo said, still not dropping his hand, "we could go to the fire station and eat even more powdered doughnuts."

Michaela felt something in her reaching out. She had not felt that in a very long time. So long a time she could not even properly place it.

"I'm already sick of those doughnuts," she said. She let herself fit under his arm, press into his wet side, make her way with him toward home.

Maggie was starting to wish for nothing more than her parents' old habits, the very ones she'd been loathing before all this began. When she saw her father standing in the kitchen cutting bananas into batter, she felt almost optimistic. The rain beating against the windows sounded less threatening and made Maggie want to stay right here with her family, cozy and secure inside. She smiled and practically chirped, "Good morning, everyone!"

When her father announced, "Tonight is a big family night," Maggie even began to settle into the possibility that somehow her parents had made up.

"My play!" Kate shouted. For days she'd been walking around in a harem outfit. She looked cute, Maggie decided.

Her mother came up the basement steps, frowning. "Poor Cuddles," she said. "These storms have her so terrified she's hiding down there."

Kate was singing "A Whole New World."

Maggie hated that stupid song. But she just ate her breakfast. Her father had made banana waffles, Kate's favorite. The day had the taste of their old life in it. Maggie almost considered returning to school.

When her father bent to kiss her good-bye, she caught a strong whiff of cologne.

"You stink," she said.

"Hey," he told her, deflated, "this is very expensive stuff."

"Could have fooled me," Maggie said.

He swooped Kate into his arms in a rustle of chiffon. "What do you think, Princess Jasmine? Does your daddy smell good?"

Kate giggled and took a deep breath. "You smell delicious," she said.

"That's my girl," he said. He put her down and started out the door. "Maybe we could all go together?" he said. He was talking to their mother.

She nodded.

Were her eyes puffy? Maggie thought. But it was morning. Eyes were puffy in the morning. She smiled and sipped her orange juice and Kate started to sing again.

And for a brief time, everything seemed normal.

Michaela wanted Josie to go down to the river and help sandbag. "We need people," she'd said. The authority with which she spoke surprised Josie, who had come to think of her sister as selfish and mostly stoned, not a person to organize a flood watch. Josie's excuse for not coming were weak—her rib still ached, she had insurance forms to fill out. Michaela was brusque with her. "Fine," she'd said. "If you change your mind, go to the fire station." But what Josie did was get in the car and go to the mall to follow Will, to catch him with Bonnie. On her way there, she saw everyone in donated rain slickers at the river. She heard a man's voice giving orders through a megaphone. For a moment she considered stopping there, donning one of those yellow slickers, getting to work. But she couldn't. How could she help save East Essex when she seemed unable to save herself?

At the mall, she circled the parking lot until she spotted Bonnie's bright blue car. It was sporty and low-slung, and reminded Josie of a jockstrap. She parked right beside it, then went and peeked in the windows. Like Will's, the car was spotless. Josie even wondered if he kept it that way for Bonnie, using the Dust Buster, the upholstery polish, Windexing the windows, the way he used to clean her car on Sunday afternoons. Bonnie's tapes were neatly lined up in a case. No stray cassettes on the floor. Josie read the titles: *Elvis' Love Songs, The Beatles' Love Songs.* She stepped away from the car. Bonnie was obviously in love. With my husband, Josie thought.

Like her carjacker, Will's face receded, grew fuzzy. Would she forget him too, someday? Forget the way his eyes looked either blue or green, depending on the weather? Forget that he had a small round scar on the inside of his thigh from the time his hand slipped as he chipped away at a block of ice with an ice pick? Despite the rain, Josie leaned against Bonnie's car, clutching her umbrella with both hands. She was reduced to this, to sneaking around after her husband instead of helping out at the river. With the river rising this way, there was sure to be a new water mark on the stone down there. This could be her flood story to tell someday, to tell her grandchildren how she helped to save the town. Instead, she was slinking around a parking lot at the mall like a criminal.

A group of women stood in front of her. With their faces half-hidden by umbrellas it took Josie a moment to see that Bonnie was there, and Sheila, and the new manager of Appliances, Maureen.

Bonnie took a small step forward, her car keys dangling from her hand.

"Were you waiting to talk to me?" she said, her voice steady.

Josie wished she were the type of woman to step forward and say yes, to demand answers. Why were you with my husband, looking so familiar? But to say it loud would move things forward in a way that Josie was not ready for. She tried to tell herself that the intimacy she saw between Will and Bonnie could be exaggerated. We've been together forever, she reminded herself. She thought of their wedding—all the white pillar candles, the white roses, her white dress with its train and veil and handsewn beads.

"I came to talk to my husband," Josie said, and she leveled her own steady gaze at Bonnie.

Bonnie blinked a few times, small rapid blinks like a mole forced into light. Her eyes were the unnatural blue of tinted contact lenses.

Maureen took Bonnie by the elbow and urged her toward the car.

"He's inside," Maureen said with the false brightness of a liar.

Josie waited until they drove off before she got into her own car and sat, hands trembling, wondering what to do next. From nowhere, she remembered her wedding again. Will had almost fainted. They'd had to stop right before they recited their vows and he sat, his head dropped between his knees, breathing slow, deep breaths. One of his fraternity brothers had shouted, "It's not too late, William!" and everyone had laughed. Josie had laughed too. Because she had known they were in love and that they would be together forever. For better and worse. In sickness and in health. She thought of her parents, of her mother changing roles, taking charge. This was the worst part, she thought. And, really, what did she have for evidence, anyway? None of it had to add up to an affair. Josie sighed. She had never been good with puzzles. They frustrated her.

What she needed, she decided, was to not think about herself and her problems. She would go down to the river and help out. Her hand rested on the gear shift, ready to back out. Then she leaned across it and lifted the mat on the floor of the passenger's side, running her hands across the bumpy carpeting. Maybe Bonnie had left behind a clue, a tube of lipstick or lone earring. She wore large chunky ones, Josie knew. She called them art jewelry and bought them at craft fairs and small boutiques near the beach. Perhaps there was one shard of Austrian crystal somewhere in Will's car, one fat piece of jaspar that had broken loose. Josie slid her hand under the seat, between the seat and the center console, feeling desperate, feeling lost. What am I doing? she thought, her hand searching, searching, coming up empty. What am I doing?

When she got to the fire station, they told her to man the coffee.

"But I want to go to the river and do something," she said.

The person in charge looked slightly crazy to her, all bushy eyebrows and wet curly hair and intense eyes.

"Right now," he said, "we need someone here. We've got a lot of cold, wet people coming in from the river and they'll want hot coffee."

He walked away before she could argue. It seemed like a ridiculous task. But she joined an elderly woman behind the coffee urn and began filling cups.

"Josie Jericho?" the woman said. "Alice Petrarca. You went to school with my kids. I saw your Aunt Beatrice here earlier. I guess your mother can't leave your dad alone these days, hmmm?"

Josie swallowed hard, didn't answer. She kept filling cups, trying to think of something to say. She was thankful when the people who'd been sandbagging came in, and happy that the man had been right—they were eager, even grateful, for the coffee. When she spotted Michaela coming through the door, Josie waved. But Michaela looked right past her and went instead to the wild-looking man. He reached over and began massaging her sister's shoulders.

Alice Petrarca nudged Josie in the side with her elbow.

"Catastrophe can bring people together," she said. Josie thought she sounded smug.

The man picked up the megaphone. "For those of you on the five o'clock shift, there are dry slickers against the far wall . . ."

"Five o'clock?" Josie said. "I've got to go. Kate's play is at six-thirty."

But Alice was already gossiping with another woman. Josie looked around for Michaela. She wanted her sister to know she had come after all. But the fire station was so full that even the bright red of Michaela's hair got lost.

There was a note from Maggie: MEET YOU THERE. Then, PS DAD CALLED. HE'LL MEET YOU THERE TOO. Then, PPS HE'S GOT KATE. Some family night, Josie had thought. Everyone coming from different places. Will scooping up Kate, taking her where to get ready? Last year, Bonnie had had a Halloween party at her apartment. She had removed all the furniture and brought in cornstalks and bales of hay, covered the floors with sawdust. Her costume, Josie remembered, was a black widow spider. She'd woven an intricate web and devised a system to move all of her thick black spider legs up and down, like a marionette. Will had not wanted to go. We sort of have to, he'd said. Josie had dressed as Raggedy Ann, and made a Raggedy Andy costume for Will, a red yarn wig and striped shirt. No way, he'd laughed, and put on jeans and an orange T-shirt he'd bought that said THIS IS MY COSTUME instead.

Had he acted differently then? Josie tried to remember, folding Maggie's note into small, tight accordion pleats. Or maybe that's when it started. Maybe he had looked at his wife dressed, ridiculously, like a giant rag doll, and at Bonnie with her black leotard and prim veiled hat, manipulating all those spider legs, and come to some kind of decision. She tried to remember back to last fall—just six months earlier. They had bought pumpkins, carved them into jack-o-lanterns, worried over the maniacal face Maggie cut into hers. Josie frowned. No. *She* had taken the girls out to that farm in Exeter for pumpkins and apples and fresh-pressed cider. *She* was the one fretting over Maggie's jack-o-lantern, all wicked eyes and ugly, gaping mouth. Will hadn't been there at all. She tried to remember back even further—two autumns, three. She saw herself, lugging heavy pumpkins from the car—one year she had even dropped one, spilled pumpkin guts all over the breezeway—dressing the front steps with cornstalks, with Christmas lights, the American flag.

Maggie's note was as thin as a cigarette, and Josie slowly unfurled it. HE'S GOT KATE. She imagined Kate getting ready in Bonnie's apartment—empty except for sawdust and hay. Maggie had written the message in one of Kate's dull crayons, but still the message was clear.

When the phone rang, Josie almost didn't answer it. The simple courtesies of talking on the telephone eluded her. Hello, she was supposed to say. How are you? But the words seemed enormous. Maybe it was Will. She didn't need courtesy then. She needed only to yell at him. How could you? she would say. When did this all begin?

She clutched Maggie's note like it was evidence as she went to answer the phone.

It was Dog McGovern.

"Uh," he said. "We're waiting."

That was when Josie remembered. The line-up. She glanced at the copper-teapot clock on the kitchen wall. Six-twenty.

"I'll be right there," she said. She ran out without her handbag, hoping Kate's performance would be in the second half.

Josie was surprised to find Barb, her old Aqua Aerobics instructor, sitting on one of the benches in the lobby. She didn't expect Barb to remember her. After all, she'd only seen Josie in an old bathing suit at the pool. And not at all for some time now.

But Barb gave her a half smile, a polite wave. Josie remembered the rumors she'd heard. Raped, they'd all whispered. Maybe even by the same man. Josie hesitated, then sat down next to Barb on the bench. The bench felt like a church pew.

"I'm sorry about what happened to you," Josie said. They were the words she most wanted to hear but never did.

Barb grabbed her hand and her face scrunched up, ready to cry. "It was awful," she said. "But I think they caught the bastard."

Josie found that she was clutching Barb's hand just as hard. "They did?"

"I just saw him," Barb said. She was crying, her eyeliner running in bright blue streams down her cheeks. "In the line-up."

Such a strong sense of relief washed over Josie that she felt light-headed. They had caught him. She would look at the men in the line-up and remember his face. Josie was surprised that she had started crying too.

"Whoa!" Dog called from across the room. "Witnesses can't talk. Did you tell her the guy's number you identified?"

Barb shook her head.

"You sure?" Dog said, trying to decide what to do.

"Yes," Barb said. In Aqua Aerobics, her voice was loud and strong, like a sergeant at boot camp. But here it sounded soft, almost breathy.

"Okay," Dog said, "good. Then, Josie, you'll follow me. No more girl talk."

Josie began to follow Dog down the corridor, to somewhere in the back, but she turned and looked at Barb, hoping that Barb would give her the right answer. But Barb had her eyes closed, her bottom lip trembled. She was trying to get control of herself.

Dog and Josie went into a room where two other policemen sat at a wooden table. There was a big window against one wall.

"Okay," Dog said again. "There are six people behind that two-way mirror and they're each holding a number and when you see your guy you'll tell us his number. Right?"

Josie nodded. But she was thinking, Six? Six was so many. She closed her eyes, tried to remember what he looked like. She saw the fluorescent parking lot light, the beige windbreaker. She remembered the smell of soap and mint.

Dog was saying she could have any of them step forward, turn around. "Whatever," he said.

Josie nodded again and stepped up to the glass.

Someone hit a switch and a wash of light spread across six men. Josie pressed her fingers to the glass. They looked, all of them, innocent. But she remembered how her carjacker had seemed innocent too, in Jordan Marsh. Slowly, she stared into each of their faces. Number one was too old. Number two seemed too fat. Number three. When she looked at him a strange sense of fear filled her. But he seemed no more familiar than numbers four, five, or six.

Dog cleared his throat.

"Number one is too old," Josie said, just to show them she knew something.

"So you're eliminating number one?" Dog asked her.

"Yes," Josie said. "And number two also. I can eliminate him." She was almost happy with her certainty at that at least.

Number five had a pencil-thin mustache. Number four looked vaguely familiar, but not the way she would describe her attacker. There was something about number three. Josie asked if he could step forward. He did. She asked if he could turn to the side. He did. She wished she could make them take him to the mall parking lot tonight and stand him in that spot under the light. Even now she could vividly recall the feeling of his foot kicking her side.

"I don't know," she heard herself say.

The three policemen looked at each other.

"I just don't know," Josie said.

Number six seemed to be looking right at her. She had to stop herself from accusing him, just to find someone to blame.

Dog told them they could all go, and she watched them file out, heads bent. Then number three lifted his head and glanced back, nervously.

"It might be him," she said. "Number three."

Dog told them to come back, to line up again.

"You know," one of the other policemen told her, "you'd have to identify him in court. Under oath."

Josie chewed her bottom lip. Then she shook her head.

"I just don't know," she said again.

This time she didn't watch them go. Instead, she left the room quickly, walked down the hallway, her own shoes seeming to echo against the stone floor. In the lobby, Barb was still sitting on the bench. But when she saw Josie she stood, excited, and Josie realized Barb had been waiting for her.

"You got him, right?" Barb said. "Number three?"

Her face with the smudged makeup looked so hopeful.

"I wasn't sure," Josie said. "I thought it was him, but I wasn't sure."

Barb stared at her, unbelieving. Her lips began to tremble again.

"I'm sorry," Josie said. As she walked out of the police station into the rain, the face of number three loomed in her mind. Even then, even after knowing, Josie still wasn't sure.

▪ ▪ ▪

It was the smell of a school that made Maggie feel strange. The chalk dust and disinfectant and paste and bread smell. Even here at Kate's school, a school that looked like a house, that smell clung to everything and reminded Maggie that she had been absent for sixteen consecutive days. She followed her father into a row of people, bumping their knees as she pushed past, and found herself feeling almost nostalgic for school. But as she settled into a seat, Maggie realized that it wasn't just school she missed. It was her old life, the same life she'd scorned not that long ago. She thought of cheerleading practice, the whoosh of pompoms at her ears, the hard thump that she landed with after a jump. She thought of study hall and tightly folded notes in lavender ink. In her locker there was a half-finished history project on Vietnam, a now overdue copy of *Marjorie Morningstar,* her sketchpad full of charcoal drawings. By now her art class had probably moved on to watercolors.

Maggie's father nudged her with his elbow.

"What?" she said.

"You're making weird little noises," he said. He opened the xeroxed program and began to read, moving a finger along each line.

"No, I'm not," Maggie said, and slumped down in her seat.

She wondered how hard it would be to catch up on all the work she'd missed. She wondered how many days a person had to miss before they were kept back. A long line of all her perfect attendance cards danced in her mind.

"Ssshhh," her father said and nudged her again.

Maggie opened her program too. At least Kate was on first. Maybe Maggie could leave afterwards and go home and start to read textbooks. Could she teach herself sixteen days' worth of chemistry? Geometry? Watercolors?

The lights dimmed and there were the sounds of people

quieting—a cough, shuffling feet, the squeak of chairs—then silence.

"I can't believe your mother is not here," her father said.

Even though his teeth were gritted, his voice sounded enormous.

"Ssshhh," Maggie whispered.

A small boy came out with a big flashlight and moved its beam around the room. The dark blue curtain opened stiffly and there on a mattress covered with red satin, sat Kate as Princess Jasmine and a little boy as Ali. The music didn't start on time, and there was an awkward moment of confused silence until the song came on. Then children dressed as stars and planets took their spots as Kate and the boy were dragged among them on the mattress. It was the first time Maggie had seen Kate looking like her old self since the carjacking. She sat straight and still, pointing to certain stars and planets, all wide-eyed and smiling, until she spotted Maggie and her father and the empty chair where her mother should have been. Kate's smile disappeared and, as if uncertain what to do, her hand turned away from the fake sky and pointed right at Maggie. The children sang "A Whole New World" and the mattress made a sharp turn, headed for the Taj Mahal painted on a backdrop. Instead of looking at that, Kate whipped her head around and half-stood, searching the faces in front of her for her mother. Ali tugged on her veil and she turned back toward the Taj Mahal. But seeing the look on Kate's face in that moment, Maggie realized that in her whole life, she—Maggie Jericho Hunter—had never felt disappointment like that.

Until they saw her mother rushing across the school parking lot after the play, they acted like nothing was out of place, as if their mother had been there like she was supposed to be.

"You were better than the real Princess Jasmine," her father told Kate.

And even Maggie, who could not leave early after seeing the look on her sister's face, had said she was terrific.

"I made a mistake," Kate said.

"You did?" her father said. "No one even noticed."

"I made a mistake," Kate said again.

When Maggie spotted her mother running toward the school, she said, "See, Kate? She's here."

Kate stopped walking. "You're late!" she screamed.

The people around them stopped walking too.

"You missed me," Kate yelled. She started to cry. "You missed me, Mommy," she said, dropping to the ground.

Everyone seemed to be whispering and staring. Maggie tried to pull Kate to her feet, but couldn't budge her.

Their father moved toward their mother, who stood, frozen, under a streetlight. She seemed to be alone on a stage under a bright spotlight, poised for something.

Parents moved their children along, speaking to them in hushed voices.

To Maggie, her parents looked like strangers, like people she had never seen before. In such a bright light, she could see that her mother had put on makeup, hastily, so that her cheeks were too pink, her lipstick crooked, like the crazy people who rode the bus downtown. And her father with his new mustache, unaware of everyone watching, clenched his fists, like a man ready to fight someone. Veins bulged on his neck.

"Can't you do anything right?" he shouted.

"Take it home, buddy," a man said. "Come on, now."

No one looked at them. They walked past with their heads bent, embarrassed.

Their father said, quieter now, "What the fuck is wrong with you?"

The disgust in his voice made Maggie stand up straight,

made her whole body stiffen. In that small instant she saw time reel forward, out of control. Her parents were going to get divorced, she realized. Her father did not love her mother anymore. She struggled to remember a tender moment between them—a hand placed on the inside of a thigh, a tousling of hair, even a kind word. She zigzagged like a drunk, thinking she might throw up.

Then Kate screamed, "What the fuck is wrong with you?"

It sounded to Maggie like everyone gasped in unison. She wished she could somehow disappear. Like a movie playing too fast, she saw all of her recitals—ballet, chorus, a whole line of years' worth of them. Her parents' proud faces right up front. Banana splits at Newport Creamery later. The flash of a camera to capture her in her costume and the strange feel of makeup on her face and eyes.

Maggie reached down and gathered Kate into her arms. The last time she'd held her sister, Kate was still a baby, hardly even walking yet. Then she had seemed small, fragile. But now she was like a spider, all spindly arms and legs. Still, Maggie held on, and moved slowly, clumsily, toward their parents.

They were almost an hour late and the secretary, Mrs. O'Rourke, made them wait in the nurse's office.

"It's truancy day," she told them. "All the parents are here and it's very chaotic." Mrs. O'Rourke was very old and had a kind of hunchback. She had been the school secretary when Maggie's mother went to East Essex High. Maggie was surprised her mother didn't tell her a story about her as soon as she walked away. Usually that's what Maggie would have to listen to, how this person had to have a colostomy, how that person's husband died mysteriously.

The nurse's office smelled like someone had thrown up in it a few days ago. Maggie knew that kids who wanted to go home snuck in there when the nurse was teaching Health and stuck their fingers down their throats so they'd throw up and get sent home.

"It always smells like this," Maggie said.

She was going to tell her mother the trick to getting sent home, but her mother just said, "Mmmm," and leafed through a pamphlet on drug abuse.

They weren't in there long when the door opened. Of course Maggie expected it to be Mrs. O'Rourke, so when she looked up and saw Miles Pfeiffer standing there, she actually gasped.

Her mother gasped too. And said, "Oh, dear," like an old woman.

Maggie wondered if Miles had reported her for following him, for breaking into September's house, for telling her aunt he sold drugs. My life is over, Maggie thought. She tried to smile but it came out like a grimace. Miles wasn't looking at her anyway. He was looking at the man with him, an older guy who looked like he'd lived the kind of life where he didn't get enough sleep.

"Man," Miles was saying, "it stinks in here."

Despite everything, Maggie wished she had her little notebook. She had never been this close to Miles Pfeiffer. She could see the hair on his arms. She could smell him. Maggie sat down on the nurse's couch.

The man with Miles looked at her mother and said, "Hello, Josie."

Her mother sat on the couch next to her. She was still holding the drug abuse pamphlet. The cover had a picture of an egg frying.

"Don't tell me you've been cutting school too?" the man said to Maggie. Then to Josie he added, "What a pair, huh?"

Her mother smiled a fake smile.

"Hey," the man said. "Do you two know each other?"

Maggie nodded.

"No," Miles said.

The man smiled back at her mother, but his wasn't fake. It was nice, like Miles's. That was when Maggie remembered. Her aunt had told her she'd loved Miles's father. Maggie couldn't see this guy with her aunt. He had on gold jewelry and a fat ring. She would have imagined her aunt with a guy on a motorcycle. Or maybe with her mother's carjacker.

"You know my aunt, right?" Maggie said.

Miles's father didn't even act surprised. "I know your whole family," he said.

He sounded like he was being interviewed on TV. Maggie decided she didn't like him. He was too smooth.

Mrs. O'Rourke came back.

"Hunter," she said.

Maggie and her mother followed Mrs. O'Rourke out. At the door, Maggie turned around. Her mouth felt dry, like the time she ate the corsage. She took a few steps toward Miles and looked right at him.

"I'm Maggie," she said, as if just stating it would make her more real.

When Michaela walked in to her parents' house for a hot bath and a change of clothes on Wednesday afternoon, she found three strangers walking around the kitchen. One of them, a slender Chinese man with a short, stubby ponytail, had his eyes closed, his arms outstretched.

"Excuse me?" Michaela said, aware that she must look odd, her hair wet and matted, the dark circles under her eyes, the dank river smell that clung to her.

When the woman turned and looked full face at her, Michaela got a strong sense of déjà vu—the woman was an older, very pregnant version of Cynthia Pullman, her high school friend. Cynthia's hair was still long and thick and hung in one braid down her back. She was short, and her bulging stomach made her seem almost penguin-like as she moved, smiling placidly, toward Michaela. Her glasses were held together on one side with a piece of masking tape.

"Cynthia Pullman?" Michaela said, letting herself be hugged. "What are you doing in my mother's kitchen?"

"My kitchen," Cynthia said. She stepped away from Michaela and pointed to the tall, too-skinny man with the salt-and-pepper beard. "That's my husband, Rich Laboissonaire. And that's our fu shei, Harry. We bought this house. And Harry is here to help us set it up."

Understanding the purpose of the fu shei was easy for Michaela. But Cynthia Pullman—married? pregnant?—moving into Michaela's own childhood home was something else. She and Cynthia had first smoked pot right upstairs, a wet towel rolled up and placed under the door of Michaela's bedroom. They had put on their first tampons in the bathroom here. Had once snuck their boyfriends upstairs for an overnight when Michaela's parents were away on a vacation to the Poconos.

"You're going to live here?" Michaela finally managed to say.

Harry and Rich went into the living room, their heads bent in serious discussion.

"I wanted to track you down," Cynthia said. "What with you back, and Oliver back, and all that's past."

It had been upstairs in that same bedroom that Cynthia had given Michaela the name of a doctor in Puerto Rico who would do an abortion. Cynthia's father had been a dentist and could afford such a trip. Still, it had been Cynthia who had known; she had gone through it herself the winter before. Yet here she was, married, pregnant. She had gone to Sarah Lawrence and studied theater.

"How have you been?" she was asking Michaela.

Without thinking about it, Michaela said, "All these years, and my only regret was that I wish Ollie had discussed it."

Cynthia frowned, took Michaela's hand in hers. For a small woman, Cynthia had large hands. They were hands that had known work, too. Tough hands, Michaela thought.

"You should have no regrets," she was saying. "We had no choice then. But you should know that he didn't want a baby. He came to me and said he wanted nothing more than to play professional baseball. He said he would sacrifice everything."

"We were just kids," Michaela said, as if finally realizing that. "It's funny," she said, letting her hand rest comfortably in Cynthia's now, "the myths we create, the stories we tell ourselves to get by."

Cynthia waddled toward the stairs, taking Michaela with her. "Oh," she said, "the stories these rooms could tell."

Sitting at the kitchen table, Josie realized she had never taken down Kate's HAPPY BIRTHDAY banner. It still hung there, limp and torn. Outside, the sky had darkened and raindrops splattered the windows. Everything looked depressing to Josie. The rain on the window made her think of bugs smashing against a windshield. Upstairs she could hear Maggie pounding something. Her feet? Her head? What could she possibly be doing up there? In the meeting at the school, Josie had sat, her hands folded in her lap, legs crossed at the ankle, in her lemon yellow pantsuit, the one she'd found at the back of her closet. Even though the pants fit her snug across her hips, she felt confident in that suit. Optimistic. She'd worn lip gloss, small gold seashell earrings. See? she had thought. I'm a mother who cares. But when they began to talk about Maggie, totaling all the days she'd missed school, all the work she had to make up, when they'd used words like summer school, repeating the year, special counseling, Josie had started to sweat. She remembered one of the reasons the suit was in the back of the closet was the way it took to perspiration—big wet circles began to form under her arms, to spread out.

"But Maggie is in the Gifted Program," Josie had said.

"The point is that she hasn't been in school," the guidance counselor said. Unkindly, Josie thought. Especially for a guidance counselor. "For weeks," she added.

She didn't look very professional. Her dress was like Maggie's, a granny dress with small flowers on it, and she wore big black combat boots. Josie turned to the principal, Mr. Blaise. He had been a math teacher when she was in high school, though she'd never had him. He had taught the slower groups and even now spoke to everyone like they weren't very bright. Still, he was the one in charge.

"Mr. Blaise," Josie said, "Maggie's under a lot of stress at home. I was . . . attacked, you know. At the mall." She hoped Maggie appreciated what it took for her to tell these people, this small woman in a dress and combat boots and Mr. Blaise. She felt the circles under her arms growing larger, damper. "I haven't been very supportive. Emotionally. Not the way I . . ." Josie hesitated. Not the way she should be? Used to be? She started to feel dizzy and bent her head. But that was wrong. Face pale, she thought, raise the tail. "May I go back in the nurse's office and lie down?" she said.

They all looked at her, confused.

Josie didn't wait for an answer. She just went out the door, through the outer office and back into the nurse's office with its comforting smell of vomit and strawberry-scented disinfectant. When Maggie came to get her, she'd whispered fiercely, "You look ridiculous. Like Big Bird."

Josie caught sight of Kate's birthday banner again. She sighed and climbed up on the kitchen table to pull it down. Usually she saved all the party and holiday decorations, carefully folded and stored in the basement. But she climbed off the table and threw the HAPPY BIRTHDAY banner into the trash. Above her, music blasted from Maggie's room. More songs she did not recognize. The strong bass thumped on the ceiling. Where did Maggie get this stuff? Josie thought. Every day she discovered how little she really knew about the people she loved. Will. Michaela. Maggie. She did not even know where her daughter went each morning when she pretended to go off to school.

Josie didn't even realize she had put her head down until she heard her sister's voice from above her.

"What are you doing?" Michaela was saying. "And what in the world are you wearing?" She reached out and felt the sleeve of Josie's jacket. "Is that polyester?"

"And cotton," Josie said. "It's a blend."

"Are you all right?" Michaela said.

Josie had not yet re-adjusted to her sister's way of jumping from topic to topic without warning. "Maggie said I look like Big Bird."

"Is he polyester?"

"Where have you been?" Josie said. "He's a huge yellow bird. From *Sesame Street.*"

"Sue me," Michaela said. "I'm not up on kids' television shows. Once, I asked you if you read the *Voice* and you had never heard of it."

"What?" Josie said, wishing her sister would go back to California.

"*The Village Voice.* You had never heard of it."

"It is impossible to talk to you," Josie said. She said it so her words would hurt. Wasn't this the time when she should be talking to her sister? The time to climb in bed with her on a starry night and whisper secrets? My husband doesn't love me, I missed Kate's recital, I was carjacked for Christ's sake will someone listen to me? Josie was afraid she had actually spoken out loud, but Michaela had not noticed. She was moving toward the door.

"Mom and Dad are in the car waiting," Michaela said. "They want you to come."

"I can't leave Maggie. You cannot imagine what she's been doing."

But Michaela was already on her way out. Josie glanced upward. At least the pounding has stopped. Maggie would probably not even notice she was gone.

"Don't you look pretty?" her father said when Josie got in the car.

Her mother was frowning into the rearview mirror. "Is that new?"

"I don't even think they sell polyester anymore," Michaela said. "I think it's illegal."

"It is not illegal," Josie mumbled. At least the underarms had dried.

"It is," Michaela said. "I think it's flammable."

Their father was turned around in his seat, grinning. "You look like a great big gumdrop," he said.

"Thanks a lot," Josie told him.

"Dan, turn around," their mother said. "Buckle up."

It was raining hard now, and even though it was mid-afternoon, the dark sky and pounding rain made it seem to Josie like they were driving at night. "I should have brought my umbrella," she said.

Michaela laughed. "You would use an umbrella."

"What is that supposed to mean?" Josie said. With it dark like this, she imagined it could be twenty years earlier, all of them off somewhere. Every Sunday they used to pile in one of her father's fancy dealer cars and drive off—to the ocean or an apple orchard or to the Jamestown ferry and from there to Newport.

"I don't know," Michaela was saying, "I mean, umbrellas." She laughed again. "Galoshes. Macintoshes."

Their father spun around again. "Is this a game?" he said. "Things you wear in the rain. Right?"

Josie tried to catch someone's eye. But her mother was hunched over the steering wheel, concentrating on negotiating the curves in the bad weather and Michaela had turned her attention to something out her window—the peculiar dip of branches suddenly made heavy by wind and rain, perhaps. There was just her father, as blank-faced and hopeful as a newborn, peering back at her.

Until a few years ago, these back roads held nothing but woods and old stone walls and small cemeteries, family plots with broken, half-buried gravestones. The stone walls had been built by the Pottowamicut Indians and formed a border long ago made irrelevant. Still, those borders were honored even today, so that the land was irregular pieces that were hard to build on. The Gallagher brothers had figured out a way. They tore up the old cemeteries, cut down the trees, and built condominiums within the stone walls. A SECLUDED COMMUNITY, they called it. But, really, there was no seclusion. All around were just more condos and uneven yards. Josie remembered the Gallagher brothers as two in a series of dull-eyed boys who took over family businesses in town—contractors, jewelry stores, gas stations. It was no surprise that they had come up with these dull buildings. They looked like the Big Bad Wolf could blow them all down without too much huffing and puffing.

When her mother pulled up to one set, Michaela groaned. "God, these are ugly."

Claire backed out and turned into another strange-shaped area. "Shit," she muttered, "this isn't it either." She backed out again, jerkily.

"Are we looking for something in particular?" Josie said.

They were already at another row of condos. Real secluded, Josie thought.

"Here," Claire said. "The one on the corner."

The gray sky and heavy rain made them look even more fragile. Wind chimes, hung at someone's back door, clanked without melody.

"I bought that one at the end," Claire said. She sounded surprised.

"You bought one of these?" Josie gasped.

"Yes," Claire said, her voice little more than a whisper.

"Other people move to Florida," Michaela said. "Arizona."

Josie turned to her, happy to finally have someone else on her side. "Do you know who built these? The Gallagher brothers."

"Robert and Raymond? My God, they're dumb as stones," Michaela said, and gazed out at the row of condos in front of them. "No wonder they're so ugly," she added. "I mean, Raymond Gallagher used to pronounce *Beowulf* 'Baying Wolf.' He even flunked shop."

"You should have told me," Josie said to her mother, who still hugged the steering wheel. "I would have looked at places with you."

"But they all had problems," Claire said. She was hanging on to that steering wheel, inching forward, so that it seemed at any moment she might crawl onto the dashboard or out the window. "Sliding glass doors or steep stairs. There's a whole group near the river. I had to do something. I had to think of the safest place for your father."

Dan turned around to face his daughters again, with the

same simple blank-faced cheeriness. "I have something," he told them. "But I can't remember." His face started to contort, with worry or confusion. "It's something bad," he said. "Something scary."

"No," Josie said, reaching her hand out to her father. "No. You're fine."

He was frustrated, his face as puckered as seersucker. "They told me what it was but I forgot."

"No," Josie said again.

Her mother's gaze was waiting for her in the rearview mirror, steady, sure.

"So everything is settled," she said. "We move in thirty days."

Josie woke on Thursday morning to the sound of a baby crying. Or was it a cat? she thought, stumbling from bed, heading downstairs. Her mouth and head were both thick and fuzzy. She thought of cotton, of angora sweaters. She had a headache. The night before, Josie had gone to a liquor store and spent eleven dollars on a bottle of white wine. After walking up and down the aisles, confused by all the choices, she'd grabbed the one with a tag hanging in front of its display which said: "Buttery and smooth, with a hint of peach and vanilla." None of those things came to mind when Josie thought of wine. Maybe that would be a new skill she'd acquire, knowing fine wines, recognizing subtle tastes. Wasn't that what divorcees did—went to wine-tasting classes to meet divorced men in dark suits? Men who were brokenhearted just like her, who would take her to some dark restaurant in Providence, maybe an Italian one somewhere on Federal Hill, or one of those new ones where they cooked everything on a wood stove in the middle of the restaurant. She had tried to imagine it, looking across a candlelit table at someone other than Will, and right there in the wine store she'd started to cry. She hadn't cried this much since she'd had Kate and her body went into a hormonal crash.

Maggie and Kate were sitting in front of the television when she got home, eating potato chips straight from the bag. They ignored her. Josie went straight upstairs with her bottle of wine and a corkscrew, climbed into bed, started to cry all over again when she imagined Will never coming back, or no one in this bed with her ever again, or someone new beside her, someone with a hairy back or pasty skin or skinny legs, someone different, a stranger. She drank all of the wine. She did not taste butter or peaches or vanilla. She did get very drunk, and she lay there and cried until she fell asleep.

Her dreams had been frightening. Although she could not recall the details, she remembered that in each of them she had been lost—at the mall, in the streets of East Essex, here in her own house. What numbers would her aunts tell her to play? she wondered. Her grandmother's system did not allow for malls or loneliness. Josie considered sneaking past her daughters, who sat in front of the television as if they hadn't moved from last night. She needed aspirin, coffee. Maybe even to throw up.

But Kate spotted her and began to shout. "There's a flood! Look!" She pointed to the television, jabbing at it with her finger.

The screen showed flooded streets, water rushing past, cars submerged. It all looked unfamiliar at first, but then, as she watched, Josie began to recognize East Essex. Water almost completely covered DiGuiliano's Drugs, an old drugstore close to the river where her mother used to take her for cherry Cokes. Mrs. Murphy passed by the television camera in a small rubber raft filled with dogs.

"They've shown pictures of the other floods," Maggie said. "Grandma's and the one that shut down the Pippin Mill."

"My God," Josie said, as an aerial view of the rising river and all that it was sweeping away filled the television.

Even the air in the living room smelled swampy.

"Shit," Josie said, remembering the sump pump, the basement that filled so easily with water.

She ran to the basement door, Maggie and Kate close behind her. When she opened it, her nostrils filled with wet river smell. Afraid to turn on the light, she made her way carefully down the steps, ordering the girls to stay behind.

It was flooded.

Josie stepped off the bottom step and into knee-deep water, thinking: Damn you, Will, you son of a bitch. Looking around, at everything that was damaged or lost, Josie could not even begin to imagine that at some future time, perhaps in a year or two, she would be a different person, changed by the events of these weeks, the accidents of time and circumstance. She could only know that she must begin to take charge of the scattered pieces of a lifetime.

In the distance, the sump pump sighed from exhaustion, then stopped working. She saw her neatly labeled boxes—Christmas ornaments, baby clothes, summer curtains. Canned food floated by, all her tomato soup and chicken broth and artichoke hearts, bought in bulk at Sam's Discount Warehouse on Route 2. She looked at all the disintegrating cardboard, the way the still-rising water sloshed over a new row of boxes. Once, in her advanced science class, Maggie had made a transparency of the human body. Each page that was lifted revealed yet another system at work, muscles, organs, until finally there was just a skeleton. That was what Josie wished she could do, lift each level away and see what was inside so she could know what to save and what to leave behind.

Thinking that, she realized she should be trying to save something, at least. Certainly not the light summer curtains that were growing muddy right in front of her eyes. But her—

and Will's, she thought—mementos from childhood. Yearbooks and report cards and A+ term papers. Still, she didn't know where to begin. Josie reached for one of the boxes that was completely covered by water, imagining carefully folded baby blankets, the small mint and yellow sweaters that Aunt Tiny had knitted for Maggie, and later for Kate. When she thrust her hands into it, they did settle on soft wet wool and Josie began frantically to try to save what was inside.

Josie gasped when she looked down at what she had found. Not those baby things at all. Instead, she found herself cradling Cuddles. The poor cat must have hidden in the box, trying to escape the water, and drowned.

"Mom?" Maggie was calling to her. "Can we come down?"

"No!" Josie shouted back, lifting the wet box with the dead cat inside to higher ground.

Looking around at all that was destroyed, Josie was uncertain what to do next. Her eyes settled on a box labeled family photo albums. She lifted that one, held it against her chest as she moved across the slippery floor, and handed it up to Maggie on the stairs. She did the same with her wedding dress, and the safe-deposit box of important documents.

Maggie said, "Shouldn't Dad be here helping?"

"I suppose so," Josie said, turning back to survey the basement. Boxes of microwave popcorn swirled at her legs.

"Will the water come up and up and up and drown us all?" Kate asked, her eyes wide with fright.

"Of course not," Josie said. But she was not certain how high the water would go, how safe they really were.

Dan Jericho looked at his wife and said simply, "I love you. You know that, don't you?"

In that instant Claire knew that it was all much worse than she'd thought. That this moment of lucidity was one of Dan's last. And she knew that he realized it too. She could almost see it, the thin thread of memory fraying, growing more narrow, until it was finally gone.

That morning, when the storm watch was at its peak, Claire had driven to Rhode Island Hospital for a meeting with Doctor Isabella French, the expert there on Alzheimer's. She had the results of Dan's CAT scan, which peered down at them on a screen behind her head. Doctor French took careful notes as Claire talked, oddly relieved to finally tell someone all of it. The doctor had long salt-and-pepper hair, a wide face, serious gray eyes. When Claire finished, Doctor French cleared her throat, then told her, without apology or sympathy, the terrible facts. Dan's case was advanced; it was moving rapidly. She produced brochures for nursing homes, for family counseling, for explanations. The latter had detailed illustrations of a brain.

Looking at her husband, Claire knew that she was already grieving his fate. And her own loneliness.

"I love you too," she said.

Dan smiled his new, absent smile. "The basement is flooded," he said.

Claire frowned. "Flooded?"

He nodded and opened the basement door.

Together they made their way down the stairs. Claire saw that they had already lost a lot. She had the urge to dive in and try to save everything, but she didn't. Instead, she stood and surveyed the damage.

"Remember the last flood?" she said. She could feel his breath on the back of her neck.

"I lifted you up and carried you to the washing machine and made love to you right there, on top of it," Dan said. "With the whole world falling apart around us."

"We were newlyweds," Claire said.

She let Dan's arms circle her waist, let herself fall into his embrace, and watched.

■ ■ ■

The flood had Will terrified in a vague, uncomfortable way. He stretched in Bonnie's bed and tried to calm himself. There was that sump pump in the basement. He was worried about that not working and the cellar flooding. There were the children getting scared. Bonnie rolled toward him, throwing one leg over both of his, seductively. But he inched away, feigning sleep.

There was Josie, home alone with the river rising. When he imagined it, his heart lurched. Somehow, over all these years, he had come to think of her as incapable. But really, Will thought, she wasn't. And he was hit with the powerful memory of Josie in childbirth, bearing the pain of both of those girls being born. She had even cracked jokes during the worst of it, walking up and down the halls of the hospital, leaning heavily on his arm. He remembered when she was having Maggie, how the doctor had ordered her to push, finally, and she had raised herself up on both elbows and bore down, grunting, pushing their daughter out of her. When the doctor had handed him the scissors to cut the umbilical cord, his hands had shook. But Josie took their daughter in her arms with great authority and sureness. Look, she'd said to him. Look what we made.

What was it that he wanted, that was driving him away from them? The feel of a carefully tended, shaved and lotioned soft leg of someone else? Yesterday he had gone back to Saint Teresa's and slipped into the confessional.

"It's me," he'd whispered to Father McKenna. "It's Will Hunter. I lied to you."

"Yes," the priest had said, without judgment.

"I have . . . I am committing adultery." Then Will had added, "I'm a no-good shit."

He had called home later that night, half-hoping that Josie would answer, relieved when she didn't because he seemed to be on a wave of confession. He would have told her everything and she would not have forgiven him, or given him some route to forgiveness the way Father McKenna had in the confessional. With all this rain, he'd told Maggie on the phone, you might need me. He'd given her Bonnie's number, guiltily. And Maggie took it, repeating it back to him in a cold, hard voice that sounded older, wiser. What did she know? he had wondered.

"I should call home," he said, moving out from under Bonnie's leg.

He went into the kitchen to call, deciding as he punched in the numbers that he might go there just to check the pump, just to check his family. The line was busy. He tried again, and again, but each time got a busy signal.

In the doorway to Bonnie's bedroom, he paused, studying her long legs, the dip of her stomach between her hipbones. He wished he could redo parts of his life. He would break up with Josie back in college, take a job with IBM, live in New Jersey, fuck different women, come home ten years later and rediscover her, marry her, grow old with her.

"What are you looking at?" Bonnie said. She was a wiseguy, sassy. So unlike his wife.

"You," he said, happy she never asked the question Josie seemed to always ask: What are you thinking? He did not want to admit that he was thinking, longing in a sad and final way, for his wife.

Maggie knew where her father was. He called last night while her mother was upstairs crying and gave her an emergency number and address. "Emergency only," he had stressed. When her mother handed her that wedding dress, still wrapped in a dry cleaner's plastic bag, the bumps of beading and pearls against Maggie's arms as she carried it to safety, she decided this constituted an emergency.

"Stay out of Mom's hair," Maggie told Kate. She played with the remote until Montel Williams's face appeared. "Look what's on. A talk show."

Kate watched Maggie put on her raincoat.

"Where are you going?"

"Just watch that. Okay?" Maggie said.

The address was near the elementary school, one of a group of new town houses built practically in the playground. Funny that's where they were located, since the town houses did not rent to people with children. Thinking that, Maggie got a stab in her side. How could her father live someplace that didn't allow children? What about her and Kate?

"It's only temporary," he'd said.

Kate, listening on the extension, had asked him, "What is temporary?"

"Short term," he'd said.

"I know what it means," she'd shouted at him. "I'm asking you how long you plan on staying there."

He hadn't answered that one.

Maggie took a shortcut through the woods. When she'd been in elementary school, a man used to hide in these woods and pull out his penis when kids walked by. She'd never seen it, but Stephanie had. These woods still scared Maggie a little, even though the man had been caught. She walked faster, happy to see the pointed tips of the town houses. The complex was called Seven Gables because it had seven gabled roofs. Mostly people who never heard of the book *The House of the Seven Gables* lived there, so it seemed like an especially dumb name. Her mother called it a swinging singles place. She said it like it was terrible, even though there was a pool—slightly overflowing now, Maggie saw—and a Recreation Center with pool tables inside. Was her father now single? Maggie wondered, confused, as she walked toward Gable Two. Or worse, a swinging single?

She climbed the three short steps to the front door and rang the bell. It played some sort of little tune, and Maggie winced.

A woman in a short silk flowered nightgown and matching robe answered, surprising Maggie. It looked like something from the Victoria's Secret catalogue. Maggie's mother got those in the mail and always threw them out. Then Maggie took them from the trash and hid them in her drawers. She liked to imitate the models' sexy pout in the mirror. Maggie noticed this woman's hair was messy, her toenails painted dark red. Like blood, Maggie thought.

Instead of saying anything, the woman took a step back and looked behind her.

Maggie followed her gaze, across the beige carpeting and overstuffed beige furniture to her father, standing shirtless, in just a pair of boxer shorts, holding a bottle with gold foil on top. He seemed to be pointing the bottle right at Maggie.

The woman laughed nervously, ran her right foot up the calf of her left. "Will?" she said.

That woman was her father's right-hand man. Bonnie. The one they always talked about. Did she have a nose job? Did she dye her hair?

Maggie figured it out then. The sexy outfit. Her father mostly undressed. That bottle was champagne. Her father had left them for someone else. No children allowed. Swinging singles. She turned, stumbling on the wet stairs, and ran past the pool, the Recreation Center, toward the woods. She thought that maybe her father was calling her name, but when she stopped and listened more carefully, decided it was just the rain falling hard through the trees.

Kate was not ever, ever supposed to go in these particular woods because once a man had done something bad to a little girl here and, even though he was in jail, her mother said *you never know.* Still, she followed Maggie all the way, but by the time she caught up with her, Maggie had turned around and was heading right back through the woods, right at Kate.

"What are you doing here?" Maggie said. "I told you to stay put, didn't I? Didn't I tell you to watch Montel Williams?"

Kate couldn't think of what to say. She tried to grab hold of Maggie's hand, but her sister pushed her away.

"I don't want to talk to you," Maggie said. "I don't want to talk to anybody."

"But why did you come here?" Kate asked, tagging behind. "We're not supposed to play in these woods," she added when Maggie walked even faster.

Maggie turned around. "Leave me alone!" she screamed. "I want everybody to leave me alone!"

Kate was scared. Everybody seemed to be crazy. Maggie was starting to run, fast, and even though Kate tried to catch up, it was impossible. Even though these woods weren't the biggest ones, they were confusing. Kate tried to follow the hot pink of her sister's raincoat, but it seemed to simply disappear. She slowed down. She thought of Little Red Riding Hood and Goldilocks and how they all came to no good in the woods.

"You're not supposed to leave a little girl alone in the woods," she said, as if Maggie, or anyone, might hear.

She walked a little more.

"I feel scared," she said.

Just when she thought she was going to start to cry, she saw a clearing. Kate ran to it and looked down, frowning. This wasn't the way she had come in. From here, she saw the flooding, right below her. There were firemen, policemen, volunteers, everyone working hard. People were crying and yelling. It looked exactly like it did on TV, except bigger. Exciting, even. Kate made her way down the hill toward the river.

■ ■ ■

Michaela Jericho had found her real purpose for coming back. She was waist-deep in water, helping families to safety, lifting frightened dogs from the river. Her friend Belle always said true meanings are discovered later. Michaela thought she had come back to confront her mother, to reclaim some lost part of her. But that was not the true meaning. All of that had brought her home. She had saved herself, now she was saving others. After this flood, East Essex would have to rebuild. She imagined how it would be—the old mills turned into loft apartments, businesses, restaurants. The river clean again. Looking up she caught sight of Leo Day, shouting instructions to a group huddled beside him. Too tired for lovemaking, they had slept together in his old trailer, their arms and legs tossed around each other almost casually. In the morning, he'd brought her a cup of good strong coffee. A handful of blueberries. She felt then, and now as she watched him, that what she and Leo had together was time.

In the distance, Michaela saw a child making her way down the hill at the spot where the water was rising hardest. How did she manage to find her way there? Michaela wondered, shielding her eyes from the rain with one hand. She was certain someone had been positioned there to keep people out. The child kept her head bent until she reached the bottom. Then she looked up, and Michaela realized it was Josie's daughter Kate. That she was standing on dangerous, soft ground.

"Kate," Michaela called. But she knew the child could not hear, that her words were drowned out by rain and wind and shouting.

As if in slow motion, Michaela began to walk toward her niece. The rising water formed currents that were impossible to navigate. Still, Michaela moved forward, her arms outstretched as if she could grab Kate even at this distance.

She called to her again, hoping someone else would notice, hoping Kate would hear. Michaela kept her gaze focused on the little girl as she moved, slowly, toward her. In the instant that Kate slipped in, disappearing into the river, Michaela thought she'd let her gaze wander, had simply lost sight of the child. But no, there was the lime green hood of her rain slicker bobbing up in a flash before once again vanishing.

As soon as Josie realized that the girls were gone, she knew they must have gone down to the river. The news broadcaster advised people to stay away. There were eddies, he said. Soft ground that gave way easily, rapidly moving water. She should not have left them alone, not even for this short time. When Josie grabbed her own slicker from the mudroom, she saw both of theirs were missing.

No traffic was allowed on any streets in East Essex except for emergency vehicles. Josie had to practically run through the flooded streets that led to the river, her movements slow and clumsy. As she neared the flood area, she saw crowds of people. Some were huddled in Red Cross blankets, others stood crying near ambulances. The sense of disaster was big, terrifying. Josie passed homes that seemed to have crumbled, like those she used to make out of Popsicle sticks.

The shouts she heard took form as she got closer.

"A child fell in! A little girl is drowning!"

Some force moved Josie forward on her leaden feet. She knew in that moment that the child was hers. That it was Kate who had fallen in, captivated by the swirl of the water or something bright floating past her.

Josie began to yell for her daughter.

"Kate!" she called to her. "It's Mommy! It's Mommy!"

There were so many people, all with the sad faces of tragedy. Josie pushed past them, heard herself mumbling, "It's my baby in there," even as she tried to convince herself that she did not really know that, only felt it in her gut. She thought of their drowned cat, the matted fur, the scared expression frozen on its face.

"Kate!" she screamed again.

Someone was holding her back, strong arms on hers, as she struggled to keep moving forward toward the river.

"Please, ma'am," he said. It was one of the policemen from the line-up.

"My daughter," Josie said, pointing toward the rushing river. Could a mother really know this? Was Kate what she'd been looking for in her dreams all night, what she'd lost? From where she stood, she saw the bright red of her sister's hair. She was bent over, digging, Josie thought.

"Michaela!" Josie called.

Michaela straightened, and lifted Kate from the surging water, her lime green slicker still on, her reddish blond curls flat against her head.

Josie held out her arms, yelled, "Kate!" again.

Michaela's voice drifted up to her, carried across this short distance between them. "She's all right," Michaela was saying. "I have her. She's all right."

As Josie watched her sister hug Kate to her, she wrapped her own arms around herself, as if they both could feel her embrace, and moved toward them.

week four

—

A week ago, Josie could not have imagined East Essex looking the way it did today. As she had stood on the muddy banks of the Pottowamicut River clutching her sister and her daughter, all of them wet, trembling, afraid, it had seemed that East Essex would always be the way it looked then, gray and dangerous. But now, driving the winding road from her own house to her parents' empty one, the sun was once again bright and the new leaves that had burst into bloom glistened a silvery green. Even the debris that the flood had sent onto the roads had finally been cleared. Michaela and Leo Day had organized a clean-up crew and put all the objects that had turned up in the basement of Saint Teresa's.

By the time she pulled up to her parents' house, Josie caught herself humming. Just that morning she had gotten a call from Dog McGovern. Her carjacker had confessed. "You're safe," Dog had told her. Then the check from the insurance company came in today's mail. Josie had made a list: Go to Saint Teresa's and adopt one of the homeless cats from the flood, go car shopping, see a lawyer.

When she walked past the SOLD sign to the back door of

her parents', Josie paused. From inside, she heard voices, laughter. It struck her as strange that she would no longer be coming to this house every day, that it was no longer home. She imagined driving Kate by it in years to come, telling her, "This is where I grew up." It struck her as odd that perhaps she had shaped some form of history this past month, that maybe she would have a story to tell her children and her grandchildren, a story that would show them who she had been, how she had lived. Beside the door Josie noticed two smudges of new paint—one lilac, one teal. She'd heard that the new owners were going to change the house's color, paint a bright trim, add shutters with cutouts of animals on them.

When Josie walked inside, she was not surprised by the house's emptiness, even though she saw that it appeared much roomier with the furniture gone. Instead, it was the familiar smell of freshly perked coffee and the comforting sound of voices—her aunts', her sister's, her daughters' and her mother's—that welcomed her. They sat cross-legged on the kitchen floor, right where the table had stood for so long, leaving an empty circle between them as if indeed they were still at that table.

Maggie jumped up when she saw Josie.

"Tell them, Mom," she said. "Tell them how you don't care about my nose."

A few days before, Maggie had come home with her nose pierced, a tiny gold hoop earring jutting from one nostril.

"I don't care how mad you get," Maggie had told her.

But Josie hadn't gotten angry. She had seen teenagers with dozens of pierced body parts—nipples, tongues, navels—on afternoon talk shows. But looking at her daughter, knowing her, Josie was certain that Maggie was not one of those young girls.

Josie had touched the tip of Maggie's nose, gently. "Ouch," she'd said. "That must hurt."

"No," Maggie told her, moving away, eyeing her suspiciously.

"Well," she added after a moment, "it does. A little."

And then, "Actually, it hurts a lot."

They had looked at each other for a long while before Maggie had said, "I'm sorry Daddy left you."

"Me too," Josie said.

"But maybe he'll come back?" Maggie said, her eyes narrowed again.

"Maybe I don't want him to come back," Josie said. Those words hurt to say out loud. But they were true, and feeling truer every day that she was alone, thinking about Will, and about herself.

Maggie had studied her mother again. "Maybe you shouldn't take him back. You're right."

Now, facing her family, Josie said, "I don't like a ring sticking out of her nose. But it's not the worst thing."

Aunt Tiny clucked her tongue. "Rings in your nose? It's disgusting. It must be unsanitary." She peered into Maggie's face. "Don't things get stuck in there?"

"On *Oprah,*" Kate said, her mouth full of Dunkin' Munchkins, "they had a guy with a ring through his penis."

"Where did she learn a word like that?" Aunt Tiny shrieked.

"Auntie Michaela told me that's what a boy's dingdong is supposed to be called," Kate said. She smiled at Michaela. "Right?"

"I mean, really," Michaela said. "Dingdong?"

"That's what dad called his penis," Maggie mumbled. "So pedestrian."

"Aunt Michaela saved my life," Kate said, her voice matter-of-fact.

As if everyone realized the truth of that for the first time, the room grew hushed.

"Well," Michaela said, embarrassed.

"Like in *White Christmas,*" Kate told everyone. "Bing Crosby gets his life saved by Donny Osmond—"

Maggie groaned. "Danny Kaye, not Donny Osmond."

"—and they have to be partners for the rest of their lives. They're linked together," Kate added. Her face was dusted with sugar, shiny in the sunlight that came through the curtainless windows.

Josie poured herself a cup of coffee and took her usual place at the imaginary table.

Aunt Beatrice touched her arm lightly. "Maybe Will will come back. But if he doesn't, you'll be dating other men soon. Now's the time to lay off the sweets. Get in shape. Make a fresh start."

Already, Denise had called Josie with blind-date setups. It's been two weeks, Josie told her. Give me time. But after each phone call, Josie caught herself fantasizing. She had not dated anyone except Will since she was nineteen years old. Who would she be attracted to now? she wondered. She imagined herself eating out at one of the new restaurants in Providence, where they topped pizza with goat cheese, tossed pasta with walnuts and sage. She imagined herself somehow more sophisticated, wiser. She imagined herself as someone interesting.

Reaching for the Sweet'n Low, Josie said, "You know, Aunt Beatrice, I learned at least one important lesson from Will. I have to start doing things for me."

"Duh," Maggie said. "Where have you been, Mom?"

"Like what?" Aunt Tiny said. She had eaten around the filling in a Bavarian cream doughnut and was taking long licks into the center. "I don't understand girls today. All these years, you didn't take care of yourself?"

Claire said, "We were brought up to take care of everybody else, Tiny. We brought our daughters up that way."

Maggie groaned again. "This is worse than my honors class in Women's Studies."

"Women's Studies?" Aunt Tiny said. "What is that supposed to mean?" She shook her head. "That's why you girls have so many problems. Too much studying. Too much thinking. In our day, we just did what we were supposed to."

Josie waited for Michaela's sarcastic retort. But Kate had crawled onto Michaela's lap and was singing "White Christmas" to her, softly.

"I'm going to help Michaela," Josie said, "with the river project."

"You are?" Claire said, surprised.

"I know everybody in this town, don't I? If I can't get their support nobody can," Josie said.

"Good for you," Aunt Beatrice said. "You need to keep busy."

She was going to take a wine-tasting course too. Wines of the Loire Valley. And she was going to get a job. She didn't know where or what she could even do, but she was going to do something. She saw herself in a bold-colored business suit, lowish heels, maybe even a briefcase. But Josie kept all that to herself for the time being.

"I remember when you two tried to get East Essex to open a recycling center," Claire said. Her eyes looked off at a distant spot on the bare wall. "I liked watching my two girls working together so closely."

"That project failed, though," Michaela said. "This one won't."

"You were ahead of your time," Claire said. "That's what it was. Now everyone's recycling."

Aunt Tiny reached for another doughnut. "I hate it. The

blue bin, the green bin. Colored paper, newspaper, bottles and cans. That's just my opinion but I think it's ridiculous what we have to do with garbage these days. It used to be, you threw your garbage away. Period."

"Before Auntie Michaela saved my life," Kate said, "it was like I was stuck in a fountain. All the water was gushing up over my head in big bubbles and it was freezing cold and I opened my eyes and what do you think I saw?"

"A tunnel with a white light at the end?" Maggie said, twitching her sore nose.

"No," Kate said, confused. "I saw stuff. Like wood and stones and shoes." She frowned. "I couldn't breathe."

Josie looked past her mother and Maggie to Michaela. There were no words for something like this, your sister saving your child's life. But she had remembered so much since that day last week, so much that had been good about Michaela, about them as sisters. The way they used to run, naked, under the sprinkler in the backyard every summer, the feel of Michaela's fingers combing the snarls from Josie's hair at night in the bathtub; how, at Scarborough Beach every summer, they would hold each other's hands as they rode the waves into shore.

"I had a dream last night," Josie said, suddenly recalling it with great detail.

Her mother and aunts leaned toward her, ready.

"We were children," Josie said. "Michaela and I were children. But Maggie and Kate were in it too. And we were at the beach, playing. You know, running and squealing and all of a sudden Michaela said, 'There's a big storm coming. We've got to get back.' "

"Did you see the storm?" Aunt Beatrice asked. "Because storm clouds are 55 but rain is . . . What's rain?"

"09," Claire said.

"No," Josie said, "I didn't see anything like that but I was terrified and I said, 'Back where? We have nowhere to go.' And Michaela laughed. She said, 'Home. We can always go home, silly.' "

"Were you in the water?" Aunt Tiny asked. "Because there's one number for clear water and one for murky water."

Michaela smiled. "I know what number to play. 401."

Aunt Beatrice shook her head. "No. 40 is if you dream of a wedding."

"401 Acqua Way is here," Michaela said. "It's our address here at home."

The women stopped talking and each, for a little while, turned to their own private places.

Until Josie broke the silence and said, "It wasn't a bad dream, you know."

"Beats me," Aunt Tiny said. "It doesn't hurt to play 401." She looked at Josie, frowning. "What is in your hair?"

Josie reached for the thick purple strand. "Kool-Aid," she said.

Kate laughed. "I have it too. We all put Kool-Aid in our hair last night."

Josie and Maggie and Michaela and Kate tilted their heads so the older women could see.

When Michaela had shown up last night at Josie's, Maggie had just explained the reasons why Josie should let her streak her hair with Kool-Aid—it was easy, you could do it at home, and everybody else was doing it. Michaela immediately agreed to do hers, so of course Kate had to do it too.

"Little sister?" Michaela had said, in the same challenging way she used when they were growing up. It was that tone that had led Josie to jump off the high diving board, wear a black armband in seventh grade to protest the Vietnam War and go to school in brown suede hot pants. All of those things had gotten Josie in trouble; she had missed her mark when she'd jumped from that diving board and landed too close to the edge of the pool, breaking a rib and scraping the whole left side of her body raw.

Watching Maggie mix the Kool-Aid with water, Josie had realized that Will would have hated her doing it, would have thought it foolish. She smiled and sat at the table.

"Ready," she'd said to Maggie. "I'll even go first."

Michaela had come to discuss the River Project with Josie, and she'd brought avocados and cilantro and jalapeños with her to teach them to make guacamole. She'd held up a California avocado, bumpy and brown, already gone soft, and said with great seriousness, "Never ever buy a Florida avocado. Better to go without."

Later they'd put toothpicks in the pit and put it in water. Michaela promised them an avocado plant would grow from it. Josie had been surprised with her sister, with the things she knew. California things, Josie thought. Things that Will would make fun of. The way she'd squeezed lime juice into the guacamole so it wouldn't turn brown. How she'd whispered to the pit in the glass, "Grow, sweetie. Grow big and tall for us."

"What is wrong with you girls?" Aunt Tiny was saying.

"At least it washes out," Aunt Beatrice said. "I don't even want to tell you how much Denise and Judy spend on real hair color. Just highlights, mind you, but a fortune.

"It feels sticky," Kate told them.

Josie stood and left the kitchen, moving from room to room, re-creating how they used to be, the rocking chair here, the grandfather's clock there. It was like a farewell, her visiting each empty room and filling them in one final time. She walked upstairs, anticipating each creak as she climbed. In her old bedroom, she stood in the center, and thought not only of what objects had occupied it, but of the hopes she'd had here, the things she'd dreamed lying alone in her bed with the yellow-and-white gingham bedspread.

Her life had turned out so differently than she'd imagined back then. In some ways, she thought, her life was just now beginning. Or beginning again. Downstairs, the voices hummed. She had woken up to those voices for a good part of her life, had gone to sleep with them in her ears. She imagined herself long ago, in this room, her feet snug in footie pajamas, her hair damp from her bath, the glow of the hall light sending shadows across the wall. She had gone to sleep every night as a child feeling safe, knowing her sister lay nearby, hearing the voices in the kitchen.

Standing alone in the empty room, with its walls smudged from old posters hung with tape and a burn in the floor from a failed attempt at découpage with Michaela one summer afternoon, Josie tried to catch those pieces of her old self, pieces that she could take with her. She remembered the stories she'd grown up with about the floods of East Essex. Her parents used to take her and Michaela down to the river and show them the watermarks those other floods had left behind.

The oldest mark was from a flood back in the 1700s, when Indians lived on the banks of the Pottowamicut. The story went that the white settlers could have helped rescue the women and children but didn't, in hopes of the Indians leaving the land. But the Indians retaliated by putting a curse on the town; one white child would drown in the river every year until the Indian lives had been paid back tenfold. That story had been with Josie as she'd run toward the flooding waters last week, convinced that this year that child would be Kate.

Another mark was from the flood that killed so many mill workers at the turn of the century. With all the doors locked, they couldn't escape. There were rumors when she was growing up that skeletons hung in those deserted mills, that the mills were haunted. One year, on a dare, Michaela and Ollie Pfeiffer and their friends had slept overnight in the Campbell Mill.

Michaela swore that she had heard voices and screams and the sound of running feet. Rats, Ollie had said. It's filled with water rats.

Last night, as they ate chips and the guacamole they'd made and Michaela had explained what she and Leo Day had planned for East Essex's empty mills, Josie asked her if she was afraid of ghosts there.

"You convert these old mills into living spaces and restaurants and shops and the ghosts might run you out," Josie had said. She'd tried to sound lighthearted, but she'd grown up believing those stories; it was hard to let go of them.

"I don't know," Michaela had told her. "I think you can learn to live with ghosts."

There was the flood that had stained her mother's wedding album and left watermarks on her wedding gown. When Josie got married she had wanted to wear her mother's dress, an ivory satin one with handsewn beads. But the stains could not be removed and she'd worn a new one instead. When she thought of that dress, the snow-white lace bodice, the tiny pearl buttons that lined the back of the dress, and of her wedding day, the way the candlelight elongated everything in the church, and Will beside her, both of them with clammy hands and dry mouths, Josie felt a pang of loss, of betrayal. How long would it take her, she wondered, to really move past Will and what she'd thought they had together? That wedding dress had been one of the things she'd made sure to rescue from her flooded cellar last week, despite everything.

Somehow, standing here like this, all Josie knew for certain was that she would get there, some day. The image of her daughter being lifted from that river had made her realize so much. It had restored a lost part of herself.

She looked around her childhood room one more time, then left it, finally, and moved toward the women's voices downstairs. This flood, her flood, had taken so much from her. All that she had lost these past few weeks, and all that she had discovered, would forever be entwined with the river flooding this time. The newest watermarks would always remind her. They would be her story to tell.

about the author

ANN HOOD is the author of six novels: *Somewhere Off the Coast of Maine, Waiting to Vanish, Three-Legged Horse, Something Blue, Places to Stay the Night,* and *The Properties of Water.* She writes a regular column for *Parenting* magazine, and has published her short stories, essays and book reviews in *Mademoiselle, Redbook, Seventeen, Story, Self, Cosmopolitan, McCall's, Glamour, The New York Times, The Washington Post, Chicago Tribune,* and *Los Angeles Times.* She lives in Providence with her husband and their son, Sam, and is currently at work on a new novel.